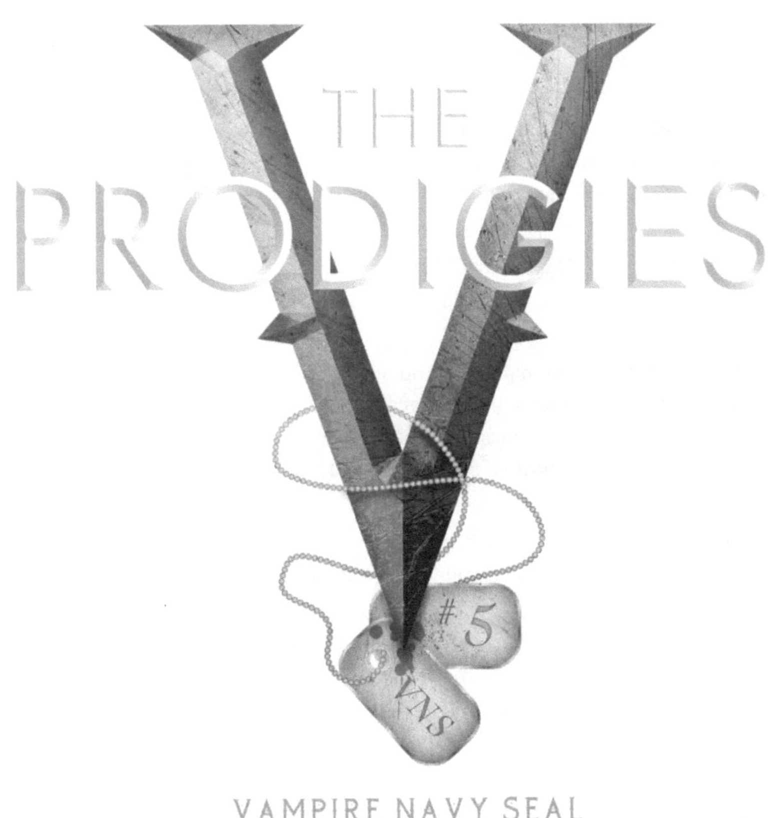

S.B. ALEXANDER

COPYRIGHT

1

SAM

My mind spun as I sat on the floor, head in my hands, rocking back and forth, reciting prayers I'd learned when I'd been human. I'd heard three of the babies cry but not the fourth. Only a minute or two had passed since one nurse had said Layla wasn't responding. Or maybe a lifetime had gone by, given the way each second was gut-wrenching, as if someone had stuck their fist into my stomach and ripped out my insides.

"Come on, baby doll," I whispered, yanking on my hair. "You can't die on me. I need you more than you know."

My breathing was all over the place as I listened intently for any sound or voice or an intake of breath. But it was either dead silent inside the operating room or I'd lost my hearing again. I opened and closed my fists, trying to rein in my emotions as the building began to rumble.

Growling under my breath, I pushed to my feet. "I need to get out of here. Otherwise, I *will* kill my wife."

And not the way Tripp thought. Several minutes ago he'd tackled me to the floor to prevent me from bursting into the OR and ordered me to stand down. "What will you do if you go in there? Think about it. You'll only prevent them from doing their job. Then Layla *will* die," he'd said.

Now, I was having a hard time controlling my elemental powers that would destroy the infirmary and everyone it.

"Good idea," Tripp said as he guarded the scrub station door.

Wife. Fuck! Would I ever again see her beautiful electric-blue eyes or kiss her full lips or see her brilliant smile when she set her gaze on me? I couldn't go down that road of thinking the worst. But it was hard not to when my feisty huntress was flatlining.

How did we get to this point? Layla had been doing well since I'd rescued her from the clutches of her grandmother, although her heart had given out while she was a prisoner at Intech. But Layla had been under extreme amounts of stress. She'd been kidnapped and involved in a car accident, then she fled her captors and spent two solid days lost in the West Virginia mountains only to be captured once again by her fucked-up sister Rianne.

For the last three months, life had been grand. Our relationship had grown by leaps and bounds. I'd finally proposed. She'd said yes, and not long afterward, we were tying the knot in a beautiful and emotional handfasting ceremony.

She hadn't shown any signs of complications, even during her checkups with Doc, who'd been watching her pregnancy closely since our kids were inhuman and Layla would deliver in six months instead of nine.

Layla's cousin-in-law Carly, a scientist who worked for Intech, had speculated that Layla's heart wouldn't be able to support four supernatural fetuses. Dr. Martin, a human ob-gyn and a good friend of Dr. Vieira's, had said the same thing.

On top of that, Doc had found a medical file in our archives on a human, Emily Crawford, who'd supposedly died during childbirth from carrying inhuman twins—a witch and vampire. But since a page was missing from Emily's file, her death was a mystery.

I stomped toward the exit, the doors rattling as my fear, anxiety, and heartbreak were about to set off an earthquake.

Four flights of stairs later, I was gulping in the balmy July air as I bent over between two military vehicles—a Hummer and a Jeep.

Tripp cleared his throat behind me. "She'll make it." His tone was ladened with sadness and not convincing at all. Plus, the worry dripping off him was hitting me like several fastballs at a batting cage.

Growling, I straightened, grabbing both sides of my head as I looked up at the moonless sky. "If she doesn't, I—"

Tripp leaned against the Jeep. "Don't finish that sentence. Dr. Vieira and Dr. Martin will not let her die. Do you hear me?" Beneath the cloak of confidence of his steady voice was a friend who was as torn up about Layla as I was.

I knew the medical team would do its best, but we didn't have any magic to bring someone back from the dead. Or did we?

Alia Costner had the ability to craft potions and magic spells. She'd taught my sister Jo and me some basic concepts. For example, my ability to compel differed from the standard way vampires had been taught. I wove a series of numbers together that caused my victims to drop into a coma-like states. Which I'd done to Rianne that night at the club when I'd first met Layla, Jordyn, and Rianne Aberdeen. Of course, Layla was officially a Mason now.

I swallowed the dryness in my throat, anchoring my nerve-trembling body against the Hummer opposite Tripp. "Have you ever heard of anyone bringing someone back from the dead?"

"No," he returned. "And again, stop thinking the worst."

I knocked on my chest at the pain stabbing me like a thousand pinpricks. "Fuck, man. It's hard not to when Layla is dying."

The cars in the parking lot wobbled on their tires.

Tripp reached over and slapped my arm. "Ease up on your powers."

I grimaced, whisking my hand through my hair. "I should be at Layla's side. If she hears my voice, maybe it will help." I started for the door.

Tripp blocked me. "No way, man. We're not going round two."

His bronze eyes flashed vampire, his inhuman gaze piercing a hole through me. "I meant what I said earlier. I'll throw you in the brig next to Jordyn." On a blink, his expression softened. "The best place for you is outside. You said yourself that if you stayed in there, you would kill your family."

I swallowed a growl as I paced up and down between the Hummer and the Jeep. The word *kill* was a punch to the gut, although he was right, and I knew it. But I had to do something. I had to keep my mind from wandering. I needed to hear anything that would give me hope. "I don't remember hearing the fourth baby cry. Did you?" Then again, the last few minutes had become one big fucking blur, as had the last two hours since I rushed Layla into the infirmary.

An earthy odor permeated the air, indicating rain was about to pour down from above. I could use a good soaking rain to wash away not only the sweat from my body but to wake me from the hell that was suffocating me.

"I was too busy keeping you from doing something stupid," he said. "So, what names did you and Layla decide on for the kids?"

I looked at him like he had ten heads despite knowing he was trying to distract me. I couldn't think about names. I was having a difficult time keeping air in my lungs.

Biting a thumbnail, I paced like a madman. "We've gone back and forth on a few." What was I saying? We had a list as long as my arm full of names and meanings. I liked Liam for a boy, and Layla adored Luna if we had a girl. "But we decided only last week that we would wait until we saw their faces before picking names."

You will see all four of your children, a small voice whispered in the back of my mind. Fuck, I wanted to believe that. I had to believe that. I also had to believe that this wasn't the end for Layla. We'd just gotten married. I wanted to fulfill her dream of living by the ocean and give her everything she'd ever desired.

My pulse sped up as I waited for another voice in my head to tell me I would see my beautiful huntress again. But none came.

Tripp lingered next to the entrance into the infirmary as if he knew exactly what I was thinking.

I stabbed a thumb at the door. "I need to know if Layla is alive." My voice cracked in several places. I wasn't a medical expert, but I knew that the doctors only had a small window of time to revive a human without any complications, like the patient becoming brain-dead.

I hated to even think that, and in that moment, I would give my soul to the devil to turn Layla into a vampire. Of course, that was impossible unless I wanted her to become a monster like her cousin Noah. He'd been injected with his cousin-in-law Carly Aberdeen's serum that had turned him into a god-awful creature—a cross between a vampire and shifter.

I came to an abrupt halt directly in front of Tripp when a screwed-up idea flashed before me.

"What's your brilliant mind thinking?" Tripp asked.

I guffawed, zeroing in on my best bud and superior officer. "There's nothing brilliant about changing Layla into one of us."

He reared back, almost hitting his head on the metal door. "Are you seriously thinking of a serum like your uncle's or Carly's? That's suicide."

I fisted my hands, ready to punch a car, the building—fuck, anything—which was my way of dealing with my emotions. I was angry, helpless, and gutted.

"I know." I pushed out an exasperated breath. "But like Matthew Costner, she has vampire blood running in her family. Look at him. His transformation from human to vampire was seamless."

Tripp tucked his hands into the pockets of his cargo pants. "Sam, Layla would cut off your gonads and stuff them in your mouth if she woke up like Noah. And her vampire bloodline is probably several generations removed, whereas Matthew's isn't. His grandfather Victor is a vampire. Therefore, you can't compare apples to oranges."

I hated that he was right. Layla *would* cut off my nuts if she woke up as a monster. Besides, I would never take that chance or make a life-changing decision for her.

I'd lost my humanity and not by choice. I'd been on my deathbed, thanks to my uncle Patrick. When I woke up, I was a crazed vampire. I'd been furious with my sister and father for turning me. But if they hadn't, I wouldn't be alive. But none of that mattered because we didn't have a way to turn Layla.

I clenched my teeth. "I will die without her." I was 100 percent certain my heart would stop if she didn't make it through this.

Tripp's phone rang as sirens blared and began wailing every two seconds, signifying we had a threat.

Motherfucker.

Tripp yanked his phone out of the side pocket of his cargo pants. "What?" he snapped as he answered.

I jogged to the end of the building and scanned the area. The road to my left led to military housing. The road directly ahead wound around for about a half mile to the main gate. But all was quiet.

I ran to the front entrance, where Petty Officer Dawson was standing guard outside the lobby doors. I glanced up toward the roof. Two more sentries, one at each corner of the building, searched the compound.

Less than two minutes since I'd left Tripp's side, a military Jeep careened around the corner and skidded to a halt.

"Sam, get in," Tripp ordered through the open passenger window.

I hopped in. "What's going on?"

He slammed the gas pedal, and the Jeep jerked forward. "Someone drove through the south gate. Petty Officer Allan said the driver seems drunk and disoriented and looks like a woman, but he couldn't tell for sure. He thinks someone was chasing her. We're checking the security cameras."

The south gate was locked and chained and only used by military personnel and for deliveries. When Layla and I left and returned from Maine, I had to use the south gate to bypass the media crowd at the main entrance. Since the hospital incident months ago when Roman and his men had kidnapped Layla, I'd had my fangs on display for a parking lot packed with humans. Not intentionally, but I couldn't react fast enough to tuck them away. Videos and pictures were taken. Not only of me but of my SEAL brother Hawk and a few of Roman's men. Yet somehow I'd become the celebrity vampire. Nevertheless, someone had leaked my whereabouts. Now news stations, paranormal junkies, and curious humans camped out along the road leading into our main entrance.

Cocking my head, I leaned into the passenger-side window as Tripp sped around a curve. "As in, barreled down the electric gate?"

Actually, sections of our perimeter had electrified fencing, and those areas that didn't were barricaded by fifteen-foot stone walls, except for the shoreline. But we had that protected with underwater nets and traps to prevent any enemy from reaching the shore.

"Seems so." Tripp sped through the dark tree-lined road that wound around behind military housing.

The handheld radio crackled before a gruff voice came through. "Command center, this is Charlie four. Come in."

"Go, Charlie four," Petty Officer Hawk responded.

"Need reinforcements," Petty Officer Allan returned.

"There's a team heading your way," Hawk said.

I braced my hand on the dashboard. "You said it was a woman. I wonder if it's Rianne." The crazy Aberdeen sister had the female balls to storm a military installation. "If it is, I will kill her. Well, I will if she's alive."

During the showdown at Intech, I'd driven a dagger into Rianne's stomach, not once but twice. Then I'd flung her across Intech's property. She'd landed against the building hard. Sadly, the bitch had still been breathing when Layla and I had managed to flee —unless Rianne had bled out later. I could only hope.

Tripp's jaw was rock solid. "If she's the perp, you might have to fight me to see who kills her." His hatred for Rianne was coming through loud and clear.

Rianne was seriously fucked in the head. She was salivating to give up her humanity for the sole purpose of besting me. She believed the only way to kill me was to be like me. Well, that wasn't fucking happening. Engineering an exact replica of Sam Mason would never come to fruition. Not in my lifetime. Or at least I hoped not.

2

SAM

Silence followed us as the headlights bounced, lighting up the darkened road. Tripp was well over the base speed limit of twenty-five miles per hour, navigating the winding curves like an expert NASCAR driver.

Luckily it was four in the morning, so most base personnel and their families were asleep. We weren't in danger of running anyone over, though I'd seen people jogging in the early-morning hours along this stretch of the dense tree-lined road. Hell, I even ran this route on occasion during my workouts.

I rolled down the window and sharpened my senses. The July humidity swept in along with the salt air from Mt. Hope Bay. Beneath the sound of the Jeep's engine was the increasing rumble of another car's motor.

"Pull over," I said.

Tripp's knuckles were white as he gripped the steering wheel. "Why?"

"Our target is approaching, and there's only one way to stop her."

"I know how to stop her," he snapped as he drove into the other lane.

My eyebrows knitted. "A head-on collision? Fuck no. If the intruder is a reporter, we'll have bigger problems on our hands. Or the woman could be drunk and innocent, or someone is chasing her."

He sighed through a growl. "When did you grow a conscience?" He wheeled back into his lane, taking his foot off the gas, then pumped the brakes before pulling off the road.

"And when did you become me?" I retorted.

His nostrils flared. "I really want Rianne to be in that car."

I chuckled. "I'm with you on that, dude."

Our target's engine grew louder, so we both climbed out.

I found a spot in the lane of the oncoming vehicle. "I'll wave her down. But if she doesn't stop, I'll use my elemental powers to short-circuit the engine. That should slow her down enough to roll to a stop. Afterward, I'll erase the driver's memory just in case she sees me using my powers." Unless Rianne was behind the wheel. Then I wanted her to remember me ripping out her throat.

I waved my arms in a crisscross fashion as the car swerved at a high speed. This was definitely our intruder, who either couldn't drive, was asleep, or was drunk.

"She's not stopping or slowing," Tripp said.

Motherfucker.

I quickly stretched out my arms as lightning flashed in the distance. *Perfect.* Just the type of weather to fuel my powers. Though I still had enough juice in me from the lightning storm in West Virginia the night I'd rescued Layla.

I bowed my head, keeping my eyes on the target. "Come a little closer," I said, not that she could hear me.

Once the driver was twenty feet ahead of me, I pushed out my right arm, pointing my hand at the car as I discharged the electrical energy much like I had when I'd zapped Noah inside Intech's building. Once again, the car zigzagged, and the beam of blue light hit the right headlight.

Fuck.

"Sam," Tripp warned.

I inhaled before releasing a loud roar, then stomped once, feeling the earth's energy fill me. As the car drew even closer, I whipped my arms from back to front and unleashed every ounce of power I had.

Streams of blue light landed on the hood of the car before lifting it off the ground.

The earth shook. The wind howled, and the trees on both sides of me swayed.

As I started to ease up on my elemental energy, movement to my left followed by a branch snapping broke my concentration. The tires touched the ground, and the driver lost control, heading off the road in front of Tripp and the Jeep.

Well, that didn't go as planned.

A husky dude holding a camera came into full view as fury held my powers steady. I was tired of fucking with reporters who had phones or video cameras glued to them as if it was another limb on their bodies. The fear in the man's wide brown eyes infused my hunger with such intensity he would be lucky if he left here alive.

I sprinted up to him as he backtracked with the camera shaking in his hands. My gums throbbed as my fangs slid out, slow and deadly. I didn't care that he'd seen me in my true form because his camera was about to be disintegrated.

Please run. I do love a good chase. And my bloodthirst is growing stronger by the second.

He sucked in air, sweat soaking his T-shirt as he kept walking backward. "Don't hurt me."

His stench grew stronger as I drew closer. He had to have snuck in after our intruder drove through the gate. Or maybe he'd been the one chasing our driver. If that were true, then where was his car?

I snarled at him.

The whites of his eyes glowed in the darkness. "You're a vampire. So you really do exist."

"This is my Halloween costume that I wear year-round." My tone dripped with sarcasm. After I was done with him, he wouldn't remember a fucking thing he'd seen or anything I'd said.

The sound of metal crunching competed with the peal of thunder.

The husky dude flinched before he ran but didn't get far before he tripped over a branch and fell. "My camera. Where did it go?" He crawled on his hands and knees, searching the ground and dense brush around him.

The area was shadowed by my tall form that was backlit by the Jeep's headlights.

I grabbed his neck from behind and lifted him as if I was picking up a dog by the scruff.

He struggled against my hold. "Don't hurt me." Sheets of fear slid off him as he squealed. "I don't want to be a vampire."

I laughed, setting him on his feet. I wasn't about to go into detail about our genetic makeup and how we were born, not made. "You could never be a vampire." Well, that wasn't entirely true. He could become a monster if he was injected with Carly's SS2, as she'd dubbed her serum. Still, he wouldn't be a true vampire like me. "And you're not leaving here with your camera. Actually, you're not leaving until we call the civilian police. You know, it's a crime to trespass on government property."

A vehicle behind me screeched to a halt. I didn't have to look to know our guards were on the scene.

I gripped the chubby dude's arm, retracting my fangs. "What's your name?" I all but dragged him with me as Webb hopped out of the military Hummer, looking pissed off as hell.

"Vince," he said as he came with me willingly.

"Well, Vince, you won't remember anything after you leave here."

Webb's gaze landed on Vince, and his blue eyes shuttered to black as he banked his vampire side.

Petty Officer Hawk exited the Hummer on the driver's side, taking in the scene. "Commander London, sir. There's the other trespasser."

Webb and I followed Hawk's line of sight.

Petty Officer Byron Lynch, who was assigned to the master-at-arms command, or military police on base, escorted a female from the wooded area across the road. Byron was a tall and broad vampire, wearing blue fatigues and a reflective armband with the letters MP on it. "She was videotaping." He held up her phone. "She and her partner sped through behind our intruder. They hid their vehicle off the road about a half klick back."

The petite brunette stuck out her chest, oozing courage and a bravado that dared us to fuck with her. Her cocksure attitude kind of reminded me of Layla. She'd had that same attitude when we'd first met at the nightclub. But like Layla, this woman wasn't fooling me. Fear was one of the hardest emotions to conceal. I could taste it, smell it, and I bathed in her fear. Not to mention, her pulse was skyrocketing as she shuffled closer to Vince and me.

"Vince, did you get any of that on tape?" she asked him with smugness etched on her pale face.

"It doesn't matter, Letty." He fired the words over his shoulder like a rapid round of gunfire. "They'll destroy my equipment."

I shoved Vince. "You're right. The content on the camera is now the property of the US government."

Hawk ran up and grabbed hold of Vince.

Petty Officer Lynch handed Letty's phone to Webb. "I'll take them to a holding room. We have a team en route to help Petty Officer Allan barricade the entrance until we can fix the gate," he said to Webb.

Letty protested. "We have rights. If we disappear, my news station knows we're here."

Chuckling, I rolled my eyes, wanting to explain that we weren't the type of vampires who murdered innocent humans. Though she wasn't innocent. She and Vince had committed a crime but not one that was punishable by death.

I was about to tell Webb I would erase their memories once we were done questioning them when Tripp shouted, "Sam! Get over here."

Webb whipped his head in Tripp's direction, as did I.

The white Ford Taurus was scrunched against a tree with steam oozing out from the engine.

"I'll be there in a minute," Webb said before he addressed Hawk and Lynch.

I darted over to Tripp as he tossed me a flashlight he'd been holding. "Take a look inside."

"Do I want to?" I glanced in at a passed-out woman with a gash on her forehead. "What the fuck?"

3

LAYLA

I was spiraling down a long metal tube with darkness all around me until a tiny ray of light trickled through it. My stomach pitched and rolled, making me feel like I was free-falling out of an airplane.

"You need to go back, Layla," a familiar female voice said.

I lost the ability to breathe. "Mom?"

I could barely see anything, and I had no control and was unable to stop myself from falling.

"Yes, it's me," she said. "Please go back. You can't be here."

I laughed out of nerves, swinging out my arms to latch onto anything to help put the brakes on. But all I felt was air. The farther I fell, the brighter the light became, spraying yellow and orange hues at me like laser beams.

"Mom, are you still there? How do I stop myself?"

"Believe in living. Fight like the warrior I know you to be, Layla."

"Am I dead?" Please say no. I couldn't die. I had children to raise. I had a husband to love and cherish. I had so many things I wanted to do with Sam and our kids.

"You will be if you don't fight," Mom said, her voice shaky.

I was tired of fighting. I wasn't one to give up, but everyone had a breaking point.

15

"It's not your time, Layla," she said, loud and harsh, reminding me of the times as a little girl when she would reprimand me for disobeying her.

Fear overpowered my senses, and I couldn't think straight or fast enough. But the closer I got to the beautiful light, the stronger the feeling of weightlessness and euphoria enveloped me. Suddenly, I didn't want to go back. I was beginning to feel free—free of pain, free of enemies, free of darkness.

"Layla, please," my mom begged.

"I'm sorry," I replied. "The light is too strong." When the last word left my mouth, a meadow of wildflowers materialized.

Then, as if some imaginary being was guiding me, I floated to the ground before my bare feet sank into the soft, damp earth. I blinked several times, taking in a deep breath and the scene before me. A myriad of sweet, flowery scents floated in the air. Fluffy clouds dotted the deep blue sky, and a boarded-up farmhouse sat at the base of the mountain range in the distance. It took me a beat to realize that I was standing on my home turf in Montana. The farmhouse was the same one my sisters and I had grown up in. The barn next to it was where we'd kept our horses.

Instantly, memories of happier days accosted me. Mom teaching Jordyn, Rianne, and me how to ride a horse. My sisters and I watching Dad in his woodworking shop as he made the rocking chairs that Mom and Dad loved to spend time in on the porch in the evenings.

"Layla." Mom's soft voice drew me out of my reverie.

I spun around and gasped. My mother stood before me, looking more beautiful than I remembered. Her dark wavy hair fell to her shoulders, touching the yellow fabric of her sundress. Her cheeks were rosy. Her brown eyes swam with love, and an ethereal glow surrounded her.

"Sam needs you, Layla."

I froze. "You know Sam?" That shouldn't have been my first question. Then again, I didn't even know where to begin. I had so many things to ask her. Still, given vampire blood ran through her family, it wouldn't surprise me if she'd at least have heard of the Masons.

She smiled as if proud of my choice in men. "Of course not. But I've been watching over you. Plus, when I was alive, I had visions of him and you."

I stiffened even more. "As in, you had magical abilities?" Holy shit. I'd had visions too.

She closed the distance between us and grasped my hands. The moment she did, a warm feeling traveled up my arms and spread throughout my chest. "If you want to call visions magical, then yes."

I knitted my eyebrows. "So you knew I would fall in love with a vampire?"

"Not until a few months before I passed away. As I was approaching death, I began to have the same recurring dreams. At first, it was you meeting Sam at the nightclub. But each night, a little more of the dream played out until he was telling you he loved you. I didn't want to believe it. I'd worked hard since my teenage years to make sure no one knew about my supernatural past, and truthfully, I despised bloodsuckers. After I witnessed a group of vampires killing three humans one night on my way home from a school dance, I chose to do everything in my power to make sure a human didn't have to suffer at the hands of those creatures again."

"So you married a vampire hunter," I stated.

"I didn't seek your father out, if that's what you're implying. I believe fate drew us together."

"But why wait until you were on your deathbed to tell Dad about your heritage? I mean, I understand why you kept it from him. The Aberdeens would've murdered you. I don't believe Dad would've, though. Still, why tell Dad at all? Maybe Dad wouldn't be dead if you hadn't told him. His brothers believe a vampire named Kendra killed him."

She flattened a hand on my cheek. "I told him because I was afraid for you. I wanted him to make sure you and Sam never met. But your father didn't believe me. He thought I was hallucinating from the drugs. Also, Kendra didn't kill your father."

"Then who? If you know, tell me, so I can seek justice."

She was glancing around as if she was about to tell me a secret when dark clouds rolled in. "You must return to Sam and your babies, Layla. They need you. The world needs you."

I could feel my eyebrows drawing down. "The world?" What the fuck did that mean?

"You and Sam are instrumental in making sure humanity survives."

Confusion snaked through me. "You mean it's up to him and me to stop the genetic engineering?"

She tilted her head slightly, frowning. "Yes, and…" Again, her gaze darted in all directions. "One of your children is prophesied to change the course of humankind, which will have a ripple effect that upsets the balance of the world."

A shiver racked my body as I listed to one side. "Come again?" I'd heard her, but I had to make sure because my brain was having a hard time processing what she'd just said.

She quickly looked at the sky. "I've told you all I can. You must go. The door between the living and the dead is about to close."

Oh, fuck no. "Mom," I bit out. "You can't leave me hanging like this. I need to know which of my children you speak of."

She pulled me in for a hug and whispered, "Find Kendra." Then she released me. "I love you. Now, close your eyes and envision your beautiful babies and Sam."

Hell no! I couldn't leave. I needed to know more. Not only that, but what did Kendra have to do with anything? My mind was a jumbled pile of puzzle pieces.

Before I could open my mouth to fire off questions, she pressed a hand to my heart.

Instantly, a jolt of electricity zapped me as she faded. "You're strong and resilient, Layla," she said, her voice growing softer and softer.

Suddenly, the sky darkened even more, the flowers wilted, and the farmhouse vanished. Then a jarring pain clutched my chest, making it hard to breathe. I sucked in air, tears stinging my eyes. Once again, I began spiraling as if I were inside a tornado funnel.

Only, I was now heading into complete darkness. Whatever was about to happen, I prayed like hell she was wrong about the prophecy.

4

SAM

Squatting down, I reached into the mangled Ford Taurus and slapped Carly Aberdeen—or at least the monster who resembled her—a few times.

"That is Carly Aberdeen, right?"

I felt Tripp's shock as if it were my own.

"Yep." I studied her intently, examining her fingers, lifting her lips, then her eyelids like I was a doctor. All signs screamed that she had taken her own crazy juice. Her cheekbones and forehead jutted outward. Her nails were sharp and long, curling toward her fingertips. Her brown eyes were a deep red just like Noah Aberdeen's, and the only things missing were fangs.

"What the fuck is she doing here?" Tripp asked.

Million-dollar question. If she was here for our help, we had none—no magic potion to reverse the DNA, or at least not that I knew of. Though wouldn't that be a screwed-up twist on genetics? Especially if vampires like me could become human again. Not that I would want to. I was cool with who I was and what I was.

"And why did she drink her own serum?" I asked, knowing neither Tripp nor I had the answer yet.

Though I doubted she had done so willingly. Carly had experimented on voluntary participants—those dying from incurable diseases and who had signed a contract.

I tapped her face again, but she wasn't moving even though her heart was beating. I pushed to my feet. "I wouldn't put it past Rianne to have done this to Carly." Rianne Aberdeen and Carly despised each other. "This was probably Rianne's way of punishing her cousin-in-law for helping us rescue Layla." I briefly closed my eyes, pleading with fate that my wife would be okay. She had to be.

Standing behind the driver's side door, Tripp scratched his chin. "I feel like we've traveled back in time. This is the Edmund Rain shit all over again." Aggravation wove through his tone. "We'll bandage her up then throw her in a cell for now."

Thunder boomed before a flash of lightning lit up the darkened area. Mother Nature was about to unleash her wrath as the wind kicked up dead leaves and rustled trees.

Webb came over, frustration steeped in his blue eyes. "Motherfucker. This shit has to stop. Who's in the car?"

"Carly Aberdeen." I moved out of the way so he could take a look.

Webb's fangs lowered as his eyes shifted to black. "You're kidding." One glance at her, and he jerked backward. "For fuck's sake. When are people going to learn that turning humans into a perfect replica of us isn't going to work?"

"Probably never," I muttered, standing next to Tripp.

Now that humans were warming up to the idea that vampires could exist, we would be battling humanity's thirst for immortality for eons to come. If my old man couldn't quell the media—then we were royally fucked. Anarchy would sweep across the planet in record time.

Webb's lips thinned. "I'll add one more problem to the mix. The reporter Letty sent the video she'd taken of Sam to her boss at the news station before Lynch nabbed her."

He pinned me with a glare. "I have Sawyer working on trying to hack into the news station servers to delete it."

I briefly closed my eyes as several swear words fired off like a rocket launcher in my head. I would like to hope he was kidding, but Webb never joked about anything.

My old man would have ten cows over this one. But he might be the least of my worries.

Motherfucker!

I was racking up infractions of our vampire laws by showing humans we existed. If the Council of Elders didn't want my head on a platter before now, they would if that video leaked out.

My old man had been able to talk the elders, his colleagues, off the ledge when it came to Hawk and me. It also helped that I was off the hook for killing a cop at the hospital the day Roman had kidnapped Layla. A bystander had caught the cop's murder on video. The culprit was none other than Scarface. The same asshole who'd been chasing Layla that day and had also killed my SEAL team brother Lane. But Scarface was dead thanks to Victor Costner. After Roman's men had stormed Victor's estate, Victor sliced off Scarface's head.

Still, a major reason humans were running in fear or curious to confirm if vampires were real was that the cop's murder had gone viral, showing how Scarface ripped out the police officer's jugular. If we continued to show the public who we were and what we were capable of, then pandemonium would sweep across the world.

Tripp came to my rescue. "It's not Sam's fault. It was the only way to stop Carly. She was speeding and swerving."

Webb held up his hand. "I'm not blaming anyone. But with the media in our faces, we have to be extremely cautious with our powers and our actions even on base. Clear?"

Tripp and I said in unison, "Crystal."

"By the way, has my dad returned from Montana?" I couldn't remember when he was due home. He'd left last week to meet with Jack Aberdeen.

Jack had decided to join us to take down his niece and mother. Sadly, he couldn't help his son Noah, and I doubted he could convince his mother, Harriet Aberdeen, to find a quiet place to die. The evil grandmother had joined Adam Emery's team to help build supernatural soldiers to hunt vampires. She had a twisted idea that it was the best way to rid the planet of my kind. But the main reason she'd trekked back to the United States from her home in Fiji was her health. She had an incurable blood cancer. She thought that by genetically altering her DNA, she could rid herself of her disease.

Webb looked at his watch. "He called me when you rushed Layla to the infirmary a couple of hours ago. He should be landing at the city airport as we speak. And you should know that Jack, Victor, and your father were able to come to a deal with Claude Irving. So he won't be a problem for Jack."

Not long after I'd been kidnapped by Intech at the abandoned airport outside of Chicago, Jack had taken his family into hiding. His mother, Harriet, had been one reason, but the deadlier one was Claude Irving.

Claude owned a chain of casinos, including one in Montana that Ray Aberdeen had frequented when was alive. Ray had a gambling addiction that had caused the Aberdeens to shut down their vampire hunting business about two years back. Good for my kind. Bad for Ray since he'd racked up one mondo bill at Claude's casino. Once Claude got wind that Ray was dead, he'd paid Jack a visit—or rather, sent his goons to collect on Ray's debt.

"Will Irving be a problem for us?" Tripp asked.

"Doubtful," Webb said. "Steven compelled Claude to forget Jack and Ray Aberdeen. So Jack's family should be safe."

"Speaking of Aberdeens, are we bringing Noah back here?" I asked.

Noah had been captured by our team in West Virginia in April. I thought he would've died by now since he was feral, but he was still kicking, although he was losing his mind. I wasn't surprised. My uncle Patrick's first test subject, Blake Turner, had suffered the same fate. We should put Noah down, but we hadn't because Doc wanted to run tests on him whenever we brought Noah in.

Webb had opened his mouth to speak when movement from inside the car had us jerking our attention to Carly.

She moaned as she brought her hand to the gash on her forehead.

Tripp and I exchanged a what-the-fuck look.

Webb, who was standing next to the back seat door, raised an eyebrow as he peeked at Carly. "She lost her monstrous features. And the gash on her head is closing up. That's odd."

Engineered humans other than Matthew Costner didn't return to human form, and they didn't heal either. But Matthew was a product of my uncle Patrick's experiments. His concoction had been whipped up with Jo's DNA and mine.

On the other hand, I would guess Carly's genetic-altering solution was a mixture of my DNA and Dane Gray's, the alpha shifter. I hated to think her serum might work on pure humans who had no supernatural blood in their lineage.

Nevertheless, Carly had some similarities to my SEAL brother Ben Jackson, who was half human and half vampire. Ben didn't have fangs, his eyes changed to red, and he had the ability to heal, although not from a wolf bite. Still, Ben didn't grow talons nor did his facial features change. Doc would be fascinated when he learned of Carly. He was constantly trying to figure out Ben's DNA makeup since Ben had no vampires in his family—at least that he knew of.

Carly pushed the airbag in as she moved to climb out of the car, and then she squinted at me. "Sam, is that you?" Her eye color had returned to its normal brown.

Stepping toward her, I raised my hand. "I suggest you stay put. You've been in an accident."

Hawk jogged halfway toward us, his green eyes lanterns in the dark. "Commander London, sir. We have two problems. We have the civilian police at the south gate, and there's a man at the main gate, asking to see the person in charge. He says the reporter and the cameraman we have in custody work for him. He's demanding we let them go."

Webb growled. "I'll be right there." Then he addressed us. "Tripp, we need to do a sweep of the immediate area surrounding the base. If Carly is here, others from her camp might be as well. We need to deal with her. We'll meet later." He hurried to join Hawk.

Carly rubbed her temple, wincing. "Those cops at the gate are probably here for me."

"Did you steal this car?" Tripp asked.

She gave him a nod. "I did. I would've called, except… It's a long story. I promise, I came alone. No one from Intech knows where I am."

I crossed my arms over my chest. "Why are you *here*?" I got the vibe that she was telling the truth. "What is your boss, Adam, up to?"

"I'll tell you everything. But first I need to see my husband."

Tripp and I swapped a knowing look.

Normally, I was that asshole who got his rocks off by hurting the enemy, but I liked Carly. Sure, I'd wanted to kill her many times over, but she'd grown on me, and she had the moral fortitude not to experiment on Layla. None of that meant she was off the hook though.

"What is it?" she asked, her pulse racing. "Is Junior okay?"

My phone rang, and my heartbeat kicked into overdrive. More so when I plucked my cell from my jean pocket and saw my sister's name on the screen. Then a big-ass boulder dropped into the pit of my stomach.

"Sis, please tell me you have great news about Layla," I rushed out as I answered.

"I need you in here now, Sam." Jo sounded exhausted, worried, and sad.

I pressed my knuckles into my chest as if I could stop my heart from ramming against my ribs. "Is Layla alive? Tell me, Jo."

Tripp's eyes widened.

Carly jerked away.

Jo sniffled. "We managed to stabilize her. Just get here, and I'll explain." Then she hung up.

I let out a small amount of air. "Layla's stable," I said to Tripp.

"Go." He waved me off. "I'll handle Carly."

I sprinted for my fucking life—or rather, Layla's. She was not dying on me. I didn't give two fucks if I had to hunt down every witch on this planet for a spell. I would find a way to bring my huntress back.

5

———————

SAM

Barely five minutes later, I was pushing through the double doors into the new wing of the infirmary, sweating my ass off as my heart clawed out of my chest.

Jo stood in the hallway with panic swimming in her silver eyes. "Hurry, please. I need to take your blood."

"Doesn't Doc have a supply?" Normally, he made sure he didn't run out. Then again, Layla had been downing my blood like water as the babies grew.

"We don't have any left." She dashed into the scrub room with me on her heels.

"Talk to me, sis."

Snagging nitrile gloves off the counter by the double sinks, she said, "When you brought Layla into the infirmary, her heart rate had been dropping. Her human body couldn't handle carrying the babies anymore. She coded while we were waiting for Dr. Martin."

Jo made quick work of drawing my blood. "We were able to revive Layla long enough for her to deliver your three daughters. But we had problems with your son. The umbilical cord was

26

wrapped around his neck. The longer it took us to deliver him, the worse Layla got, and she flatlined once again."

She switched out a filled vial for an empty one.

I swayed to one side, my heart beating erratically. "Are they okay? On the phone, you said Layla was stable."

"They're breathing, but their vitals aren't improving. Layla's body has been through the wringer. She might need time and fluids. As for your son, we think he needs your blood. After all, the babies needed it while they were growing in the womb. So it makes sense they would after they were born."

Air punched from my lungs as I almost collapsed in relief on the floor. "Maybe my blood would help Layla too."

She finished filling the second vial. "Possibly. I know this has been rough, brother. But on a good note, you have three beautiful baby girls, and they're doing fine."

Elation wrapped around me like a warm blanket on a snowy winter day, easing some of my panic. I couldn't celebrate quite yet. Not until Doc gave Layla and our son a clean bill of health.

"Three girls and a boy," I mumbled, more to ground myself in reality. "Layla dreamt we would have at least a boy and a girl."

Dr. Martin had struck out on identifying the sex because of the way they were positioned inside Layla. Regardless, I had three daughters and a son. Knowing Layla and I were having quadruplets was one thing. But now I was truly a father. Me. Sam Mason. I'd never thought I would have kids. Hell, I never saw myself getting married. Yet I had a gorgeous auburn-haired goddess as my bride and four newborns. Fate had gotten something right.

Someone knocked on the window over the double sinks to my right.

Jo looked to her left.

Doc's tired brown eyes met my green ones. "I need that blood stat, Jo. The boy's vitals are dropping." Fear was stamped on his face, causing my pulse to skyrocket as Doc disappeared from view.

Jo collected the two vials and darted into the OR.

I found a spot in front of the sink, intent on getting a glimpse of Layla or my son and daughters, when a nurse said, "We're losing him again."

Alarmed, Doc added, "Layla's heart rate is spiraling downward."

My vision blurred, my pulse pounding in my ears like the little drummer boy on speed. I clutched onto the stainless steel sink as my insides churned and the walls closed in. The sound of metal crunching did nothing to zap the shock running through my veins. I couldn't move, couldn't think, couldn't even breathe. The scrub room spun, and a sense of death clung to my exposed skin, sinking deep into my pores before spreading out like fissures in the earth, scorching a path straight to my heart.

I couldn't track the flurry of activity through the window. I blinked several times to clear the haziness, and on my last blink, I zeroed in on Doc holding the paddles of the crash cart over Layla.

I gasped, fisting a hand to my mouth as bile shot to my throat.

Layla's dead. Dead. My wife isn't breathing. Where is my son?

The lights flickered on and off as misery bled from my soul. My elemental powers were on the precipice of destroying everything around me.

I bolted out into the hallway, stumbling in the process, then bent over and gulped in air. I pounded on my chest, then rubbed as hard as I could to curb the piercing pain that was sucking the life out of me.

Outside air. Blood. I needed both of those to quench the fire and the suffocating feeling burning my lungs.

I ran down the hall like a drunken sailor, pushed through the doors into the lab of the old part of the infirmary, and plowed into my father.

His green eyes were brimming with sadness. "Tripp filled me in. I'm here for you, son."

I threw myself at him like a boy running scared. I'd never needed my father like I did in that moment. I berated myself as I cried. I was Sam Mason, strong and powerful, and hardly anything screwed with my head. The word weak wasn't in my vocabulary. Sure, I had flaws. Flying scared the fuck out of me. But I still got on a plane. Yet there I was, afraid and seeking solace from my dad, which I'd never done in my life. I mean, I'd never cried in his arms.

My father didn't stand for weak individuals. As a military man in charge of the Vampire Navy SEALs, he whipped weaklings into shape. Those that didn't fit the mold, he would send packing. However, this wasn't about my stamina as a soldier but as a husband and father. If anyone understood how it felt to lose someone, it was him. After all, he'd lost his wife and my mother.

"My wife and son are dying again," I choked out as my soul ripped into a million fucking pieces.

He rubbed my back. "Samuel, you need to calm down." He gently eased away, held on to the sides of my arms, and gave me a tender but somewhat stern look as we stood eye to eye.

He never called me Samuel, except when he wanted to make a point or was angry with me. He wasn't mad, but his tone was firm, which belied the emotional pain washing over him.

His Adam's apple bobbed. "You know, Dr. Vieira will not let Layla or your son die," he said, as sure as my pulse throbbed in my ears. Then he went over to the fridge and snagged a bottle of blood.

I wiped the tears off my face and anchored my body against one of two lab benches.

He returned and handed me an open bottle. "Drink. You're white as a ghost."

I chugged the processed blood like a thirsty fool on a hot summer day, staring at my father. He looked like I felt—drained and weary. Dark circles colored the area beneath his green eyes, he had a day-old beard, and his black hair was damp but so was the blue buttoned-up shirt he was wearing, which meant it was raining. Nevertheless, I got the feeling he'd had a hell of a time with Jack Aberdeen.

I was about to ask how his Montana trip had gone when Jo

glided through the double doors from the new wing, wiping sweat off her forehead. As an empath, I could feel others' emotions, but I was striking out. My guess was my panic was blocking my otherworldly ability.

Her chest lifted and deflated on a sigh. "Your blood did the trick for your son. What's weird is, as soon as his vitals improved, so did Layla's."

I set the empty bottle on the bench beside me. "Thank fuck," I muttered, expelling the oppressive feeling caught in my chest.

My dad cleared his throat. "Are Layla and the boy connected?" His tone was more inquisitive than surprised.

That would be strange but not out of the realm of possibility in the world of magic.

Jo went over to our father. "Hey, Dad." She kissed him on the cheek. "It's probably just a coincidence. Dr. Vieira had been using the crash cart at the same time I was giving Sam's blood to his son."

Coincidence or not, all that mattered was they were alive.

My father's phone rang, and he excused himself, swearing under his breath as he stalked down the aisle between the lab benches, fishing his phone from his pants pocket. I never wanted to be in his shoes. Dealing with politics and trying to keep our existence a secret was more than enough to drain the energy out of a vampire.

"I want to see my family," I said to Jo.

She massaged her shoulder. "You will. But not right now. Dr. Vieira and Dr. Martin will be running tests. The nurses are cleaning up Layla and the babies. Doc is also whipping up a batch of his healing potion with Abbey's blood and shifter blood for Layla. That should help her recover quicker. Look, Sam—take some time to relax. I'll call you when you can see them. And if anything goes awry, I'll definitely hunt you down." Her confident tone was helping to loosen my muscles.

I especially liked the fact that Doc was giving Layla his healing potion. I wanted my huntress upright, breathing, and chasing my ass around a beach somewhere with our kids playing in the sand. Or her and me rolling around in bed, tangled together, fucking like bunnies. Or just sitting by a fire while I held her in my arms.

I hugged my sister. "Thank you, sis." I also had to thank everyone in the OR.

She squeezed me before shrugging out of my hold, tears clouding her silver eyes. "No need, brother. It's our job. I have to get back in there." She tapped her chest twice. A signal we'd used since we were kids to let the other know we had each other's backs and loved one another. Then she started to leave.

"Jo Mason London, you're going to be an amazing doctor."

She was close to finishing her studies in genetics and hematology. She'd always been curious and inquisitive about how things worked and ticked in this world. But she was fascinated with vampire genetics, and after the Edmund Rain and Patrick Mason era of genetic engineering, Jo had made it her mission to learn how humans differed from us. She would definitely be excited to study Carly.

She gave me a warm smile.

"Oh, and Jo—Carly Aberdeen is here and not human anymore. You and Doc might want to do some testing when you have a chance after we interrogate her." Which I had time to do now since I couldn't see Layla.

Her face lit up like a little girl's on Christmas morning who had opened the biggest present under the tree. "Are you serious?"

"Maybe you can read her mind too," I said.

"I'll try, but I couldn't read Fred Emery's. I don't know if Carly developed a blocking serum like Alia's or if those at Intech learned how to keep someone like me out of their heads." She stabbed a thumb at the doors leading to the new wing. "Layla and my nieces and nephew come first."

"Damn straight," I said. They would always come first.

Once she was gone, I slumped my shoulders, feeling numb from head to toe. It was five in the morning, and at least three hours had passed since Layla collapsed in the apartment. I swore she had because of her sister. If Jordyn hadn't been trying to skirt past a prison guard, Layla might not have died. I shivered, knowing my wife had actually died—not once, not twice, but three fucking times.

It felt as though I'd lived a thousand years in that time, without any sleep. But I didn't have time to rest. I was itching to find out why Carly was here, and I wanted to be sure I erased Vince and Letty's memories of what they'd seen earlier. Plus, I was antsy to talk to Jordyn and ream her ass.

I turned on my heel to find my old man pacing at the other end of the lab with his phone glued to his ear.

Tension crawled up the wide aisle between the lab benches from him to me. He was furious about something he was hearing from his caller, and I would bet I was the topic of that conversation as well as the video Letty had taken of me using my elemental powers.

The hackles on my neck rose, and I zeroed in on his conversation when he yelled, "No fucking way."

I might as well take my licks now. I marched in his direction like a soldier going to war. The closer I got to him, the more his anger scorched the fuck out of me. It seemed my empath ability had returned.

Nevertheless, I licked my dry lips, prepared to explain what had happened, when he lowered his phone and said, "We're fucked."

I held up my hands. "I'm sorry, Pops. The only way to stop Carly was to use my powers."

He angled his head. "What are you talking about?"

"I guess I should ask you the same thing."

"That was Webb on the phone," he said. "Our tech team learned that Adam Emery called a press conference outside his companies in Chicago to announce a new project. The fucker is about to go live shortly."

I didn't have to speculate on what this new project entailed. I would bet my vamp ass it had something to do with a brain-to-machine interface or BMI device that could control a person. I would like to say the technology didn't work, but I knew firsthand that it did. I'd almost killed my wife, gone temporarily blind, and lost my acute vamp hearing for a stint, and all because of that fucking chip.

Thank fuck we had Peter Landon in our court. The scientist had originally developed the chip for the handicapped community until Adam hired Peter under false pretenses. Still, Peter had been successful in removing the device from my skull.

"You think this new project of his is, what? Super soldiers with chips in their heads?"

Adam was salivating to build an army of super soldiers. In fact, he wanted me to lead the charge.

"Possibly," he said. "But I have a bad feeling it's more than that."

My blood gelled as a conversation my father had had with Jack Aberdeen months ago brightened in my memory like spotlights on a black-as-sin night.

"Seems you have a ton of shit to handle with the media as well," Jack said to my dad.

My father's response was, "One of the reasons the war will be here faster than you think. Intech will use the media to its advantage."

I'd gotten pissed at my dad for that comment he'd made in front of Layla. She'd taken my dad's statement to mean that Intech would use my notoriety with the public to Intech's advantage, going as far as to put a contract out on my head.

"As in, you think he'll put a contract on my head?" I asked.

"Maybe," he replied through clenched teeth. "Whatever it is, I have a feeling there's no coming back from this one."

If Adam was about to use the media to his advantage related in some way to super soldiers and genetic engineering, then my dad was right. We were fucked.

6

SAM

On the way to the war room, I filled my father in on what had happened earlier with Carly, the cameraman, and the reporter.

Surprisingly, he didn't yell or respond in any way, except to swear a ton. I was sure my feet would be held to the fire once he wasn't so focused on Adam Emery's news conference. Or maybe he was treating me with kid gloves given what I'd been through with Layla and my son. Though my father wasn't the type to dance around anyone or anything.

"I'll be there in a second," I said as he opened the door to the war room. "I need to text Jo." I hadn't had a chance since we bolted out of the infirmary so quickly. I wanted to make sure she knew I was close by in case she needed me.

After a quick stiff nod, he went inside.

In addition to a war brewing, a storm was coming that had my father's name written all over it. He was as powerful as I was or more so, and I pitied anyone who got in his way. His patience had grown in the five years since the war with Edmund Rain. My father had been more reserved, professional, and levelheaded, and made damn sure he'd done things by the rule of the Council of Elders. Sure, he was an elder, and even when he hadn't been, he'd always abided by our laws and certainly held the SEALs accountable. My gut was telling me my old man was about to take matters into his own hands and ditch the council rule.

I believed the entire SEAL team was ready to follow suit. Those of us who had fought Edmund Rain weren't jumping on a train to travel down those tracks again. The genetic engineering bullshit was yesterday's news. But as SEALs and soldiers, fighting was our job. We had to protect mankind. Humans played an important role in the evolution of every species. Like them, vampires were born not made. We arose from a species of organisms that developed through the natural selection process—just like humans, or animals, for that matter. All living things had a purpose in the evolutionary process. My father believed our kind was born to keep the peace so humans could thrive, reproduce, and survive. In turn, our kind would too.

The door groaned open, yanking me out of my thoughts.

Tripp came out. "Dude, everything okay? Your father said Layla and the babies were fine."

I gave him a quick nod. "They're on the road to recovery." I prayed they were. Otherwise, I wouldn't be able to function. I needed my wits about me to hear what Adam Emery had to say. Whatever came out of his mouth wouldn't be good. That much I was certain of.

I tapped out a quick message to my sister: *Let me know as soon as I can see my family, please. I'm in the war room with Pops. Something big is going down.*

No sooner than I pocketed my phone, Tripp was giving me a bro hug. "Everything is going to work out with them. I can feel it."

"Thanks, man. I seriously don't know what I would do without you." Or without any of my SEAL brothers, who were also family.

"I'll always have your back," he said as we went inside.

Webb, my father, and Sawyer were standing in front of the

movie screen with their shoulders hunched as the air crackled with tension in the theater-style room.

"This blows," Tripp said, climbing down the steps alongside me. "We should be drinking beer and smoking cigars, but instead, this fucker had to overshadow such a celebratory occasion."

I believed in karma and had every confidence that dickwad Adam's kingdom would fall.

"Where is Carly? Did she talk? Any sign of her counterparts hiding in the shadows?" Her presence raised many questions. One in particular—Carly was Adam's star scientist. So who did Adam have at the helm of genetic engineering?

"She's in a cell," he said. "I told her that her husband, Junior, is dead. She didn't take it well. We'll question her when we have time. Right now, the master-at-arms command is handling the civilian police, but we have to deal with the reporters."

"Just say the word, and I'll erase their memories," I offered.

"Webb doesn't want you to do that. It would raise red flags," he said.

I guessed it didn't exactly matter. Trying to erase memories would be like trying to hit a Whac-A-Mole.

The commercial ended, and the lead-in music to the cable news network announced that it was showtime. As Tripp and I approached Sawyer, Webb, and my dad, an aerial view of Chicago's cityscape flashed on-screen.

My gut twisted in anticipation and not in a good way. My father had every right to be fuming and worried. The problems were stacking up higher than the Himalayas. The media was in our faces. Vampire Matthew Costner and shifters Ross Gray and Tucker Whyte were missing. Plus, Roman Brown, Adam Emery, and Harriet Aberdeen had been quiet for the last three months, which meant they were scheming and regrouping.

Sawyer, who was perpendicular to Webb's left shoulder, bobbed his head at me with a grin. "Congrats, Sam."

I bypassed my father and stood on Webb's left between him and Sawyer. "Thanks," I said to Sawyer.

Webb gave me a quick hug, and he also congratulated me. "Sorry we're not celebrating, but we will."

I hadn't had a chance to fill my brother-in-law in on Layla and what had been going on. Tripp probably had though. I was just stoked that my family was alive. Still, I would be lying if I said I wasn't fucking pissed that such a momentous occasion was eclipsed by the shit flying at us.

An anchorman adjusted his moss-green tie as he looked directly into the camera. "Good morning, folks. I'm Dick Hurtz, and I'll be with you for the next hour, sharing all the top headlines. But first, we have breaking news. In just a few minutes, we'll be hearing from owner and CEO Adam Emery of Camden Industries and Intech Corporation. Our sources tell us Adam will be announcing a new endeavor that will impact every American in this country."

My father swore. "I don't like this one fucking bit."

The tension in the room escalated at breakneck speed.

Dick continued. "Both Camden Industries and Intech Corporation are well-known entities among the military community. Both companies employ approximately one hundred thousand people in total worldwide and are principally engaged in the research, design, development, and integration of advanced technologies in weapons and computer systems for the Department of Defense." Dick pressed on his ear. "We're going live to our lead correspondent, Timothy Cox, who is outside Camden's headquarters. Tim, what's the mood on the ground there?"

Tim pierced the camera with his brown gaze as he stood midway on the steps leading up to a podium in front of a set of glass doors and flags flying high on the flagpoles flanking the entrance. "Well, Dick, there are rumors that Adam will speak about the folklore surrounding vampires. We tried to contact those close to Adam to gain a better sense of what to expect from his speech but weren't successful. As you know from interviews we've conducted, as well as those of our colleagues and competitors, humans are chomping at the bit to know if vampires are truth or fiction."

"So, Tim," Dick said. "What do you think humans will do if truth wins out over fiction?"

Webb growled. "Fucking chaos."

Behind Tim, six men dressed in SWAT gear emerged, loaded with weapons on their hips and around their legs. Each of them scanned the area before one of them waved at the glass doors.

Tim's voice faded as the camera panned in on Adam Emery strutting up to the podium with an arrogant attitude, as if he'd already won the war.

I silently laughed as the fuckwad swept his brown gaze from right to left. He hadn't won a fucking thing.

"You think his security team are vampires?" Sawyer asked.

It was hard to tell, since we weren't there, but the answer might be a resounding yes when none other than asshole Roman Brown sauntered out of the building and sidled up to Adam.

The head of one of the largest blood cartels smiled, looking smugger than Adam. But Roman's cocksureness fit his personality. He had a love for flair and shiny new cars, and he devoured attention like a hungry bear. He also loved to fuck with people's minds, and staying true to his fashion sense, he was wearing a black pinstriped three-piece suit. Probably the same one he'd worn to the fight when he'd stormed our compound in early February. Little did the blond-haired and blue-eyed vampire know that he would have little time left on this planet when he and I finally met in battle.

Anger weaved a knot in my stomach as my fangs lowered. I would give anything for the magical ability to teleport. Because if I could, my hands would be around Roman's neck in a flash.

Adam adjusted the microphone, placed his hands on the podium, and rolled back his shoulders. "Thank you all for coming out at such an early hour. As you know, Camden Industries and Intech Corporation have a long-standing relationship with our US government, helping and serving the needs of our military to combat our enemies."

The camera angle swept over the reporters. Some were holding out their phones, others had a pen and notepad in their hands, while others held microphones.

Adam stood up taller. "I'm proud to announce that Intech Corporation is branching out to develop a revolutionary prototype to combat a new enemy we have right here on our soil. And you know exactly what I'm talking about. You've been reporting on the topic for months."

"Vampires," a woman among the media shouted.

The camera zoomed in on Adam.

"That's right," Adam confirmed, with sweat dripping down his temples.

"The question you keep asking yourself is"—Adam eyed Roman, who in turn nodded—"are vampires real?" He picked up a glass of water from the podium and took a sip.

My father, who had stepped out from between Tripp and Webb, was pacing on the other side of Tripp. "This is fucking insane." His hands were fisted at his sides, his face tomato-red, and his nostrils were flaring.

That storm named Steven Mason was about to wipe out anyone in his path.

"*Are* they real?" a male reporter asked.

My father came to an abrupt halt and focused once again on the screen.

"Billion-dollar question," another person piped up.

The buzz of voices grew louder, the eagerness and excitement mingling among them.

Adam raised his hands in an attempt to quiet the crowd. "I can tell you firsthand that vampires are definitely among us. They've been coexisting in the shadows for centuries."

"Prove it," someone shouted.

"That's bullshit," another person yelled. "Those images we've seen on TV of Sam Mason are probably photoshopped."

I cringed at the mention of my name. I didn't need any more public attention.

Adam shook his head. "There is nothing fake about Sam Mason. In fact, he's the one each of you should be worried about. He's the most lethal of them all." He placed a hand on his chest as though he was about to say the Pledge of Allegiance. "As I stand before you today, Sam Mason and his team are holding my brother, Fred, in a dungeon on the naval base in Massachusetts. They've probably drained his blood." He looked into the camera like he was glaring daggers directly at me. "Sam Mason, if you're listening, I implore you to release my brother. He's done nothing wrong." He sounded like he was about to cry.

"Fuuuuuck!" I roared, grabbing my head as fury whipped around my throat and strangled me.

I would never be able to live freely anymore. Not that I could at the moment, but Adam had just stuck a nail in my coffin, sealing the fucking thing shut forever along with those of every other vampire on the planet.

My dad had been right when he told Jack Aberdeen that Adam would use the media to his advantage, and he was putting on a great show. He solidified his fake demeanor by plucking a handkerchief from the breast pocket of his suit jacket then wiped his eyes.

I opened and closed my fists, desperately in need of punching something, preferably the nose off Adam's ugly face.

A brunette reporter held out her microphone with her station's logo, CBC 4. "Mr. Emery, are you saying your brother was captured by vampires in our military for his blood?" Her voice had risen an octave.

The four of us were riveted to the screen. I couldn't speak for my counterparts, but I was anxious as hell to hear Adam's response.

Instead, Roman's mouth curled on one side as he leaned in toward the podium. "As Adam said a moment ago, vampires coexist among us, even in our military. Some higher echelons within the human government have known about them for eons."

"So, a secret group," the CBC 4 reporter said. "I heard they're Navy SEALs."

I would like to know who the culprit was broadcasting this factual information. "Do we have a mole?" I asked, even though Roman could've very well leaked that to the press.

"Shoot me if we do," Tripp piped in.

"Rumor also has it they protect humanity," the CBC 4 reporter said.

"Fuck me sideways," I belted out. "We need to look within our ranks. Roman wouldn't offer up that type of Goody Two-shoes information."

Swear words buzzed left and right, humming to a loud roar.

My father's face was bloodred. "The council will be up in arms, as will the Secretary of the Navy."

The secretary was one human within the DOD chain of command who knew about us. Though he and his undersecretary might not be able to shield us from their colleagues any longer.

Tim Cox angled his microphone at Roman and Adam. "So is this revolutionary prototype you mentioned the weapon to kill these vampires like Sam Mason?"

"Why do they have to keep saying my fucking name?" I asked no one.

Adam patted his forehead with his handkerchief. "I believe the only way to stop this type of enemy is to fight fire with fire." He glanced at Roman as if seeking his permission.

Maybe Adam wasn't king in this freak show.

The crowd of reporters began launching questions at Adam.

"Are you saying you're building a vampire?"

"Are you one of them?"

That brunette reporter from CBC 4 spoke up again. "I don't understand. If vampires like Sam protect humans, why would you want to kill the military vampires?"

I made a mental note to find out who she was. Maybe she could tell me who her informant was. Plus, she sounded as if she was digging the idea of what we did for humans.

The media was getting out of control, which was a prelude into how other humans would react. Chaos, for fucking sure.

Adam raised his hands. "Everyone, I'll answer as much as I can, but please, one person at a time." He swallowed, still sweating like a pig. "As I said earlier, Sam is evil, but there are many others like him roaming the planet. They're predators. High up on the food chain. Would you want to sit next to one in a restaurant? Or have your child go to school with one?"

The asswipe was controlling the narrative quite well, instilling fear in the minds of whoever was watching and listening.

An idea occurred to me but was quickly squashed when two people came into view behind Adam.

Two lingering questions were answered. Rianne Aberdeen and Matthew Costner were alive. Holy fuck! Both were dressed in black suits and white shirts as if their attire was the uniform of the day. Rianne had a shaved head like she was in military boot camp, and Matthew appeared to be happy, as if he was proud to be part of the team.

The five of us swapped what-the-fuck looks with wide eyes and open mouths.

"Are they your prototypes?" Tim Cox asked.

From my vantage point, I was having a difficult time grasping that Alia Costner's son had been kidnapped by Roman Brown. Matthew smiled at the camera as his blue eyes sparkled.

I checked on the others next to me just to be sure they were breathing.

Sawyer was frozen solid. Tripp's bronze eyes were wide as he glued his gaze to the screen. The muscle in Webb's jaw was like a jumping bean on steroids. As for my old man— well, his fury was rattling that table in front of us.

As for me, I was numb. Every limb on me was locked tight.

"This isn't happening." Webb shook his head hard, strands of his brown hair coming loose from his low ponytail.

"I wonder if Rianne was injected with Carly's SS2 serum?" I asked.

"Maybe we're about to find out," Sawyer murmured.

I had to sit down, so I dropped into one of the seats in the front row.

Sawyer joined me. "There's no coming back from this."

We'd hidden our existence from the world ever since our species evolved long ago. Sure, we had humans who knew about us, worked with us, kept our secret—and for very good reasons. Chaos being the top one. History was about to be made but not in our favor. From this day forward, the landscape of the world would change and become dark and dystopian. Humans would run and hide. Others would form massive armies of hunters. And still others, the curious ones, would want to study us or even want to become vampires.

My dad was an ice sculpture, his shoulders hunched to his ears.

Tripp and Webb sat down on my right.

The media went silent.

"Before we demonstrate," Adam said. "I want you to know that you're safe. It's also important to note that this young man and woman signed up for this program of their own free will. We haven't forced them in any way, and we can prove that with the contracts they've signed." Adam whispered to Rianne and Matthew before Matthew traded places with Adam.

I had to give Adam props for having the balls to use the media as a weapon against us. Or maybe I should be giving Roman the credit. After all, he had a twisted mind and loved to fuck with people's heads. The criminal vampire was an intelligent adversary. He held several degrees in the fields of chemistry, law, and business. He'd even worked for a pharmaceutical company that made one of the raw ingredients in some drug used in operating rooms.

"I would bet Roman's calling the shots," I said. Adam had

looked to Roman a couple of times for either encouragement or approval. "Roman told me he had his own plan brewing. This is it." I would bet my vamp ass I was right.

My dad crossed his arms over his chest. "Doesn't matter who's running this horror show. I can't fix this. The council can't either. And I doubt the Secretary of the Navy can. If anything, the secretary might wash his hands of us."

"And I will be blamed," I muttered. I was reaching for straws, but I wouldn't put it past the ancient elders to somehow blame me or use me as a scapegoat. As an elder himself, my old man would never let that happen, but if he was voted down, I was screwed.

Webb leaned close to Tripp. "Once this is over, pull out our emergency plan. We'll need to start with the families on base. Let's get them moved to a safe location. Also, call the team in from West Virginia. There's no point in monitoring activity at that facility. We need all hands on deck here."

We had a disaster preparedness guide ready in the event something like this happened. We'd been fortunate that we had never had to flip that switch.

"Before we push the emergency plan button," my dad said. "I need to talk to the council. But start getting things in place. And definitely bring our men and women in from West Virginia. Also, engage Viking II, and we'll need the help of the Special Forces."

"Sir, we need to alert the supernatural community," Tripp said. "It's not just vampires in this war anymore."

"For sure," Sawyer said. "My mom knows a few witch covens."

Webb sighed. "First and foremost, we deal with our own on this base. Their safety is our priority. I'm sure news like this will spread like wildfire, which means supernaturals will find out before we have the chance to talk to them."

I'd been listening to the conversation around me while watching the screen. Matthew had been ready to speak until Roman pulled him aside and the two began talking privately. My gut had a sudden queasy feeling that Matthew was of sound mind and knew Roman too well.

After Matthew nodded at Roman, he went up to the podium once again. "My name is Matthew, and what you've heard so far is true. Vampires have coexisted among humans for centuries. But what you don't know is, those vampires were born with a recessive gene, which means pure humans can't turn into one of them by drinking their blood. What you read in books and see on TV shows is folklore. I know firsthand because my ancestors were vampires."

"I can't tell if Matthew is trying to help us by reducing mass hysteria or if he's helping Roman and Adam in some way," Tripp said.

"Doesn't matter. It's still not going to stop anarchy," my father added.

"Matthew, are you a vampire?" Tim Cox asked.

"I am, but I wasn't born with the recessive gene. I was made in a lab," Matthew replied. "But I'm considered a success because I have the right DNA markers to become inhuman."

No lie there.

"Is anyone getting the feeling Matthew is there of his own free will?" Webb asked.

"He doesn't seem robotic or under duress like he has a chip in his head," I said.

When I had a chip attached to my brain, I'd been a monster programmed to kill, and not of sound mind. But maybe if Matthew had that BMI device in his skull, it was programmed for him to say whatever Adam and Roman wanted him to say.

Matthew squared his shoulders as his fangs elongated, his blue eyes swirling to black.

Screams and squeals blared through the speakers as reporters scurried down the steps and away from Matthew, with the exception of Tim Cox and the brunette from CBC 4. Both looked shocked and awed but didn't seem afraid.

I dug my elbows into my knees, watching a horror movie—or

what seemed like one. Even more so when Rianne traded places with Matthew.

She waved her hands. "Folks, no need to be afraid. He's not going to hurt you. If you don't believe anything you've heard or seen so far, I would like to drive a point home."

The murmurs from the fearful crowd died down as I gritted my teeth.

Rianne glanced into the camera as a tear slid down her cheek.

I rolled my eyes. "This should be one for the books."

"Adam mentioned that the military vampires are holding his brother. Well, they've also taken my sisters." She sniffled. "That's why I've signed up. I want to fight them. I want to save my sisters."

"Oh my fucking God," I shouted.

"Who are you?" Tim Cox asked. "And are you like Matthew?"

"My name is Rianne Aberdeen. My family has hunted vampires for centuries. I know how to kill them, but as a human, I don't stand a chance against someone as powerful as Sam Mason. That's why I'm a willing participant. And no, I've not made the change yet. But I will. I have to. My older sister, Layla, has been compelled by Sam Mason to fall in love with him. She's even pregnant by him. My grandmother is distraught over this. Layla, if you're listening, please come home. Granny needs you. *I* need you." She dashed a tear away.

I flew off the chair, roaring as I lunged for the table and threw the fucking thing across the room.

Webb, Tripp, and Sawyer surrounded me.

"I hope what you've heard and seen demonstrated today helps you understand the need for a like-minded enemy," Adam said. "To build prototypes like Matthew, we're looking for those humans who have any type of supernatural ancestors in their lineage. If you fall into that category and want to make a difference in protecting humanity, call the number on the bottom of your screen. We're giving each individual one hundred thousand dollars as a signing bonus."

I pushed through my comrades. The need to kill Rianne Aberdeen burned through my veins hotter than ever before. "I need to see my wife and kids."

If I thought my father would blow the roof off the building, I was wrong. I would be the one to cause mass destruction.

7

SAM

A baby's cry, a balm to my frayed nerves, echoed in the hallway as I passed the scrub room on my way to the birthing suites.

No sooner than I'd bolted out of the war room, Jo had texted me that Layla and my kids were doing well.

Thank fuck.

Best news ever.

I blew out what felt like a mountain of air, trying to shake the nerves, the rage, the need to destroy something. My family didn't need to see me angry. This was supposed to be a special day and not one darkened by the likes of Roman Brown, Adam Emery, Rianne Aberdeen, and Matthew Costner. Although I was pushing Matthew to the side for now. I found it hard to believe he would side with the enemy. He'd hated when my uncle Patrick changed him into a vampire. Roman had to have put the fear of God into Matthew. That was the only plausible reason I could latch on to.

The baby crying zapped my concentration. I came to an abrupt halt outside the entrance to the birthing suites, shoved my fingers through my hair, gave myself a pep talk, plastered on a smile, and stalked in.

A medicinal odor washed over me as I oriented my vision. I'd only seen this part of the new wing once before Layla had given birth. Doc had been excited to show off the apartment-style rooms for mothers-to-be and the nursery.

The hallway was wide and long with doors closed along the right and left with the exception of one, which I would guess was either Layla's room or the nursery. As I headed in that direction, butterflies took flight inside my stomach. I was about to meet my son and daughters. I'd been thinking about this moment since I'd found out Layla was pregnant. The curiosity was killing me. Who would they look like? What type of powers would they have? Were they vampires or witches or both?

The baby's cry grew louder, and I picked up my pace, feeling as though one of my kids was calling to me, almost as if his or her cry was saying, "Hurry, Dad. I want to meet you too." Weird and odd. But shouldn't be. My kids were inhuman.

Halfway down the hallway, Layla's siren voice tickled my eardrums, and goose bumps covered my body.

"Shhh. Here you go, little guy," she cooed.

Pure happiness flooded my veins, and as I broke out into a fast-paced walk, the baby stopped crying.

Doc waltzed out of the open door of the room, wearing a goofy smile. "I thought I heard footsteps."

His grin was a far cry from the panic he'd had earlier. *Halle-fuck-ing-lujah.*

Still, I had to ask, "Everyone is fine?"

He tucked his hands into his lab coat pockets. "Surprisingly so. The healing blood I gave Layla worked wonders. She bounced right back within the hour. Your son too. Your blood did the trick for him."

I wrapped Doc into a bear hug. "You're fucking awesome, Doc." The man's intelligence and medical knowledge were remarkable.

I couldn't count how many times he'd saved the lives of Webb,

Jo, and the SEALs, including me. If it weren't for him, I might not be alive. A long story for another day.

"Can't breathe, Sam," he squeaked out.

I let go of him. "Sorry. I can't thank you enough. I know it's your job, but you and Dr. Martin, Jo, and the nurses deserve medals of honor." I didn't see any of the medical staff or hear them nearby either. "Where is Dr. Martin, by the way?"

"He's in my office, making some calls and following up on his other patients at the local hospital."

"Sam?" Layla called, excitement in her tone.

Doc tipped his brown head of hair at Layla's room. "Go meet your son and daughters, though the girls are sleeping."

As I stepped inside, I felt as though I'd walked out of hell and into heaven. Instantly, a magical aura blanketed the room. Four tiny hearts beat loud and strong, their blood zipping through their veins. My gaze rounded on my wife, who was sitting up in bed, beautiful, glowing, and like her children, her heart banged as though it was calling me home. I *was* home. I seriously felt like I'd died and gone to heaven. The evil world outside this room was a microcosm, and nothing belonged in here except happiness and fucking joy.

Layla's electric-blue eyes glistened beneath the soft glow from the lights above. "What are you waiting for? Cat got your tongue? Legs not working? He's stunning, vampire. He has your green eyes, black hair, and is a miniature Sam." She blinked away a tear and then another before she returned her loving gaze to our son cradled in her arms, sucking on her finger. "Your papa is here," she uttered. "He can't wait to meet you."

Tears shot free, sliding down my face like a rushing waterfall. The last several hours had been hairy, maddening, death-defying, and downright soul splitting. But now my heart was overflowing with so much love that I was feeling high and weak in the knees.

Doc came up beside me. "It's going to be a nice change to have newborns around here," he said. "They will balance out the tension we're all under."

If he'd heard Adam's speech to the nation or Rianne's fake message or even Matthew's monologue, he might change his tune. Or the fact that we might be going underground could be the thing to change it. If we couldn't keep humans from amassing an army of their own and coming through the gates, then we would either shoot to kill or run. I didn't see Doc leaving his lab or newly constructed medical wing. The vampire doctor would go down with his ship. But I wasn't about to burst his bubble.

He nudged me with his elbow. "Don't be shy."

I was far from shy. I was just taking it all in, feeling the magic tingling along my arms, absorbing Layla's happiness as it seeped into my pores, and imprinting the image of her holding our son into my memory so I could replay it again and again.

"Your daughters are sleeping, Papa," she said. "And each of the babies weighs about four pounds each, give or take a few ounces."

My gaze landed on the four bassinets along one side of her bed.

"We're not sure what our daughters are yet, but this little guy is a vampire," she cooed.

I assumed so since he was sucking on her finger. But I asked just the same. "Are you giving him your blood?"

"She is," Doc said in a rush of zeal, zest coloring his tone.

"We tried formula," Layla added. "But he wanted nothing of it so far. We'll need to mix your blood or mine with his formula."

"We'll need to make sure the portion is mostly Sam's," Doc responded. "It's essential that a young vampire feeds on his father's blood. I'll go into more detail about that later. I'll also run a full DNA workup on them. For now, I'll leave you two alone." He patted me on the back before he left.

When the door clicked shut, I snapped out of my drunken bubble and crossed the mini apartment-style room. Doc had thought of everything in designing the birthing suite. In addition to the standard hospital equipment and furniture, there were rocking gliders, a small kitchenette with an under-counter fridge, a TV, a bathroom, and other amenities scattered about. Doc had also made sure the new dad had a pullout couch to bunk on.

"Can you wash your hands before you hold any of them?" Layla asked.

I ducked into the bathroom directly to my left. I needed to splash water on my face to rid myself of the hours of sweat, anyway. Once inside, I made quick work of cleaning up. I didn't dwell on the horror that I saw in the mirror—dark circles beneath my dull green eyes or my day-old beard that made me look like an ogre. I snarled at myself. I would probably scare my kids. But I couldn't worry about that right now. I dampened my hair, then tied it back into a low ponytail at my nape with a leather strap I had on my wrist. I finished with a thorough scrubbing of my hands. Now I was decent and clean enough to hold my kids.

I strutted out as the steady *bang, bang, bang* of my heart kept time with each step I took.

She beamed at me. "You're tired, vampire. I can see it in your eyes."

I sidled up to her bedside. "I don't matter. You do." I bent over, captured her face in my hands, and ghosted my lips over hers. "I want to devour you, hold you, and never let you go. You scared the living crap out of me." A tear fell from me and landed on her nose. "I love you so freaking much, Layla. I don't know what I would've done if I'd lost you."

"You can't get rid of me, vampire," she teased, seemingly trying not to burst into tears herself.

"Never plan to, baby doll." I straightened, laying eyes on my boy, and my knees buckled—black hair, green eyes, and staring up at his mom as though she was his everything.

"Do you want to hold him?" she asked.

"Fuck yeah." I wasn't ignoring my daughters, but they were asleep. I could see them on the other side of the bed and hear their tiny hearts beating.

She removed her finger from our son's mouth.

Immediately, he started crying again.

She gently handed him to me, and the moment he was in my arms, a wave of energy whooshed over me, and suddenly I could feel the magic stringing us together, a thick rope bonding father and son. No doubt he was inhuman.

I couldn't thread words together to describe the bevy of emotions coursing through me except that my mind, body, and soul overflowed with a deep sense of love so strong, it brought tears to my eyes. I loved Layla to no end, but the way I felt for my son was a different kind of love. I was beginning to understand something my old man had told me over the years. *Jo and you are my life. I would die if anything happened to you two.*

I completely understood him now. I would literally burn, gut, carve, scratch, rip, shred, and slice and dice anyone who dared try to hurt my children. That was a fact, and I wouldn't care who they were or who they were related to.

My fangs clicked into place, and I punctured the tip of my finger before inserting it into his mouth. He latched on, sucking like he was starving.

He stared at me with his shamrock-colored eyes as if he were peering directly into my soul.

As he suckled, I was mesmerized. "I don't think you look like a Liam."

"I agree," Layla said. "Your mom believed in the mysticism and symbolism of the stars and planets. So, what do you think of the names Apollo or Orion? Those were both on our list. I vote for Orion."

I tucked my fangs away. "Mm. Orion is the brightest and most popular constellation in the night sky, and it also means the hunter. It kind of fits him since it's who we are."

She toyed with her necklace that was holding her ruby engagement ring. "My husband the astronomer. And I didn't know that Orion meant hunter. But I'm glad we're in agreement. Orion Mason it is, then."

The name definitely had a nice ring to it. "What do you think, Orion?" I asked him as his eyelids became heavy.

Removing my finger from his mouth, I turned around and sat in the glider next to the bed and rocked.

"You're a natural with him, Sam," she said, sounding content. "How did I get so lucky?"

"I'm the one who is lucky, baby doll. Fate got it right with us again."

Layla glanced at our daughters. "For sure. I can't believe they came out of me. But fate better not fuck with them."

The press conference returned with a vengeance, clouding my mind. Layla would freak out when I told her about her sister Rianne.

I closed my eyes, swearing left and right in my head. The whole fucking world now knew we had a child but not quadruplets. Layla had never told Rianne she was having more than one. Regardless of the number, we would be hunted, more so than I'd ever thought. I had to do everything in my power to shield my children from the evil about to rain down, even if that meant giving my life to make it happen.

More importantly, the quicker Layla was on her feet, the faster she could train. The road ahead was about to become darker than I'd ever seen it.

8

LAYLA

For the first time in ages, I felt pure, sheer happiness. I couldn't remember the last time I'd felt this content. In the four years since my mom died of breast cancer, life had been one roller-coaster ride after another. My dad had been murdered, supposedly by a vampire. I'd met Sam, and then whoa. What a journey of epic proportions—physical, emotional, magical, and supernatural.

I also learned that my mom had vampires and witches in her family. I'd found out I carried the unique blood type to get impregnated by a vampire. My grandmother had turned evil. My crazy sister Rianne had joined her along with my cousin Noah. Sam had been kidnapped. I'd been taken as well. I'd gotten married in a handfasting ceremony. Then to add the cherry on top, I'd given birth to four tiny inhuman babies.

As much turmoil as Sam and I had been through, the journey up to this point had been worth it. Sam and I had made four precious and beautiful creatures. Fate had gotten it right, and for the moment, I wanted to bask in the love floating around the room and not dwell on whether one of my children had the ability to upset the balance of mankind.

My daughters were sound asleep, swaddled in pink wraps and beanies. One girl had black hair like her brother. The other two had red to reddish-brown hair. I had yet to hold them, but I didn't want to disturb them. Truth be told, I'd only come out of surgery just over an hour ago. The fact that I was sitting up and ready to start the new chapter in my life was amazing, thanks to the magical elixir Dr. Vieira had given me. My healing process would be cut down by more than half.

Hallelujah. That meant I could get back into fighting shape sooner rather than later. I would need more energy than ever before to keep up with four littles and, of course, my hot-as-sin vampire husband—a chiseled beauty whose rough exterior was softened by his adorable son.

Sam bonding with his tiny look-alike was a moment to behold. Sam's long lashes had swept downward as he fixated on Orion, a tear cascading down his face, with a loving grin that had my heart soaring and my stomach fluttering. I wished I had my phone to capture the heartwarming picture of father and son.

I couldn't imagine what my husband had gone through. Doc and Jo had filled me in on what had happened during my delivery. I'd cried when I heard Orion had a rough start, then I was shocked to learn I died three times. Magic and miracles did happen, and I was grateful for the incredible medical team but also for the supernatural world I was now part of.

I was also relieved that I hadn't suffered the same fate as Emily Crawford. She was the only human before me who had been pregnant with inhuman babies. Doc had been worried I would follow the same path, and I had but with some differences. She gave birth to twins not quadruplets, and while I'd died during childbirth, I'd returned to the living. As far as we knew, Emily *was* dead, at least according to her medical record, although pages were missing. But just like her pregnancy, our babies grew faster in the womb and were born at five and a half months instead of nine.

Since I didn't have my phone, I mentally imprinted the tender and loving scene into my psyche as I clutched on to my ruby engagement ring that was hanging from my necklace. It was a habit I'd developed from the moment Sam had clasped the chain around my neck. At first, I'd been afraid I might lose the gemstone, but as time passed, I clung to it whenever I was nervous or deep in thought.

The longer I stared at my babies, the more happy tears began to flow. I was so in love with Sam and now our new family. I wanted to steal them away and not subject them to the world, at least not until we could find peace. If my mom was right about the prophecy or my grandmother continued her quest or if my crazy sister Rianne was still alive— and the list went on—then living a blissful existence was a pipe dream.

But for the moment, in this room, among our babies, the prophecy and everything else could go fuck itself. I wanted to cherish every second I could before life walked through the door. I wanted to absorb the love peppering the air, swallow it, feel it, and bottle it up.

I gazed at my daughters, and joy bloomed like a bed of wildflowers on a warm summer day. I swung my legs over the bed on the side closest to the bassinets.

"What are you doing?" Sam asked in a gruff voice. "You need rest."

I eyed him over my shoulder. "I need to hold my girls."

Sam rose from the rocker. "I'll bring them to you. Get back in bed." His tone permitted no argument.

I snarled. "I'm perfectly fine." I dug my palms into the mattress and pushed myself up, and dizziness washed over me. Well, shit. I guess it wasn't a good idea to pop out of bed, so I sat back down. "Okay, you're right."

Mentally, I was ready to work out, kick some ass, and fend for myself, something I hadn't done in months. Physically, I couldn't do any of those things yet, and that pissed me off.

Easy, girl. The magical elixir is working, but Doc said you won't heal instantly like a vampire.

Sam set Orion in the empty bassinet farthest from me. Then he came over, helped me back into bed, and kissed me on the head.

I flattened my hand on his unshaven face. "I never thought I would say this, but immortality would be nice right about now. That way I would heal as fast as you do and also spend eternity with you and the kids."

As if I'd triggered a demonic memory, he flinched, his brow creasing.

Then it dawned on stupid me. "I don't mean genetic engineering." I would bet his mind had gone down that road. "I want to live by your side forever. But I would never take the serum."

I shuddered at the memory of when Rianne had hooked me up to an IV bag filled with the crazy juice. Luckily the stars had aligned that horrific day in Intech's lab when I'd woken up and ripped the needle from my hand. I'd learned later on that not enough of the serum had gone into me to turn me into a monster.

Sam's broad shoulders slumped, losing that ten-ton weight he'd been carrying since he'd walked into the room.

Suddenly, one of the girls started crying.

He whisked a hand over his black hair, then picked up our daughter closest to us.

The minute she was in his arms, she quieted as if her daddy was the baby whisperer.

Instantly, the color returned to his ashen and tired face as his dimples emerged, his lopsided grin awakening the butterflies in my stomach. "What shall we name you?"

Goose bumps sprinted along my arms as warmth bloomed in my chest. "We have Luna, Bianca, Elara, Phoebe, Danica, and Aurora on the list." The names had various meanings but mostly aligned with the stars and planets, which was important to Sam.

I'd never been interested in any of the sciences or had given much credence to what a name meant. Growing up, I was more interested in how to hunt and kill vampires than the constellations. Nevertheless, I loved the names we'd come up with, especially Luna.

He rocked his upper torso. "You have your momma's blue eyes. And do I see some reddish strands poking out of the pink beanie? How about Bianca or Elara?"

"Isn't Elara the moon around Jupiter?" We'd researched names, argued over some, tossed some out, and in the end, we had several we both liked. I was dead set on using the name Luna, but the girl in his arms didn't strike me as a Luna. To me, our daughter with black hair did. Maybe because her hair was the color of night, and Luna meant goddess of the moon. "Your middle name is Jupiter. Elara seems fitting, and we can call her Ellie for short or El."

"Then Elara it is," he said just as the other two girls woke up, crying.

Sam's eyes grew wide.

I broke out into a laugh. "This is only the beginning, vampire. Feeding time will be quite the task." As would changing diapers and everything else that came with raising quadruplets.

I'd decided not to breastfeed. Four mouths would be hard to juggle. Of course, it was doable, but I was concerned the supernatural aspect might bring on its own challenges. Fangs came to mind. I didn't mind Sam's fangs in my thighs or neck, but my nipples—not so much. Supernatural aspects aside, the easiest course to take was bottle-feeding.

"But we have Jordyn to help us," I added.

My sister agreed to be our nanny since she wasn't working on Sawyer's tech team. The SEALs had suspended her for sneaking off with our now-deceased cousin Junior. Jordyn had the notion that she could bargain with our nutty grandmother for my life. She'd convinced Junior to take her to Intech's facility in West Virginia, the place where I had been held against my will. Tragically, they'd gotten into a car accident that had taken Junior's life.

A chill crept down my spine as something occurred to me. "Is

Jordyn okay? I remembered she was trying to get into the prison before I blacked out."

He cringed slightly as he handed me Elara.

She became fussy the second she was in my arms. Maybe because I was wound tight, waiting for Sam to answer me. After all, my husband was an empath, and I had no doubt one of our children would have that special ability.

"Tell me, Sam. How is my sister?" My voice hitched. She hadn't been herself since she and Junior had gotten into a car accident.

He picked up our black-haired beauty and gazed down at her. But he wasn't beaming like he had with Elara, and a muscle jumped along his jaw. I doubted his ire had anything to do with his daughter and a lot to do with Jordyn. But whatever was plaguing Sam had to wait.

"They're hungry." I stabbed a thumb behind the bassinets at the bottles on the counter by the sink. "The nurses made up bottles of formula."

Sam collected two bottles and handed me one. The second we began feeding Elara and her sister, they quieted, but their other sister was bawling.

Taking care of four babies would be a challenge, but once I got them home, I'd planned out a schedule to feed them thirty minutes apart. Hopefully, the routine would work.

The door opened, and Jo glided in. Her black hair was damp and free about her shoulders. She'd changed out of her scrubs and into a blue blouse, black cotton slacks, cute silver flats, and a lab coat with her name stitched into the chest.

"I was just coming to check on you. Perfect timing," she said with pep in her step, eager to hold one of her nieces or her nephew.

Before I could track her movements, our third daughter was in her arms. "Auntie Jo is here. Let's get you a bottle."

Sam went over to the glider and dropped down into it, a sigh escaping him.

I giggled. "Are you ready for all this, vampire?"

Despite the exhaustion plaguing him, he said without hesitation, "One hundred fucking percent."

I fell in love with him all over again.

The minute our third daughter had a bottle in her mouth, silence reigned.

We certainly had a busy life ahead of us, but one day at a time.

Jo sat in the other rocker next to Sam. "Have you named them yet?"

I bobbed my head. "Only two so far. I'm holding Elara. And our son is Orion." I loved the name Luna, and Sam and I had agreed on that name. But we also wanted to see their faces before we made the final decision.

Sam removed his daughter's pink beanie. "Whoa! She has a head of black hair like Orion." He stared at his daughter, who was sucking down the contents of her bottle in his arms. "I don't think I've ever seen violet eyes on anyone except Jo when she's in vampire mode. But this precious girl has a medium shade of purple. That has to mean something, right?" He regarded his sister.

Jo shrugged, seemingly entranced by her niece. "Like with us, maybe it's a sign of power."

Ordinary vampires had black eyes when they turned into full-on scary bloodsuckers with fangs. But not Sam, Jo, and Steven. Jo's pretty silver eyes morphed to violet, and Sam and his dad had green orbs that swirled to a liquid silver when their beastly sides emerged. The implication of their eye color was strength and power, which included the ability to wield all four elements.

Or maybe my daughter was the one who was prophesied to change the course of humankind that would upset the balance of the world. My heart kick-started in the wrong direction as the hair on my arms stood at attention.

Sam's head shot up. "Baby doll, what's wrong? Your pulse just propelled into outer space."

"Nothing," I lied. I wasn't ready to articulate my conversation with my dead mother.

Then I remembered Jo could read minds. If she was listening to my thoughts or however she got into people's heads, she wasn't saying anything, which was odd. Normally, Jo was always quick to regurgitate whatever she read in someone's mind.

But right now, she was tracing her niece's temple. "This one has mahogany-colored eyes."

I sighed, relieved that Jo hadn't taken a hike through my thoughts. Eventually, I would tell Sam about my time with my dead mom, but we were deciding on names, and I wasn't ready to open up a can of worms. The minute I did, it would become real.

Sam's attention was still glued to me.

I gave him an award-winning smile to show him I was okay. "The remaining names on the list to choose from for those two"—I nodded at the girls in their arms—"are Luna, Bianca, Phoebe, Danica, and Aurora. Sam, I say we name her Luna." Jo could weigh in, but she had no skin in our naming game.

Sam beamed at the black-haired beauty in his arms. "She has a Roman goddess of the moon vibe."

"Exactly," I said. "Her violet eyes would light up the night sky. Just like the moon."

"Luna Mason. That has a ring to it too," he murmured.

I was relieved we had done our homework well before they were born. Otherwise, our children might not have names for a while.

"One more to go," I said.

Sam rose and got up close to our daughter who was in Jo's arms. "Maybe this one is a Bianca." The vampire was pushing for Bianca. Sure, we both liked the name, but I wasn't convinced.

"I would like to hold her," I said. "Better yet, I would like to sit in a rocker."

We shuffled babies around, and I had to laugh because it was only the beginning.

Jo now had Luna. I was in the rocker beside her with our nameless daughter, Ellie and Orion were in their bassinets, and Sam stood next to me.

As I fed my daughter, I stared into her mahogany-colored eyes. "There's nothing about her that says she's a Bianca, vampire."

Bianca was a celestial name and a pretty one. But I couldn't remember the meaning. It didn't matter. I wasn't agreeing to Bianca. That left Phoebe, Danica, or Aurora. "She reminds me of sunshine." I swore I could see fireballs in her eyes. "My choice is Aurora."

The last thing I wanted to do was argue, but he hadn't been fond of the name Aurora only because he felt it wasn't a strong name like Bianca or Danica.

He stared at Ms. Sunshine.

"What do you think, Jo?" I asked, not that she had a say, but like Sam and their mother, Jo was of the same belief that the celestial bodies exerted forces and exhibited personalities of a person.

She raised her hands. "I'm not getting in the middle of an argument."

Sam growled. "We're not arguing."

Jo laughed. "You're about to."

He snarled at his sister. "Stop reading my mind."

I pressed on. "Sam, Aurora is the goddess of dawn or sunrise. Look at her eyes. There's fire in them. And we can call her Rorie."

A long tense silence stretched between my husband and me.

Finally, he pushed out a sigh. "I like Rorie."

"Is that a yes?" I wholeheartedly agreed that naming our children was important and had to have meaning. But we both had to agree.

His dimples emerged. "Yes. The more I look at her, the more I can see her as Aurora."

"It's settled. Elara or Ellie, Orion, Luna, and Aurora or Rorie Mason," I said in a yawn. Ellie and Rorie were our redheads, and Luna and Orion had hair as dark as a starless night.

Sam patted my head. "You should rest. I'll help you back in bed."

"No. Not yet. I'm fine." I was enjoying my daughter, who was still sucking down formula. "You're the one who needs sleep, vampire. Jordyn can help me."

Jo rose, glancing at Sam as if they were speaking telepathically, then walked around the room, burping Luna like Jo had several kids under her belt.

"What have I missed?" I felt compelled to ask. Sam still hadn't answered me about whether Jordyn was okay. What could've happened in the middle of the night other than my sister wandering the compound to sneak into the prison to exact revenge on Fred Emery?

9

LAYLA

Sam sat in the rocker Jo had been in and clutched the back of his neck with both hands.

The fact that neither Sam nor Jo was answering my question was beginning to stir my ire. I wasn't pregnant with a weak heart anymore. The days of dancing around me, afraid I might croak, were over. If Sam had any plans to treat me with kid gloves, I would squeeze his nuts until he was doubled over in pain.

"Look, you two," I said in a scolding tone, "here's the skinny. Don't either of you dare keep anything from me. Especially about my sister. I can't tell you how maddening that is. I'm a big girl, and don't forget I grew up killing vampires. Not that I'm threatening anyone here." I was quick to add. "Just making a point that I can handle shit."

Sam chuckled, sitting back in the rocker. "We're not keeping things from you. And I don't plan to either. But you just came out of surgery, and I wanted to meet my children before I brought you up to speed on what has happened."

I suddenly felt like a bratty bitch. That wasn't who I was. "I'm sorry. When you speak to each other telepathically, it's unnerving. And months of coddling me drove me insane." Truth.

Jo regarded me from her spot near the bassinets. "No need to apologize, Layla. Your hormones are out of whack."

They had been for the last few months, and I was sure they would still be for a while. Doc's healing elixir took care of wounds, not hormones. And come to think of it, my mom had suffered from postpartum depression with my sisters and me.

Fun times ahead.

Jo gently set Luna in her bassinet, then kissed her niece. "I'll give you two some space. I'll be back to help with my nieces and nephew." Then she was out the door as if an explosion was about to happen.

"Jordyn. Is she okay?" I'd been rocking Rorie, and the motion was making me sleepy like it had my daughter.

Sam studied me. "Jordyn is in a prison cell."

I flinched hard as if he'd dropped a bomb. He had, in a way. "For real? Why? Please tell me she didn't kill anyone." I hadn't forgotten that she wanted to cut off Fred Emery's head.

His hard green gaze pinned me to the chair. "She pulled the fire alarm as I was rushing you up here."

I locked my jaw in retaliation—like that would hurt Sam. I couldn't react the way I wanted to with Rorie in my arms. "That isn't a crime." Or was it?

"Layla." His tone was abrasive. "Whether it is or not, I believe she was the cause of you passing out. And when alarms go off on base, we shut down the gates. That means people like Dr. Martin can't come in. Luckily, Tripp jumped into action, and Dr. Martin was able to get through but not in time before you died." His voice cracked on the last word. "What she did is unacceptable."

He came over to me, crouched down, and grasped my hand. Instantly, a bolt of electricity zipped up my arm, and I wasn't talking goose bumps and flutters and gooeyness from holding my husband's hand. Rather, it was a feeling of magic and mayhem and a connection that could probably fry everything in this room to a crisp.

His eyebrows slashed down. "Did you feel that?"

Mine shot upward. "I know you're upset, vampire." His anger always brought out his elemental powers. Or was it Rorie giving off magic?

"I am, but our connection is more than that. Are you still feeling the energy?"

I nodded. "But it's you, not me. Or is it our daughter?" It felt like a million electrical pulses throbbed along my arm.

He studied our conjoined hands, then glanced at Rorie. "It's not me. My powers only go one way. You're the one zapping me. Or maybe it is Rorie feeding you power."

"I could understand if she was. After all, the babies had given me my banshee scream and mind control abilities." I wondered if I would continue to have those magical powers.

Sam stood up, and the electrical charge vanished. "It's happened twice before. Once when I joined hands with you at Intech's loading dock in Chicago and again at Intech's lab when I rescued you. But then, you were pregnant."

"Why do I get the feeling you're worried about this?" It wasn't a big deal. I hoped I continued to have powers. If my mom was right and Sam and I were the ones to ensure humanity survived, then I would need a magical ability or two.

"You mistake my worry for curiosity. Is it your power or Rorie's?" He gave me a thigh-squeezing grin. "I hope it's you *and* her. I want each of you to have a way to protect yourself. Not that she can yet. And I can't help but wonder if you have any dormant magic in you that the pregnancy might have kick-started. After all, your Vel-negative blood type indicates you come from a line of witches."

I was digging that idea, which wasn't out of the realm of possibility. My mom had visions on her deathbed. Did that mean she had witch magic all along but never used it?

He resumed sitting in the rocker. "If in fact you are the one with power and it's not Rorie, then our connection will have the same impact as when Jo and I join hands. Our enemies won't know what hit them." His excitement was bleeding through his words and gleaming in his forest-green eyes.

I licked my lips. "What can you and Jo do together?" His enthusiasm was heightening my own.

"Remember when Roman stormed the base?"

"How could I forget," I said, conjuring up that snowy morning in early February. "You were mind-blowingly scary."

Jordyn had been wrapped in C4. Roman Brown had sliced off my uncle Ray's thumb, and I'd seen Sam in all his elemental glory. The earth had shaken like a strong earthquake, and the wind whipped around like a Category 3 hurricane. Then Sam raised his arms high above his head and unleashed his fury—an elemental storm unlike anything I'd ever seen, and Roman was smack-dab in the middle as he clutched his throat, laboring for oxygen, barricaded by a ring of fire. I'd learned afterward that Sam had gone easy on Roman.

"Then multiply my powers from that day by five. That's how powerful Jo and I are together," Sam said.

If my eyes weren't somewhere in the back of my head from the initial zap of electricity, they were now. "Surely, you're not saying you and I can have an impact like you and Jo?"

He shrugged. "Anything is possible."

Ever since I had started living in his world, that statement had never been truer. "Then we should practice to see if I have any magic in me."

"We have work to do. You need to physically train, including with weapons, and we'll test your magical abilities for sure. First, you need to heal." A frown marred his handsome features.

I made a move to stand up, and Sam was right in front of me, taking Rorie from me. After he set her in her bassinet, he returned to help me out of the chair.

"You know I can walk," I teased.

He wrapped me in his strong, protective arms and buried his nose in my hair. "Maybe I want to hold my wife."

I sighed as I inhaled his woodsy scent, craning my neck upward. "No complaints here. I love you, Sam. You're my safe anchor and will always be no matter the storm." I rose on my toes and ghosted my lips over his. Lips that promised heated nights of wicked sensuality and gentle, loving butterfly kisses dipped in love and devotion. A contrast for sure but one that Sam delivered in spades whenever we were naked between the sheets. Though it had been a long time since we had any nights of passion. "I'm ready for our new beginning."

He threaded his fingers through my hair as his green eyes sparked with concern. Not the reaction I was going for.

I flattened my hand on his chest. His heart was beating furiously, which only caused mine to do the same. "What's wrong? Did I miss something other than my sister's stunt?"

He studied me. "Rianne's alive."

Blood rushed through my veins as I gasped. We knew she could be, but I was retraumatized at the thought that she could be here. "Is she on base?"

He kept me securely in his embrace. Good thing. My legs were trembling. "She's not anywhere remotely close. Rianne just spoke at Adam's press conference outside Intech in Chicago. She told the nation that you've been compelled to fall in love with me and have my baby."

Sam's lips were moving, but I could barely hear what he was saying over the loud buzzing noise in my head. My brain froze. My heart stopped, and my blood solidified into gel. I took back what I said earlier—that I didn't want Sam or anyone to treat me with kid gloves. I was wrong. I wasn't ready to face my enemies—in particular, my deranged sister—at least not until I was in fighting shape.

"You're saying she spoke on national television? Like, she was pleading with the public?"

He blinked on a nod.

"I need to lie down." My fucking sister was a piece of work. I still couldn't figure out what had gone wrong with her. Her hatred for Sam was mind-boggling. Or was it her jealousy? Regardless, she'd just sealed our fates, especially if she had humans believing I was being held captive.

He helped me into bed, then adjusted my pillow.

"We'll be hunted, and not by Adam, my grandmother, or Roman, but by humans," I said.

He flattened his huge palm on my face. "I didn't want to tell you. But the press conference has changed the game and drastically. This is no longer a war with just Intech but the fucking universe."

Understatement of the millennium.

His phone beeped, and this was the one time I needed a distraction. Anything to not have to deal with my sick family. The more I thought about Rianne, the stronger the desire I had to end my sister once and for all. How freaking sad was that? I had as much hunger to kill Rianne as Jordyn had to murder Fred Emery.

He read the text. "Tripp needs my help at the prison building. I'll talk to him about releasing Jordyn."

My sister seemed like the least of our worries, though we needed her help now more than ever, and not just to help me take care of our children but to fight if need be. Above that, to protect my children.

"We need Jordyn, Sam, especially in light of what you just told me."

Sighing, he kissed my forehead. "Agreed. There's more to the press conference that you should know, but right now, I need to go."

His phone buzzed again.

Jo glided in, shock and awe written on her pretty face.

"You must've seen the news," Sam said to her.

She was a deer in the headlights as she bobbed her head at Sam.

"Go," I said to Sam. "Jo can fill me in on the press conference."

He gave me a quick peck on the lip. "Love you, baby doll."

Whatever Adam had announced had to be horrifying. Maybe I didn't want to know.

10

SAM

My brain was on overload as I left Layla's room. It broke my black heart to tell her about Rianne and destroy the protective bubble we'd wrapped ourselves in. The only thing I'd wanted to do when she was pressed against me, her long lashes fluttering, her eyes full of desire, was to take, possess, and love every inch of her.

I hated to leave her without giving her a blow-by-blow of what had gone down at Adam's eye-opening press conference. I'd been tempted to also tell her about Carly, but she was in shock over Rianne. I didn't want to push her heart to the brink of destruction, since as fast as it had been beating, one more dreadful piece of news would've put her in a coma.

But I agreed with her that we needed Jordyn. Whatever came next would require boatloads of help.

I read Tripp's message again as I walked.

Tripp: *Your father has orders from the council to release Fred Emery. They're afraid we'll have a mutiny on our hands. I need you ASAP to deal with Jordyn. She's driving the prison guards mad.*

I typed a text to Tripp: *I'm on my way. But just let Jordyn go.*

He responded quickly: *Jordyn wants to talk to Fred Emery. Says if she does, she promises she won't pull any more stunts.*

Me: *Then let her say her piece. I'll be there to help referee. Layla and I need her.*

Tripp: *This is her only chance to redeem herself. She has two strikes. One more, and I will kick her off base. Webb is prepared to back me up.*

Her first strike had been leaving the base with Junior and not telling anyone where they were heading. Jordyn had made a deal with her grandmother. She would join Harriet, and in exchange, Harriet wouldn't harm Layla. I couldn't fault Jordyn for wanting to save her sister. Hell, I'd been ready to go rogue when Layla had been kidnapped. But we'd had a plan, so there was no need for Jordyn to throw herself in harm's way.

Me: *Copy that. After she reams out Fred, I'll talk to her and drive your message home. Did the council say anything about Layla?* She wasn't a prisoner like Fred, but the public didn't know that, and I had to believe my father would've shared my marriage with the council.

Tripp: *If they did, your father hasn't said. Just get here.*

I couldn't dwell on or control what the council, our enemies, or the public would do. What I could control was my family's safety, and for fuck's sake, that would be a difficult feat if Layla and our babies remained on base. I was sure the crowd had been multiplying outside the gate after that press conference.

I wanted to scream or punch something, preferably Rianne's face. But at some point, I would have my chance to end that bitch once and for all. Of that much I was certain.

I picked up the pace, laughing out loud at how fate was fucking with me again, ruining a day that should be perfect and festive. I should be handing out cigars, drinking beers, and toasting my inception into fatherhood. Instead, the world was on the brink of destruction and taking my family down in the process.

Breathe, man. Think of your beautiful children, Elara, Aurora, Luna, and Orion. They are the reasons you need to fight for a better and safer world for them to grow up in.

I wasn't fighting to protect humanity anymore but rather my family.

Heels clicking on the tiled floor broke my concentration as I approached the door from the new wing into the old.

"Sam, hold on," Jo called, running up to me.

"I thought you were filling Layla in on the news conference," I said.

"She's in the bathroom. Look, I know you don't want to hear this, but you have to go off the grid."

I snorted through a laugh. "I know. All of us might have to. Webb has Tripp on standby to engage our disaster-readiness plan." I swallowed, hoping saliva would coat the sandpaper in my throat. "The only place I can think of to shelter Layla and the babies is at your Maine house." They should be safe there. The coastal town was ruled by vampires, including the sheriff, Stan, and his deputies. Not to mention, I also implicitly trusted George, Webb's longtime family friend, who took care of Jo and Webb's place. He would guard my family with his life.

She bobbed her head. "I was thinking the same thing. I'll have George, and Stan's wife, Gina, set up a nursery in one of the guest bedrooms." Then she poked me in the chest with her pink-painted nail. "You need to leave, like, now. I'll take care of your family. The council probably has guardians on their way here to take you in. They'll throw you in the brig until they can figure out how to handle the hysteria out there."

"The thought has crossed my mind that the elders might decide to use me as a scapegoat, but Pops won't let that happen. I didn't do anything wrong." My intentions had never been premeditated. Sometimes I couldn't help when my emotions brought out my vampire side. And if I had known the reporters were filming earlier, I might not have used my powers. Then again, I hadn't seen any other way to stop Carly. "I'm more concerned about Layla than me."

My father was an elder and had taken an oath to uphold

vampire laws. But I had to believe he would fight for me. Besides, if my dead grandfather's message to my dad held any weight, then I couldn't end a war if I was in the brig. Even the ancient elders believed in messages from the dead.

Maybe, but that was before the world knew vampires exist. If they're afraid, they'll mutiny if you don't release Fred. The elders might think along those lines and make an example out of you. I growled at the devil in my head.

I clutched the sides of Jo's arms. "I love you and that you worry about me. I know time is critical, but I want to talk to Pops first. Okay?"

As strong as my sister was, tears pooled in her silver eyes. "For now. Oh, and one more thing. Matthew isn't himself. Adam has to be controlling him with one of those chips."

My sister had a soft spot for Matthew. "Do me a favor, sis. Watch Matthew's segment again. Something is off with him, and I don't mean he's being controlled. Just the opposite."

She reared back, a crease denting the space between her eyebrows. "You think he's doing this of his own free will?"

"I don't know. But even Tripp said you can't tell if Matthew is helping us or hurting us. But what if he's been working with Roman? What if he alerted Roman where Abbey was or set up the plan for Roman to kidnap him?"

"No way would he put Abbey in harm's way," she said in disbelief. "And we found Victor's mole. I read the guard's mind."

"Jo, you and I know that those who are aware of your capabilities can erect mental shields. You told me earlier that you couldn't read Fred Emery's mind. What if Victor's guard wanted you to believe it was him?"

She shook her head. "Matthew hated what Edmund and our uncle did to him. He wouldn't betray us."

My sister knew better than to be so trusting. I lowered my gaze to my flak boots, and before I could stop myself, I was transported back in time to the day I almost lost Jo to someone the entire SEAL team had trusted with their lives.

Jo and I had broken out of a room at a funeral home where Edmund Rain had been holding us hostage. We weren't his lab rats that day but rather a bargaining chip—our lives for his daughter Abbey's.

But when Jo banked left with me on her heels, she ran directly into Webb's sister Kate London. Before I could stop Kate, she'd plunged a cobalt dagger into Jo's chest. If Jo hadn't killed Kate that day, I would have in a flat second.

I lifted my gaze, blinking away the past. "Like how everyone thought Kate London could do no wrong. Yet Webb's sister was sleeping with Edmund Rain. Need I say more?"

She blanched and swallowed audibly.

I hated to play that card since my sister had a difficult time coming to terms with having killed her husband's sister. Webb had understood the stakes. He'd known his sister was the enemy and that she could die by our hands. That fact didn't make it any easier for anyone involved.

"You might have to do the same to Rianne," Jo fired back. "Are you prepared for that?"

My nostrils flared. "Really, sis? You know the answer." I'd been protecting Jo since we were five years old. During our human teenage years, I'd done a few stints in jail because a foster dad or two thought he could have his way with Jo. "But to say it out loud, you bet your ass I'm prepared to rip Rianne's head off if she touches my family. If we should be worried about anyone who was part of that press conference, it's her." I gave Jo a hug. "I have to go." I left her standing in the hall as I tore out of there.

Several minutes later, I was crossing the courtyard toward the prison. The sweet aroma of morning dew drifted on a light breeze as the sticky, humid air clung to my skin. A sign that we were in for another hot July day when the clouds finally cleared and the sun had a chance to peak at midday.

My boots scuffed the cracked pavement that separated the grassy area on one side with picnic tables on the other.

Approaching the guard, I grinned at Petty Officer Peterson like I did every time I saw the six-foot vampire with a crooked nose. He could very well snap his nose back into place with a flick of his fingers. But he didn't see the point, since he would only injure it again in one of the many boxing matches he competed in when he wasn't on duty. Plus, he'd mentioned that women found the look sexy.

He straightened, opening the heavy metal door to the oldest building on the naval base, which had once been home to a textile company. "Sir, Lieutenant Tripp is expecting you."

"Any upcoming matches?" I asked as I passed him.

"Not lately. But I'll let you know."

I gave him the thumbs-up as I entered the building. "Do that." Tripp, Ben, and I had been to a few of his matches, and I almost considered competing three years ago. But I hardly had any free time since the SEALs were constantly on missions.

I climbed the stairs two at a time to the second floor, where we housed human criminals and detainees. The door leading into the prison cells wasn't guarded, but it was locked. We didn't have many humans who broke the law on the naval base, so there wasn't a need to keep the floor heavily guarded. However, vampire offenders and enemies had the luxury of staying in the cobalt-encased cells two stories below ground and were guarded twenty-four seven. And even though Fred Emery was human, we'd thrown him in the vampire cellblock for extra protection.

When I reached the landing, I glanced up at the camera before a click and a two-second-long buzzing sound resonated, unlocking the door.

I saluted the person on the other side of the camera then strutted in.

Tripp was standing outside the second cell, texting.

Before I had a chance to open my mouth, Jordyn hopped off the cot inside her four-by-four room. "Sam."

She said my name as though I was her savior, and I was far from it. If she thought Tripp was angry with her, she was in for a rude awakening.

She flipped her brown hair over her shoulder. "You look awful. Did something happen? Does Layla know I'm in here?" She wrapped her fingers around the thick metal bars, trepidation evident in her voice.

From her questions, it was clear Tripp hadn't filled her in on Layla. But just to be certain, I opened a telepathic connection with him only because I didn't want to explain what had happened to Layla until Jordyn talked to Fred. I wanted her undivided attention and ample time to drive the seriousness of her behavior home.

Dude, I take it you didn't tell her Layla had the babies?

Still absorbed on his phone, he responded, *Nope. I was saving that announcement for you.*

I sharpened my hearing, but I didn't hear any heartbeats except Tripp's and Jordyn's—on this floor anyway.

"Layla does know you're here," I said to the youngest Aberdeen sister. I could at least share that with her. "She's not happy with you either."

Jordyn lifted her chin. "*I'm* not happy with me."

That comment was a good sign that she was coming to terms with what she'd done.

"Where's Fred or Carly?" I asked Tripp.

Jordyn gasped. "Carly is here?" She paled. "Is Rianne?"

"Your deranged sister is nowhere near the base." Tripp tucked his phone away in his cargo pants, flicking his bronze gaze to me. "Carly was taken to an interrogation room. The guards are bringing Fred up from the vampire cellblock." He rounded his attention on Jordyn, wagging his finger. "Remember what I told you. Another infraction on your part will not be tolerated. Also, under no circumstances can Fred leave here with bruises or any visible sign of duress." My lieutenant addressed me. "Don't get any ideas of compelling him or erasing his memories. We don't need more public scrutiny. Am I clear?"

I held my hands up. The last thing I wanted to do was piss off the elders.

"The only bruise I'm inflicting won't be visible to anyone," Jordyn said. "Seriously, thank you, Tripp, for giving me a chance to talk to the asshole."

She didn't have to articulate the body part she would be going after. Nevertheless, I was eager to see what she had in store for Fred Emery.

11

SAM

After a prison guard deposited Fred, handcuffed and shackled, into Jordyn's cell five minutes after I'd arrived, the guard took her leave.

Tripp and I smiled at each other.

Let the games begin.

In one corner of the cell near the window, we had Jordyn Aberdeen salivating to sink her teeth into Fred Emery. If I were able to read her mind, I would bet she was wishing upon a star for fangs like Tripp and I had.

In the other corner opposite Jordyn and just inside the cell door, we had a man about five feet ten, military-cut brown hair, sharp brown eyes, and a scar that stretched from his left ear to the corner of his mouth.

I felt as though I was at Peterson's boxing match as Tripp went over to Jordyn, and I pushed Fred deeper into the room.

The human stumbled but didn't fall as he bared his light-yellow teeth.

"You must've royally pissed someone off to get a scar like that," I said.

Fred jutted out his pointy chin, smirking. "A dead someone," he bragged. "Why am I here?" He pushed out his chest, the blue jump-suit stretching in the process.

I leaned against the cell door. "We're just having a friendly conversation."

Fred shuffled to the wall and leaned against it so he had a view of Tripp and Jordyn on his right and me on his left. His slow pulse told me he wasn't nervous in the least.

While Tripp talked to Jordyn about how much time she had, I asked Fred, "Did you kill the person who gave you the scar?"

Up until now, he hadn't talked. And as my sister had told me earlier, she hadn't been able to read his mind. But he was proud of his battle scar, and those who had a high opinion of themselves loved to boast. Plus, I was curious to know who his victim had been. Vampire? Human? More importantly, it was imperative we had more insight into what made our enemies tick. My father lived by some of Sun Tzu's teachings, and one in particular came to mind. *If you know the enemy and know yourself, you need not fear the results of a hundred battles.*

Fred sized me up. His expression was pompous, severe, and dark, like he was better than me but wanted to chop off my head. "Sam Mason. My brother has big plans for you."

"Do you mean the chip that isn't in my head anymore?" I touched the back of my skull, feeling smug. I never said I wasn't arrogant. But I also wasn't telling him top secret information.

The pretentiousness melted off his scarred face, and I gave myself mental high fives. The fucker had been out of touch with his brother's so-called plans ever since he'd been our guest after the hospital incident at the beginning of April.

I folded my arms over my chest, enjoying the verbal sparring —a welcome change to the agony I'd been through during the last several hours. "You've missed a lot over the past three months."

Jordyn stomped over, hands balled into fists, nostrils flaring.

Hellfire was about to burn Fred alive. Before he had a chance to blink, she grabbed hold of his nuts.

Air rushed out of his lungs as he cringed, his facial muscles snapping taut.

Nicely done, Jordyn Aberdeen.

She twisted his balls in one direction, smiling like she'd won the lottery.

He squealed, turning ten shades of red.

Tripp and I swapped a pained but admiring look while Tripp took up a position on the other side of Jordyn and Fred.

"If you ever come near me again, I will rip these tiny testicles right off your disgusting body." She twisted in the opposite direction. "Are we clear, asshole?"

He spat in her face.

Jordyn flinched but clung to his precious jewels like she was holding on for dear life. "Please do that again. I really want to feed your dick to the crows."

No question about who she was: an Aberdeen—feisty like Layla. I hardly saw that side of Jordyn. She was and had been the level-headed sister. The one who reasoned with people, gave them advice, and talked Layla down off a ledge many times. But Jordyn had no doubt reached her breaking point.

Fred trembled, his face dark red, pain dripping off him and saturating the air.

I was the strong empath, and Tripp was the weaker one. Which meant we could feel what Fred was going through.

I was tempted to tell Jordyn to ease up, but the show was too fucking good.

"We're"—Fred took in a breath—"clear."

She released him and wiped the spit off her cheek with her T-shirt-covered shoulder.

Fred shuddered, inhaling and exhaling. "You know, Jordyn." His high-pitched voice cracked, so he cleared his throat. "If your father were alive, he wouldn't approve of what you're doing here." He swallowed as color slowly returned to his face.

She tilted her head. "What would you know about my dad?"

"Plenty," he said rather boldly. "I know he was dating a vampire named Kendra. I know he wanted a better life for you and your sisters." The corner of his mouth curled upward. "And I know he would still be alive today if he hadn't been a fucking idiot."

It took me a second to process his last statement. Had Layla's dad been the one who had given Fred the scar?

Jordyn raised her knee, about to ram it into his gonads, when he headbutted her.

The sound of bone on bone along with a screech from Jordyn blared in the room as she floundered to stay upright.

Tripp steadied her while I grabbed Fred by the throat, my fangs front and center, primed to tear out every vein one by one.

The asshole guffawed like he was enjoying himself. "You don't scare me, Mason."

I choked off his airway, lifting him until his feet dangled. "Did you kill Jordyn's father? Is that who gave you the scar?"

"What the fuck?" Jordyn's extremely high-pitched voice was mouselike.

"Sam, let him go," Tripp warned before he came over.

Jordyn charged up on my other side. "Did you kill my father?" Venom drenched her tone.

Tripp touched my arm. "Ease up so he can talk."

I pulled him toward me before slamming his head into the wall. Fuck being careful with him. I didn't give a rat's ass if he walked out of here with black eyes, a broken nose, and a bashed-in head. The more I thought about the people at the press conference and the message they'd blasted to the world, the more my fury grew. But I wanted to hear his answer. Because if he had murdered Wayne Aberdeen, then he was just another target to kill, and I would gladly do the deed on behalf of my wife, who would be distraught and pissed to know this fucker was responsible for taking her father's life.

Tucking my fangs away, I unleashed him from my grasp and stepped backward.

He choked, slumping to the floor, laughing.

Jordyn fisted her hands, the muscles in her arms bunching. "Answer me."

"I enjoyed draining your father's blood and watching him die a slow death," Fred boasted.

Jordyn went ballistic, kicking him over and over and over again, crying and screaming, "You motherfucker, bastard, fucking asshole. I will murder you!"

Tripp and I watched, making no attempt to stop her. She needed to release her anger. Besides, no one would see the bruises on his upper thighs.

"Aren't you two going to do something with her?" he asked, not reacting to Jordyn's repeated kicking.

I slipped my hands into my jean pockets. "Nope. You'll be lucky to leave this room with your dick attached."

Tripp said telepathically, *She's going to pass out if she continues.*

As much as I was enjoying the show, Tripp was right. Jordyn's heart rate was astronomically high.

I gently grabbed her arms from behind. "Enough."

She spun around and buried her face into my chest and cried.

I held her as every one of her tears made me itch to slice and dice Fred Emery. Layla would have the same reaction, and that only increased my desire to drive a dagger straight into his heart.

"Were you trying to show the Aberdeens a vampire was responsible for his death?" Tripp asked Fred.

"It worked, didn't it?" he said in that egoistical tone that seemed to be his signature trait. "The Aberdeens think Kendra is the guilty vampire."

"Why did you kill Wayne Aberdeen?" I asked, holding Jordyn.

She sniffled and faced Fred.

In the coldest of timbres, Fred said, "Because he didn't give me what I wanted."

Jordyn made to unleash more rage, but I gripped her shoulders. "Wait."

Fred was vomiting up information or rather, bragging, and we couldn't break the momentum.

The fuckwad moved his upper body around, seemingly finding a comfortable position with his hands cuffed behind his back. "It took my brother a few years to wrap his head around Patrick Mason's genetic data, vampires, and what Patrick had been trying to do. Once he did, he decided to continue where Patrick left off."

Obviously that wasn't news to us.

Jordyn went over and sat on the cot while Tripp and I stood over Fred.

His Adam's apple bobbed. "To start, we needed vampires to study. That's where the Aberdeens came in. Patrick had a list of names, including vampire hunters. Two years ago, I met with Wayne, and we made a deal. Intech would pay him in exchange for vampires. It was going well until Kendra came into the picture. I wanted to bring the blond vampire in, but Wayne said no. We got into a heated argument one night outside the Deer and Elk Bar in Montana."

"You murdered him because he wouldn't give you Kendra?" Jordyn asked, horrified. "What's so special about her?"

"It wasn't so much about her but rather who she knew." Fred glowered at me.

I could feel my brow lifting. "I don't know Kendra." I knew of her. Jack and Ray Aberdeen had dragged her to our meeting at the abandoned airport outside of Chicago. Then she'd stayed briefly in our infirmary after Ben and Olivia found her unconscious in her hotel room, thanks to Roman Brown. I hadn't talked to her either time. My sister had but hadn't learned much except that Kendra had been in the wrong place at the wrong time.

"From the conversation I overheard between Wayne and her, Kendra seemed to know you Masons pretty well."

Tripp scraped his fingers along his jaw. "In our world, most vampires know *of* the Masons."

Popularity for being the most powerful family. A stigma I wished like fuck I didn't have.

"Then how does Kendra know about Abbey?" Fred asked.

My jaw hit the floor. Maybe my father knew Kendra. Even if he did, he wouldn't share anything about Jo's adopted daughter to anyone except those in his inner circle. He'd always been secretive about my niece. After all, he knew that if word ever spread about how she was changing into a vampire as she aged, her magical powers, and how she was prophesied to be the first female vampire to produce offspring, then she would be hunted. Which was coming to pass since Roman was salivating to get his evil paws on her. Not to mention Intech and Harriet Aberdeen.

I glared down at Fred. "Did Kendra say how she knew about her?"

"I've told you plenty," he said.

I was lunging for the fucker when Tripp's fangs lowered, and he clutched Fred's throat, then lifted his ass off the floor. "Talk, or else I'll give Jordyn my dagger so she can slice off your dick." Seething, Tripp released him.

Fred rubbed his neck. "Fuck you."

I laughed as I bowed my head, my eyes changing, my fangs sliding out, and heat crawling along my right arm until it filled my hand.

Fred jerked his attention to Tripp. "What's he doing?"

A fireball spun in my hand, growing bigger and bigger. "Either talk or I'll shove this down your throat." I didn't give a rat's ass if he was on fire when we threw him off base.

"Okay." For the first time since the guard brought Fred in, he was bathing in fear.

I snuffed out my fire element, closing my hand into a fist as Fred began to talk.

"I overheard Kendra telling Wayne about how she knew

Wayne's wife, Meredith, and her sister Vanessa. They grew up together. In a nutshell, Vanessa has a granddaughter. Kendra didn't know much about her except the little girl would be around eight years old. That conversation was two years ago. Therefore, the girl should be ten today."

Tripp tucked his fangs away. "That doesn't mean the girl is Abbey. Did Kendra tell Abbey's name to Wayne?"

Fred pushed out a suffering sigh. "No, she didn't come out and say Vanessa's granddaughter was named Abbey. But she didn't have to. In Patrick's notes, he has a family tree of the Drakes. Who's who and kids and grandkids. Apparently, Vanessa's daughter is named Rachel, who is Abbey's biological mother. We wanted Kendra to help us get our hands on Abbey."

My eyebrows disappeared into my hairline. If he was right, then Abbey and Layla were cousins—whether once removed or second, I wasn't sure.

Suddenly, a conversation I'd had with Jo sharpened to a pinpoint in front of me.

"I've been looking into Abbey's family history. It's been a challenge, but I think I found Abbey's grandfather on Rachel's side. I don't have much yet," Jo said.

"Sis, if I recall, didn't Rachel's mom die of cancer and her father in a car wreck? Also, Rachel didn't have any siblings. At least, not from what Pops told us."

"I'm trying to confirm that," she said. "And you know people keep secrets about their past for various reasons. Look at Layla's mom, Meredith. She lied about hers. Not only that, Rachel was also good at shielding Dad from reading her mind."

Fuck. The skeletons were coming out of the closet, and I wasn't sure if that was good or bad. It sucked we couldn't ask Rachel, thanks to Abbey's biological father, Edmund Rain. The asshole had killed Rachel for his own twisted reason. Nevertheless, my sister might not have to do extensive research anymore. If I recalled, she had Kendra's phone number and so did Layla. Bringing Kendra in would confirm and clear up questions about Abbey's maternal family, something Jo had been working diligently to achieve.

Tripp must've connected the dots, too, because he whipped his gaze at me.

"If you're right, then Abbey is my second cousin," Jordyn said from behind Tripp and me.

"All the more reason to study you and your sisters," Fred said. "You would be a perfect candidate for our genetic program."

"Fuck you," Jordyn spat out.

I was beginning to feel like I didn't have enough bandwidth in my brain to process this new information. But a question snaked through my synapses. When Ben had been Roman's prisoner, he'd overheard Roman talking on the phone to someone by the name of Fred.

"You're the one who hired Roman Brown to kidnap Abbey, right?" I asked Fred.

"That's right," Fred confirmed. "We paid him a lot of money to find her and bring her in. But we also wanted you, Mason. Your uncle was a wealth of information and detailed in documenting his data."

"Since you're bragging, tell us who your brother is working with other than Roman, Harriet, and the US government? Any other vampire hunters, government agencies, or supernaturals?"

We had Carly to pump for information, but she might not be privy to the business side like Fred was.

He half smiled, his recent fear replaced with a dose of courage. "If your twin can't read my mind, you're not about to trip me up, Mason. My brother and I have had a few years to learn and prepare for your kind."

"Where there's a will, there's a way," I said with no display of cockiness despite knowing we had the mad scientist in our custody. Carly might not know the details of Adam's investors, but she had read my uncle's notes.

"My dad died because Intech was trying to kidnap Abbey and

Sam. This is fucked up. My dad wanted to live in a better world where we didn't have to run and hide from bloodsuckers." Jordyn's mixture of despair, heartache, and anger rang in her voice.

"Yet here you are, living with them," Fred said matter-of-factly.

She sneered at him. "The vampires here are protecting humanity, not killing them for sport or genetically altering them into monsters. What's your motive? Money? Control? Power? Because it's not to reduce the vampire population."

"Maybe some of us want immortality," he answered. "The Masons and others like him shouldn't be the only ones who can enjoy life for as long as they want or have the power."

Tripp and I laughed.

"You're about to have your chance," I said.

Fred's brown eyes lit up. "Carly was successful?"

Tripp shoved Fred toward the door. "It's time to go."

Once Tripp and Fred were gone, I sat next to Jordyn. "This was an eye-opener."

She puffed out her cheeks. "Once again, I feel like I don't know who my family is anymore. When I first heard my mom came from vampires, I was blown away. But that news was nothing compared to what I just heard. I might be related to Abbey. What does that mean? Do I or my sisters have power like her?"

I leaned my elbows on my knees. "It's possible. However, if you do, your abilities would never be as strong as Abbey's. Your father wasn't a vampire like hers."

She shrugged. "What's important right now is to find Kendra. I want to know more about my mom."

The newfound information that Abbey and the Aberdeen sisters could be related and the fact that Fred had killed Wayne Aberdeen were indeed eye-opening, but they were not my immediate concern. Making sure Jordyn wasn't going off the deep end was.

12

SAM

Jordyn and I sat in silence. She bit her nail, and I stared at the floor, taking a beat to collect my thoughts before I brought up her fire-alarm stunt. I wasn't as angry with her now, which was good news for her.

"Am I free to go?" Jordyn asked.

"Not yet. I want to discuss that stunt you pulled."

My phone beeped with a text. I would've ignored it, but with the way things had been going since about one thirty that morning, I couldn't. Even though Layla and the babies were great when I left the room, something could've happened, especially if Layla had watched the press conference, which was probably on repeat on every cable news network.

I fished my phone from the pocket of my jeans and opened my text app.

Jordyn was reading over my shoulder.

Dad: *After we release Fred Emery, you and I need to chat.*

The conversation I had with Jo about fleeing surfaced.

Me: *We do. Ping me when you're done.*

Jordyn popped off the cot, huffing as she gathered her hair from

90

behind her and pulled it forward. "Why are you letting Fred go? You can't. He murdered my father."

Twirling my phone in my hand, I sat up straighter. "If you hadn't pulled the fire alarm, you might know."

She twisted her hair in her hand nervously. "Might know what?"

My blood began to boil for multiple reasons, but only one mattered at the moment. "You know we have rules around here."

"What's that got to do with Fred Emery?"

I rubbed my chin. "Nothing. Tell me why you pulled the fire alarm."

I knew why, but I wanted her to say it out loud.

"I hate that man," she screeched, swinging out her arm toward the open cell door. "I hated him the moment I met him at Intech. He might have been at the hospital that day to capture Layla and me, but he wanted more from me." She blinked away a tear as she clenched her fists.

My muscles tensed. "Are you saying that fucker violated you?"

She hugged herself. "Remember my interview with Intech in February? After I met with Carly, I spent time with Fred. Carly said it was part of the interview process to meet with the head of security. Anyway, during that meeting, he was leering, staring at my chest, sizing me up, and licking his lips like he wanted to attack me. I tried to rush out, but he caught me and pinned me against the door. He told me that I would be his one day." She shivered as she paled. "Now that I know he drained the blood from my father, I will hunt him down and kill him, Sam. I don't care what it takes."

Men touching women without their consent infused me with more fury than anyone was ready for. Jo had been a victim to shit like that when we were in foster care. I just might go out of my way to bring Fred back here. The fucker needed to be taught a lesson for sure.

I pocketed my phone. "When the time comes, I'll help you with Fred. But first, I need you to promise me that you won't pull any more alarms around here or put yourself in the middle of our missions. I like you, Jordyn. I don't want to see you hurt in any way. And before you tell me that you already promised Tripp, I want to hear you say it to me. Because, Jordyn, your idiotic actions could've cost Layla her life."

"What? No! Is she okay? Tripp didn't say anything to me about that. Please tell me she's alive, Sam." She raised her voice, blinking away tears. "Did her heart give out? Did she have the babies?"

I went over to the window. Blue skies peeked through the clouds that were breaking apart as they moved west. "Last night, Layla saw you trying to slip past the guard. She was on her way to stop you from doing something stupid when she lost consciousness." I regarded her. "As I was rushing her to the infirmary, the fire alarm went off, and we shut the base down. That meant Dr. Martin couldn't get in. He was finally able to, thanks to Tripp, but you get my point."

She shook her head furiously as her bottom lip wobbled.

"The last several hours have been nail-biting, harrowing, and heart-stopping," I said on a sigh. "But Layla, our daughters, and son are alive."

She ran the short distance and threw herself at me. "I'm so, so, so sorry. Please forgive me. I was desperate to get by the guards. It was a stupid move."

I peeled her off me, and as cold as I might seem, I needed to drive my message home even further. "It infuriates me what Fred has done to you, and I'm not discounting how you feel. Believe me when I say I know. Jo had to deal with foster dads like Fred. But right now I need your help. Layla and I are counting on you to help take care of your nieces and nephew. But if I can't trust you to follow orders or you're going to go off on your own, pulling shit like you did, then maybe Tripp is right. We can't have you living on base."

She flicked a tear off her face with the pads of her fingers, craning her neck up at me. "I swear on my mom and dad's graves, I will not act out anymore. From the beginning, I've always been on your side. You know that. Please, Sam, believe me. I will protect those babies with my life. I promise you. If I fail, you can lock me up and throw away the key."

I could feel her regret. Even if I couldn't, she'd sworn on her parents' graves. That had to mean something.

I raised my forefinger. "One chance, Jordyn. And understand that I will not hesitate to follow through on throwing you out of here. You won't be allowed to step foot on base again." That would hurt Layla, and I was certain Jordyn knew that. "Understood?"

She nodded quickly. "Yes. I understand."

Layla loved Jordyn dearly, but my wife wouldn't put up with Jordyn's shit either, especially if our children's lives were at stake. And for fuck's sake, after Rianne's speech, our kids were in jeopardy. Who the fuck knew what crazy people would do if they thought my children were a threat to them?

"Good. I'm glad we're on the same page."

"Can I see Layla?" she asked. "I want to shower first. Oh, and please don't tell Layla about what Fred did to me or my dad. I feel it's something I have to do."

"Of course. Come on." Jordyn was staying with Sawyer's sister, Harley, at her place, which was a quick jaunt through the woods, but the walk would give me ample time to bring her up to speed on the state of the union. "I'll walk you home and fill you in on your sister Rianne—who is alive, by the way—and why we're letting Fred go."

13

SAM

I headed back from Harley's house, using the shortcut through woods that separated a section of the military housing from the hub of the SEAL command.

Splashes of mud sprayed around my booted feet as I trudged along the muddy path, texting my sister. I was anxious to tell her about Abbey and the Aberdeen sisters and to see how Layla was doing.

Once I hit Send, I inhaled the musky-sweet aroma of the dead vegetation that hung in the air. Nothing like the scents after a hard rain. A light breeze rustled branches high above me, causing water droplets to ping off my head, when a beeping sound alerted me to a text.

I was ready to read Jo's response, but instead, a text came through from my father.

Dad: *Meet me in the war room as soon as possible.*

I would give anything for a hot shower, a bed, and a romp in the hay with my wife. However, the sweaty, tangled sex with my huntress couldn't happen until she recovered from surgery and Doc cleared her for physical activity.

In the meantime, I had to direct my energy elsewhere and settle for a punching bag. Too bad Dane Gray wasn't on-site. The wolf shifter owed me a sparring date. I hadn't seen him since I'd rescued Layla, but I had spoken to him on the phone about a week ago. He was still bunkered down with Ben, Olivia, and the Special Forces team in West Virginia, hoping to glean any sign that his brother Ross was alive and in the hands of Intech. Ross had been taken at around the time Matthew had. The question now—was Ross Gray or even the other shifter, Tucker Whyte, about to make a TV appearance? Sergeant Rebekah Whyte was just as anxious to find her brother as Dane was.

I bolted across the compound and into the back door of the command center—a shortcut to the war room. I had a sneaky suspicion my old man wanted to chat about the council. In fact, he was probably fielding calls left and right from the elders after Adam's performance at his press conference.

The hum of voices, the tapping of keys, and other subtle computer noises acted as white noise as my mind wandered until I glanced at the largest of monitors that encompassed the far wall.

Several swear words dropped from my lips as I slowed to a walk. The crowd outside our perimeter was massive, filled with humans carrying signs that read Free Layla.

Motherfucker!

Adam Emery certainly knew how to mind fuck us. Or rather Rianne, bitch extraordinaire, sure did. We should throw Carly Aberdeen to the wolves, so to speak. Put her on television and show the nation what would happen if anyone signed up for Adam's experiment. He was taking the credit for Matthew Costner when in fact the honorary award went to my uncle Patrick.

I chewed the inside of my cheek, standing near an empty cubicle. I could picture the long lines of money-hungry humans outside Intech's headquarters in Chicago. A hundred thousand dollars wasn't anything to sneeze at. I was right when I'd told Victor and Webb on the day Roman's men stormed Victor's estate that those of our kind who have chosen not to turn, like Alia, for example, were the ones Adam would target. Or humans like Matthew who had vampires in their families. The good news—Adam wasn't taking people against their will. Bad news—we might have a well-formed army of lab-born supernaturals to deal with.

Sawyer came out of Tripp's office, tucking his hands into the pockets of his green fatigues. His kaleidoscope-colored eyes lasered in on me as he approached. "Just the man I was looking for. Tripp has me working on locating Kendra. I got her number from Jo, but we also pulled her prints when Kendra was in the infirmary. I'm running a background check on her within our vampire database and also the civilian one. Since you have a full plate, Tripp instructed me to work with Jo on this. But are you cool with me bringing Layla in too? I understand from Tripp that Layla and Abbey could be related."

"Go for it. Layla wants to know more about Kendra anyway."

"Also, one more thing. Harley and I have spoken to our parents. And we would like to offer our childhood home in Vermont as a place of refuge for you and your family. There's plenty of room. Our neighbors are vampires and some are witches, and my mom can help with the babies."

My stomach dropped. Despite flipping the switch on our disaster-readiness plan, I might be leaving here before then. Yet warmth spread through my chest that Sawyer and his sister Harley were thinking about Layla and me. "I have no words." We exchanged a bro hug. "I'll keep that in mind. But let's hope it doesn't come to that."

Sawyer had always kept his head down, followed orders, and was a dedicated team member. I couldn't say I'd ever seen him worried like he was now.

"I've told Webb and Tripp," he said. "I have a space in our basement as big as this room. It's set up with computers and security systems. I would need to make some upgrades, but we could move our command center there."

I wasn't surprised. Sawyer was the epitome of a techie.

"You're a good soul, Sawyer," I said as my phone buzzed. I stabbed a thumb in the direction of the war room. "I have to run. We'll chat later."

I stalked into the war room two seconds later. My father, Tripp, and Webb were standing in a circle, dressed for battle.

I laughed. "Is this a Sam intervention or something?" I wagged a finger between Tripp and my dad. "And why aren't you two escorting Fred out the gate?"

Webb rubbed his unshaven jaw. None of us were clean-shaven, and I was the only one not in uniform.

My dad regarded me with equal parts anger and concern. "I just got a call from the Secretary of the Navy. Derrick Atkins informed me his undersecretary, Joyce Klein, is missing along with other governmental officials. He believes they were taken by Adam's goons. We're not sure why, but according to the secretary, the DOD recently voted against Adam's contract for the BMI devices."

My eyebrows slashed downward. "Adam doesn't get what he wants, so he kidnaps DOD employees?" Childish was the word that came to mind. "Is his plan to show the government how the chip works by using their officials as guinea pigs?"

Tripp stood at parade rest. "Seems that way. We also got a call from someone claiming to be an FBI agent asking if we were holding Fred Emery and Carly Aberdeen."

Oh, this just keeps getting better and better.

"Have you questioned Carly yet?" I asked.

"She won't talk to anyone but you and Layla," Webb chimed in.

"Jo could read her mind." I tipped my head at my dad. "Or you can."

"Jo's busy and tired," Webb said. "I'm not putting any more stress on her today. Besides, we have other pressing matters to take care of at the moment. I doubt Carly has anything of value to tell us after that press conference."

"That's not to say we won't question her," Tripp added. "We do need to know where your uncle's data and notes are that Carly and Adam have so we can destroy them and for good this time."

We'd thought we had burned every last piece of data after we killed Edmund and Patrick. Regardless, I wanted the Drake family tree for Layla. If Abbey and my wife were related, then Jo would be interested as well.

My dad gnawed on the inside of his cheek. "Son, Carly isn't going anywhere. We'll get to her in due time. You and I need to talk."

"Let me guess," I said. "The council is furious." That was the only reason I could think of unless he was finally about to scold me for using my elemental powers to stop Carly earlier. "Or is it about the reporters we have in custody?"

Webb and Tripp eyed my father as if to say, *I'm not telling him*.

Nausea churned in the pit of my stomach. Things were happening at warp speed.

"We released the cameraman and the reporter to the civilian police," Webb said, his jaw as hard as stone.

"What about the video Letty sent to her boss?" I asked. I didn't want that on national television.

"Unfortunately, Letty's boss isn't cooperating. He won't hand over her video. Sawyer's team is working on hacking into the news station servers," Tripp said, irritation scraping his tone.

"Gentlemen, can Sam and I have the room?" my father asked, staring at me and clearly not the least bit upset at me for using my powers in front of a reporter.

In the grand scheme of things, I guess it didn't matter. Humans had seen me on TV. What was another outburst on my part for the nation to see? It would only confirm what they were probably struggling to grasp—vampires were real.

14

SAM

Silence snaked through the war room as my father leaned against the table below the movie screen while I lingered near the first row of seats.

"Well, talk, Pops."

His green eyes appraised me, seemingly trying to figure out how to start or searching for the right words, which was confounding. My father had never been at a loss for words.

He rubbed his chin. "I'm not going to lie, son. The council is in an uproar with you. When your picture was plastered on TV the first time, I convinced them that punishing you would not solve the larger problem, but after Emery's comedy show, they feel something must be done to show the public we're dealing with our own."

I snorted. "What does that mean, Pops? Sit in a vampire prison until the media circus blows over? That won't solve shit. And you and I know what's happening outside these gates won't end."

He adjusted the dagger strapped to his leg. "I want you to start thinking of a place to hide."

I folded my arms over my chest, tucking my hands underneath

my armpits and gritting my teeth. "Sounds to me like the council has decided my fate."

He released a loud sigh. "Nothing has been decided. I know you and Hawk weren't intentionally complicit that day at the hospital. It's hard to keep your vampire side hidden when your emotions take over. The other elders know that too. But unfortunately, with your face appearing on national television for the last few months and now that you're Adam's weapon to instill fear in humans, the council is nervous. They feel they need to show our human government contacts, including the Secretary of the Navy, that we are, like I said, dealing with our own."

I laughed erratically. "How? Stone me to death in the town square?" *Oh, fuck no.* The movie screen started swaying back and forth, my anger increasing with each breath I took.

My father came over to me. "Sam, I won't let them do that or anything else to harm you. Do you understand me?" We locked eyes. "I will die before I let the council do anything of the sort." The conviction in his tone stopped my heart from banging against my ribs.

Still, as powerful as he was, he couldn't exactly take on the guardian force, and neither could I, for that matter.

I shoved my hands through my hair, on the verge of losing my shit. "The guardians will hunt me down. How will you stop them?"

Fuck! We had a damn police force in every state in the country, including scouts who helped police vampires. A special group of talented guardians with two elemental abilities were handpicked to serve the council. Fighting one or two at a time would be easy, but a group of them might be a challenge.

The electrical charge I'd emitted that morning to stop Carly was child's play. When the guardians pooled that energy together as a team, a vampire didn't stand a chance. Or their fire element would certainly light up my ass like a bonfire.

A corner of his mouth turned upward. "I have something up my sleeve. I can't talk about it right now. But again, pack your go bag."

My brow creased. "Have you been planning a coup d'état before now?" My dad had always been predictable. Something went wrong, he flew off the handle. Anyone who broke the law, punish them. Follow orders. Bow down to the rule of the vampire law. Hell, my old man had probably written the laws that governed our kind.

He rubbed the back of his neck. "I always have a backup plan, son. But since the war with Edmund Rain, the elders have refused to see that times have changed. They've been dead set on keeping to old, antiquated rules that worked a hundred or even fifty years ago. We need to evolve. I'm not saying I saw Adam Emery coming, but after what we'd gone through with Edmund Rain, it was only a matter of time before another Edmund surfaced."

Those of us who had fought during that war knew we would face something similar in the future, which was one of the reasons we kept Abbey hidden. A lot of good that had done, since my uncle Patrick's notes and genetic data had been sent to Adam Emery.

I swallowed the dryness in my throat. "Are you saying we should come out of the shadows?"

"Frankly, yes."

My eyes bugged out. "You're the last person I expected to hear that from."

He rolled back his shoulders. "Look, son. More and more humans have been learning of our kind even before Adam's news conference. But how we present ourselves to the world will be critical. First, though, we can't have Adam on national television, scaring people about how evil we are. People fear what they don't know. We need to take away their fear, which means Adam needs to be stopped any way possible, particularly before too many lives are lost through experiments. Once he's out of the picture, maybe then the hysteria will die down enough for us to discuss a path forward with the human government and not just the small group of humans who know the good we do."

I squeezed my temples and sat down, feeling like I was living in an alternate universe. In a way, I was. In a matter of hours, the landscape had changed drastically.

"You're more than sure we're ready to explain who we are to humans?" I had to ask one more time just to be sure I was hearing him correctly.

He eased into the chair next to me. "I never said we're ready. But yes, I am certain. I'm also sure of your role in ending Intech, which I will drive into the council. It would be nice to have them in my court. The last thing we need is division among our kind."

If my dead grandfather's message to him were true, then he was right about my role. "Did you get another message in one of your dreams?"

"In a way, yes. Remember I told you about the panther. Well, I've had a few more dreams of him in the last month. He's your grandfather's spirit animal, which he detailed in his dream journal. Anyway, there are many opposing forces we're up against, and the panther told me to make sure Layla is ready. She'll also play an important part. What that is, I don't know. We're facing mankind, Intech, the Aberdeens, and Roman Brown. And if the tide doesn't turn with me, then we might be fighting our own."

My brain was overloaded, my thoughts muddled, but one thing stood out like a beacon calling me home.

"The fuck? Layla?" The buzzing in my ears sounded like a colony of bees despite my plan to whip her into shape.

I'd always envisioned us fighting alongside each other. I shouldn't feel like someone had just ripped out my guts. Yet the pain was real and made me sweat. I didn't want her caught up in battles and wars. But everyone had a role to play. It was more important than ever to ensure Layla was prepared.

"While I deal with the council, Webb and Tripp will begin working on a black-ops strategy to figure out how we take out Adam. Every move on our part needs to be thought out with precision since Adam has the public's attention. We can't for one second allow the humans to assume the vampire military is behind anything that happens to him. And if we do come out of the shadows, we can't look like the predators or monsters that humans believe us to be."

I leaned my forearms on my thighs and picked at a hangnail. "What are your plans for Fred Emery?"

He adjusted the watch on his wrist. "To be determined. The council will be furious I didn't release him. I was outvoted on that one."

"There are people carrying signs outside our gates that say, Free Layla. If the council has any ideas of handing her over, they can go fuck themselves. Also, I'm moving her and the babies to Maine as soon as Doc says she can travel."

"Good idea," he said. "Also, have your go bag ready with or without Layla. If for some reason I have a hiccup in my plan, I will text you a 911. Jo will take care of moving Layla to Maine." He pinned me with a hard but soft look. "Promise me you'll bolt if it comes to that."

I pushed to my feet, swallowing a damn elephant. "I really want to know what you're up to, but I know no matter how much I try to beat it out of you, you won't budge. But I trust you implicitly, Pops."

He stood and grabbed my arms. "Son, promise me."

I stared into his green eyes, my pulse staccato. I couldn't leave my family. But they would be safer without me. It would be easier to disappear alone than with a wife and four newborns in tow. Above that, I couldn't and wouldn't allow the council to make an example out of me. Dying in battle might be an honorable soldier thing. But handing my ass over to the council so they could send a message to the human government or to anyone—no fucking way.

"It won't come to that, Pops. I have faith you'll succeed. But if not, then I'll disappear." Bile burned its way up to settle in my throat. Layla would not be on board with this, but if I knew my wife, she would understand.

My father briefly closed his eyes and released a breath. "Good, son. Good." Then he pulled me into a tight hug, his heart freaking the fuck out.

Good or not, war or no war, my father and I had reached a new pinnacle in our relationship—one that was tighter and fiercer than ever before. He'd always put the military and vampire laws before anyone. Knowing he put me first told me I wasn't out on an island alone, swimming upstream against enemy forces. I was grateful and thankful I had him, and as a dad, I understood him more now than ever before.

I hugged him. "I love you, Pops."

He squeezed me to him. "I'm proud to call you my son. I love you, Sam."

But as we broke apart and walked out of the war room, that nauseous feeling reared its ugly head. It wasn't the war, the battles, and the killing that made me sick with fear. I would gladly fight twenty-four seven. The tornado inside me was from knowing Layla had to fight. She had the drive, the attitude, the feistiness, and even the skills, given that she'd hunted and murdered vampires. But she had two things against her—one, she was human. She could die from a single bullet. And two, time wasn't on our side. I prayed I had a chance to physically prepare her.

15

LAYLA

After Sam left over two hours ago, Jo and I watched the press conference. Every news station was streaming Adam's comedy show. Newscasters were speculating about whether the vampires had drained the blood of Fred Emery and me.

I was still fixated on the TV as I sat on the couch in the birthing suite, fuming, dumbfounded, and shaking like a magnitude-five earthquake. My eyes hurt from the thousand eye rolls I'd done after watching Rianne's speech on national television. Her fake crying and words would almost have had me puking if it weren't for the rage overpowering my senses.

Adam mentioned that the military vampires are holding his brother. Well, they've also taken my sisters. That's why I've signed up. I want to fight them. I want to save my sisters.

Give me a fucking break.

My name is Rianne Aberdeen. My family has hunted vampires for centuries. I know how to kill them, but as a human, I don't stand a chance against someone as powerful as Sam Mason. That's why I'm a willing participant. And no, I've not made the change yet. But I will. I have to. My older sister, Layla, has been compelled by Sam Mason to fall in love with him. She's even pregnant by him. My grandmother is distraught over this. Layla, if you're listening, please come home. Granny needs you. I need you.

My sister was more demented than I'd ever thought possible. Yet smart as a fucking whip. Or maybe it wasn't her idea to appeal to the masses. I would guess Roman had come up with the plan. The irritating vampire had the smarts. After all, he liked to play head games. I envisioned his death by a zillion cockroaches eating him alive.

Nevertheless, Rianne said she hadn't turned, but why not? Was she afraid? If I knew my sister, she wasn't frightened. She'd boasted about becoming like Sam. She felt the only way to kill him was to be like him. As fiercely driven as I was to knock some sense into her to stop the madness, I *was* curious to see how she would fare if she turned vampire or monster. Would she resemble our cousin Noah, who looked like a cross between vampire and shifter? On top of that, I was also dying to know if her blood type was Vel negative like mine. I understood that siblings didn't necessarily share the same blood type. But it would be hilarious if Rianne got knocked up by a vampire. I was reaching for straws, but she and Matthew seemed quite chummy on TV together.

Jo had said the same thing about Rianne and Matthew. She hadn't seen the chemistry the first time she'd watched the press conference but picked it up on her second go. Even then she was just as flabbergasted. Mainly because of Matthew Costner. Apparently, Sam thought Matthew was siding with the enemy of his own free will. But the fact that he'd been kidnapped by Roman's men was throwing Jo for a loop. But she could almost accept the possibility that no one had coerced Matthew to speak on national television.

I'd heard a lot about Alia's son, but I'd never met him. My takeaway on Matthew was that he was of sound mind. If he had a chip in his head, I couldn't tell, and I knew firsthand what the chip had done to Sam. He'd been a different person, almost feral in nature.

What still had my ass glued to the couch were the people outside the naval base gate, some of them carrying signs that read Free Layla. I let out a maniacal laugh, but beneath the deranged sound, my nerves were rocking and rolling like a boat in high seas. Steven Mason had predicted Adam would use the media to his advantage. I didn't know what was worse—using weapons like daggers and guns or drawing on psychological weapons, like controlling the narrative, to infuse fear or maybe even excitement into the minds of billions of people. After all, Adam was offering one hundred thousand dollars to potential candidates for his experiments.

Icy fingers tiptoed down my spine as visions of an apocalypse danced before me. We had to start packing, moving, finding a place off the grid. Or, hell, on another planet. Sam and I would never be able to raise our kids in a peaceful environment. We would always be on the run. I was sure there were two camps of believers when it came to me. Those who felt I was in danger and others who felt I was disgusting for sleeping with a vampire. The latter probably thought it was a sacrilege to have a vampire spawn. Little did Rianne know I had quadruplets. Regardless, panic was pressing on my chest like a three-hundred-pound weight. I didn't care about me but only my babies.

I swallowed the dryness in my throat as that familiar burn increased with each breath. The one that warned I needed blood. *Weird.* Now that the babies were born, I would've assumed I didn't need any. Maybe I was addicted. Maybe I had to wean myself off the sticky red stuff.

Rubbing my throat, I went over to the fridge. I'd seen blood vials on the top shelf when I grabbed a bottle of water earlier. I pulled out a tray and sifted through six tubes, hoping one of them was Sam's. The labels had numbers and dates on them with the exception of one that had Sam's name on it. *Bingo.* I just needed enough to cool the fire. So I popped the rubber top and poured most of the contents onto my tongue. The second the candy-flavored blood slid down my throat, I moaned out a sigh.

Satisfied, I replaced the top and inserted the remains of the tube into the tray and returned it to the fridge, thinking of Jo. She'd said she would be right back when she left about fifteen minutes ago to talk to Sawyer, who'd asked her for Kendra's number. She didn't know why, but Sawyer mentioned it was important and that he would explain later.

I was more than curious about Kendra. She'd been an enigma—a mystery vampire who seemed to be in the wrong places at the wrong times. Maybe I wasn't meant to talk to her or learn her story. My uncles had accused her of murdering my father. Maybe she had, which was why I felt like she was avoiding me. We'd swapped texts right before I'd seen Jordyn trying to get into the prison building. Kendra had mentioned she wouldn't be back in the States for a few weeks.

Jo had sensed something big was going on that involved Kendra. What could possibly be bigger than what I'd just watched on TV? I would've followed Jo, but I needed clothes, and I didn't want to leave in case I had to feed the babies. The nurses had taken them down to the nursery so Doc could run more tests on them.

The walls of the birthing suite were closing in on me. Where was Sam? Was he able to free Jordyn from prison? I would call him, but I didn't have my phone either. I would venture through the building to my apartment, but I didn't have a key.

Argh! I felt helpless as annoyance had me ready to scream. Instead, I resumed my spot on the couch, my attention on the TV. The sound was off, but I didn't need to hear what they were saying. Sam's picture on-screen said it all, as did the banner on the bottom—"Truth or fiction. Are vampires real?"

I laughed out loud, sounding like a psycho when the door opened.

Jordyn sashayed in, appearing freshly showered, wearing a navy-blue-and-white flowered sundress and open-toed sandal mules, her wet brown hair hanging free and her phone glued to her hand.

She lit up when her brown gaze rounded on me. "You're up and on your feet?" She threw herself at me. "It's so good to see you. I'm so sorry. I should've been there for you." She locked her hands around the nape of my neck. "I was not in my right mind last night. It will never happen again."

I rubbed her back before untangling her from my body. "Hey, slow down. I'm alive, and the babies are healthy. They're with Doc right now."

Dashing tears off her face, she settled on the cushion beside me and set her phone in her lap.

I grasped her trembling hand. "You look good, sis."

Compared to her, I looked like death. When I'd gone to the bathroom earlier, I'd been horrified when I saw myself in the mirror, mainly at my dirty hair, and the hospital gown didn't exactly scream fashion statement. But soon enough, I would be able to fit into my old wardrobe again. I couldn't wait to get in shape either. I'd worked out early on in my pregnancy, but after I'd been kidnapped by Roman Brown on behalf of my grandmother, I hadn't exercised at all.

She sized me up. "You as well. Did you drink from the fountain of youth?" She giggled.

"I wouldn't say that, but Doc gave me a healing potion." My well-being had gone out the window when I saw Roman Brown on TV. "Have you seen the news?" I grabbed the remote off the arm of the couch and turned up the volume.

"I've only seen parts of it after Sam filled me in," she said. "This is fucked-up."

Tim Cox, a reporter, shoved a mic in Roman's face outside Intech's headquarters in Chicago. "Sir, can you tell us more about the vampire prototype?"

Roman smoothed a hand down his suit jacket as he smiled, his blue eyes lasering into the camera. "I'm sorry, Tim. I can't divulge any information. But know this. We are excited about the outpouring of candidates lining up to be part of a new era."

Cue the eye roll—a thousand and one of them.

Roman lowered his head as he beelined it to a black SUV

parked at the curb. Tim followed on his heels and again shoved his microphone at Roman. "Mr. Brown, can you then tell us more about the recessive gene vampires are born with? Or the medical science behind them?"

Roman grinned, seemingly enjoying the attention. "The answers to your questions would take hours. Just know this. What we're offering humans who qualify is a once-in-a-lifetime opportunity to become immortal—a gift of never dying." He held up his hands, shielding himself from the camera as two security guards flanking him ushered Roman into the back seat of the SUV.

Tim returned his brown gaze to the viewing audience. "That was Roman Brown, one of the scientists working for Intech."

I muted the volume as my eyebrows knitted. "Scientist? I thought Carly was running the experiments."

"Not anymore," Jordyn said as sure as we were sitting there. "Carly is on base in some interrogation room."

I jerked my head at my sister, and my neck locked. "Since when?" I massaged the knot where my neck met my spine.

She lifted her suntanned shoulders. "According to Sam, she made an action-packed appearance at about four this morning, and she's not human anymore."

I gulped in a sharp breath. "We should talk to her. I want to know about Granny. Is she still in the game? I know Rianne mentioned her, but you know Granny. She would've been part of that comedy show."

The news was showing long lines of people waiting to get inside Intech.

"Just for a few minutes, can we talk about my nieces and nephew and you?" she asked. "This crap on TV is depressing, and I'm dying to know if they're vampires. Witches? Do we know? What are their names? How are you feeling? I mean, as I said you look great. Tell me more about the healing potion." She beamed with curiosity and giddiness.

She was right. The more I watched TV, the more depressed,

angry, and obsessed I became with hunting down Rianne and ending her. But Rianne, Roman, and Adam wouldn't stop until each of them achieved their goals. Adam wanted power. Rianne wanted to kill Sam, and Roman, well, he wanted Abbey, but that wasn't the vibe he'd given me on TV. The evil and cunning vampire was enjoying the public's attention. If we had to watch anyone, it was Roman. He was the lethal one.

I withdrew my hand from hers. "I could use a reprieve from the bullshit."

"We should be celebrating the births of my nieces and nephew," she said.

I smiled from ear to ear. "You're going to adore them, Jordyn. They're the most precious beings alive. There's Orion, our son. He has black hair and green eyes just like his daddy. Luna has black hair but violet eyes. Then there's Aurora with reddish-brown hair and mahogany eyes, and Elara, who has a lighter shade of red hair with blue eyes." I adjusted my position, turning slightly toward Jordyn and bending a knee and draping my other leg over it. "We're pretty sure Orion is a vampire since he's been sucking blood off my finger and Sam's. As for the girls, the verdict is still out." I was convinced Rorie was the conduit to the power Sam and I had when we joined hands. If I was right, that meant she would be a strong witch or vampire or both.

Tears cascaded down Jordyn's rosy cheeks, her smile reaching up to her brown eyes. "They sound precious."

Orion was going to be something special. Not that my daughters wouldn't be, but the only boy among three girls would definitely add an interesting dynamic. I could see Orion protecting his sisters and scaring off boys, although he would have to get in line behind his dad. My handsome husband would be overprotective and suffocating when the girls were old enough to date. But we had years before we had to worry about that.

She mimicked my position and draped her arm on the back of the couch. "Will Orion have fangs before long? Will each of them grow faster like they did in the womb? What has Doc said about that?"

I shrugged. "Too soon to say." I decided not to tell her the play-by-play on what had happened in the delivery room. She didn't need to take on more regret. None of us did. But after what she'd done last night, I needed to take her temperature. She'd walked in happy, and maybe I didn't need to worry about her. Just the same, it was the appropriate moment to broach the topic of her psychological well-being.

Rubbing my lips together, I asked, "Jordyn, are you okay? I've been concerned about you for the last few months. I know you were struggling with the car accident, but where's your head at?"

She twisted wet strands of her hair around her fingers—a habit she had when she was nervous or deep in thought. "Sam and I had a heart-to-heart. I know what I did was stupid. It won't happen again. We don't need to rehash it. But I am still upset with myself that you almost died because of me."

"Nonsense, Jordyn. Don't you dare blame yourself. Dr. Martin and Dr. Vieira had warned me that my body might not be able to sustain the fast growth of the babies. Plus, I was close to delivering them since I was only a week away from the C-section."

"But if Dr. Martin wouldn't—"

"Stop, Jordyn." My tone was hard. "You can't keep blaming yourself for Junior's death or what happened to me. Yes, pulling the fire alarm was not your best decision, but I'm here, and the babies are healthy."

She gnawed on her bottom lip.

I wasn't ready to explain that I'd seen our mother, but if it helped her overcome the remorse stamped on her face and in her voice, then so be it. "There's always a brighter side. When I died, I got to see Mom."

She levered back. "For real? And you remember that?"

I shivered. "Every detail. You know how some people describe their brush with death as seeing a white light? That's true. It's warm and beautiful and wraps around you, making you wish you were really dead. I didn't want to wake up. I felt free, really free from the bad shit in my life." I stared at my waffle-woven textured robe. "I was in a sea of wildflowers in Montana. Remember the fields around our farmhouse?" I sighed. "The mountain range and horse barn. Anyway, Mom kept urging me to return to the living. But I couldn't, especially when I saw her. She was more beautiful than ever. Her dark, wavy hair was silky. Her brown eyes were bright and full of love, and she had this ethereal glow surrounding her."

Jordyn cried, breaking my trance. "I want to see her. I need her, Layla. We need her."

Tears began trickling out and sliding down my cheeks. "I know. But she *is* watching over us."

"What did she say? Was Dad there too?"

I frowned. "Dad wasn't." I dashed a tear away with my fingers. "When Mom was on her deathbed, she had visions of us at the nightclub, Jordyn, when we met Sam. And she saw Sam telling me he loved me." I was still grappling with seeing my mom.

Whether or not it was a dream, the state of mind between life and death, or if I'd been truly dead, I wouldn't discount the words she'd spoken. On more than one occasion, I'd been advised to pay attention to my dreams. Steven Mason had even counseled me on that very thing. *If you know what's coming, you might be able to stop it.* Yet I couldn't prevent something from happening if I didn't have the whole story, and my mother's message about the prophecy was obscure at best.

Jordyn, on the other hand, was completely engrossed and in awe —eyes wide, mouth ajar, and shoulders stiff.

So I continued. "She'd worked hard since she was a teenager to make sure no one knew about her supernatural past. She hated bloodsuckers as much as our Aberdeen family does. Apparently, Mom witnessed a group of vampires killing humans one night after a school dance. Since then, she made it her mission to hunt and kill them."

"Why did she wait until she was dying to tell Dad about her family?" Jordyn asked.

"She never planned to tell him. But after her dreams about Sam, she was afraid for me. Dad didn't believe her though. He thought she was not in her right mind because she was dying and due to the drugs she'd been taking for the pain."

Jordyn rubbed the screen of her phone as though she was doodling.

A murky silence filled every corner of the room.

"I know it's a lot to take in." I was still trying to understand the entire experience myself.

Jordyn continued fiddling with her phone. "Was that all she told you?"

I stared at my leg, the *boom, boom, boom* of my heart resounding in my ears as I debated whether or not I should tell her about the prophecy, afraid if I did, the damn thing would come true. How could a child upset the balance of the world? Until I understood the meaning behind that, I wouldn't tell anyone except Sam—and maybe Jo or Steven. They believed dreams were the windows into the future. Besides, my sister had enough on her plate. I needed her focused on helping me with feedings, diaper changes, and being there to protect her nieces and nephew, if need be.

Jordyn snapped her fingers. "Layla, she told you more. Didn't she?"

I rubbed a corner of my eye. "You know that vampire Kendra? Well, she didn't kill Dad."

She angled her head, giving me a knowing look. "Fred Emery did."

Anger, hot and fast, seared my veins as my eyebrows scrunched together. "Come again?"

She clutched her phone, her knuckles turning white. "Fuck. I didn't want to have this conversation now. Not today anyway. But before you jump down my throat, I was going to tell you later."

I laughed nervously. "Do I really want to hear this?" I asked myself more than her.

We'd enjoyed three months of solitude—boredom was a better term to describe the last part of my pregnancy. But boredom was nice. The time between when Sam rescued me from Intech until I'd given birth early that morning had allowed Sam and me time to learn more about each other. I had a chance to grow my relationship with Harley. The strawberry-blond vampire who was Webb's assistant was becoming a great friend. I'd even had an opportunity to spend some quality time with my father-in-law, Steven, which sparked a thought. He had flown out to Montana to help my uncle Jack.

Jordyn tapped my leg. "You're spacing again."

I shook off thoughts of my uncle and Harley for the moment. "How do you know Fred killed Dad? Did you talk to him?"

She pressed her lips into a thin line. "Tripp gave me the chance to say my piece. But if Sam and Tripp hadn't been in the cell with me and that disgusting creep, I would've yanked his balls from his body. Anyway, I never expected to hear the asshole brag about how he took Dad's life. The bastard drained Dad's blood to make it look like Kendra murdered him." Flames flickered in her eyes.

That fury I'd had while watching Rianne's speech pushed me to my feet in a flash, and I was out the door before Jordyn could say a word. The constant round of dreadful things happening felt like shrapnel flying at me constantly.

The long hallway seemed to go on for miles, and a hint of fresh paint hung in the air. I closed the robe I'd thrown on when I'd gotten out of bed, my bare feet slapping on the pristine, cold, white-tiled floor.

"Layla Aberdeen." Jordyn raised her voice, sounding like our mother, before she came up alongside me. "You won't find Fred."

"Oh, I will, and when I do, I'll be the one living in a prison cell." I didn't care either. "And I'm a Mason now." I shouldn't be biting her head off like a snapping turtle, but my rage was taking control of my psyche.

"Layla," Jordyn said again. "The SEALs let him go."

I jerked to a stop, the walls closing in. Suddenly, a sharp tingle swirled in my stomach and careened up into my throat. Before I could connect the dots of what was happening, my inner banshee unleashed a scream that had me expelling the madness clutching my insides.

Jordyn's body hit the floor with a thud.

What the hell? No. No. No. This can't be happening. I had powers because of the babies, who aren't in me anymore. So how is this possible?

I rushed the short distance to her as the hallway spun. I blinked several times, my body feeling like I'd been strung up over a firepit.

A squeak of a door followed by heavy footfalls trickled into my ears. I was about to drop to my knees when darkness encroached within my peripheral vision.

The last thing I heard before the lights snuffed out was Sam shouting, "Baby doll!"

16

SAM

With vampire speed, I was lifting Layla in my arms as my daughters and son wailed as if they knew something happened to their mom.

Jordyn groaned, reaching for her ears as blood dribbled out. She took one look at her sister limp in my arms and scrambled to stand up. "What happened to her? She doesn't pass out after one of her Emmy-award-winning screams."

As if I knew what had happened. But Jordyn was right, which had my nerves eating my insides. The good news—Layla's heart was beating normally. Mine, on the other hand, was ramming into my chest as if Thor was swinging his hammer against my ribs.

"Find Doc. He's probably in the nursery," I said to Jordyn.

I knew he was close by because I had checked his office and the old wing of the infirmary and came up empty.

My intent had been to ask Doc when Layla and the babies could travel. After talking with my old man, I realized the naval base wasn't the best place for my family. Particularly considering the humans waving signs to free Layla.

Jordyn hurried down the hall toward the infirmary's nursery as I carried Layla into her room and laid her on the bed.

Leaning down, I moved strands of hair from her sweat-sheened face before kissing her on the lips. "Baby doll." I tapped her on the cheek. "Wake up."

I wondered if she was having a bad reaction to the healing blood Doc had given her. Now that she wasn't pregnant anymore, maybe the blood didn't agree with her.

Doc rushed in like a gust of wind with Jordyn on his heels. "I heard her, but I was in the middle of pulling blood from Elara." Doc proceeded to listen to Layla's heart.

"I'm pretty sure the entire building heard her," I mumbled.

Jordyn stood at the foot of the bed, rubbing her ear. "I shouldn't have told her about what Fred did to our dad. I'd never seen her that angry before."

The day's events were hard to swallow, and if I'd learned someone had murdered my father or sister, I wouldn't be able to contain my rage.

"Layla would've been more furious if you hadn't told her, Jordyn," I said.

I wanted to treat my wife with kid gloves, protect and shield her from the bad shit outside these walls, but I knew I couldn't. She would be important in our battles ahead, and she would cut off my nuts if I locked her up. I had to trust in her, in her strength, her resilience, and those attributes that made Layla feisty and strong. I also had to have faith that fate had our backs.

"Doc, how are my son and daughters? I think they reacted to Layla's scream."

He was in the middle of checking her blood pressure. "Babies are doing well. The nurses are feeding them as we speak."

Which was why I didn't hear any more crying.

"I didn't think Layla would have any powers once the babies were born," Jordyn said, biting a nail.

"It might take time for them to dissipate, or maybe not," Doc said.

"Maybe she had a bad reaction to the healing blood you gave her, Doc. Or maybe she's doing too much too soon." Even vampires needed to recover after an injury.

He slid his penlight into the chest pocket of his lab coat. "Possible on both counts. But I gave her the healing elixir hours ago. If it had a negative effect, we would've seen something before now. I'll check her incision. There might be complications from the surgery." He eyed me then Jordyn.

"I'm not leaving." I appreciated Doc's professionalism about respecting Layla's privacy, but she was my wife.

"The incision won't bother me, but I want to meet my nieces and nephews. Can I see them?" Jordyn asked Doc.

Doc dipped into his lab coat pocket and produced a pair of nitrile gloves. "Of course. You can help feed them since we only have three nurses."

Smiling, Jordyn grabbed her phone off the couch and sped out.

After his hands were gloved, Doc opened Layla's robe, lifted her gown, then removed the dressing covering her incision. He studied the pinkish cut and stitches. "I knew the mixture of Abbey's blood and a shifter's did wonders but not this fast for a human. I was expecting to remove the sutures tomorrow. Normally, we would leave them in for about three days."

"That's great, Doc. But why did she pass out?"

He lowered her gown. "She's not displaying any signs of infection or internal bleeding, but I'll have Dr. Martin examine her."

Layla's eyes fluttered open. "Hey, vampire. I missed you." She reached for me with one of her ball-squeezing smiles.

I peppered kisses on the back of her hand. "You scared the fuck out of me again." Man, I couldn't take much more.

She rolled those electric-blue eyes that made my dick jerk. "I told you. I'm not dying on you." Turning toward Doc, she scrunched her face. "What happened?"

Doc chuckled. "You tell us."

"Oh shit. I still have my banshee scream. But Jordyn? Is she okay?" Layla's voice hitched.

"She's fine, baby doll. But you usually don't pass out after one of those Hollywood performances."

She giggled. "True. What's happening to me? I mean, I was so flipping mad about everything I learned today. Knowing what Fred Emery did to my father threw me over the edge."

"I'm more concerned about you passing out. Stress is a possibility. Any pain in your abdominal area or anywhere else?" Doc asked.

"Not at all," Layla said, seemingly thinking. "Oh, I did drink Sam's blood that's in the fridge. Maybe that has something to do with it."

I didn't agree. She'd been downing my blood like it was water during her pregnancy, so I was going with stress.

Doc's brow lifted. "There shouldn't be any blood in there." Removing his gloves, he pivoted on his heel, went over to the refrigerator, and pulled out a tray of vials. "Mm. The nurses were supposed to dispose of these. They were labeled wrong. That's why I was pulling more blood from the babies." He returned to Layla's bedside with one tube that had a very small amount of blood in it. "Is this the one you drank from?"

Layla read the label. "Yeah. That says *Sam.*"

I remembered my sister pulling two tubes of my blood earlier, mainly to help Orion.

"In the craziness in the OR, things got mixed up," Doc said. "This one might not be Sam's but one of the quadruplets. I'll have this tested to see whose it matches."

Layla adjusted herself, sitting upright a bit more. "Maybe now that I'm not pregnant, my body can't tolerate blood anymore even though I'm still craving it."

Doc scratched his chin. "That's quite possible. But if you couldn't keep it down, you would've been throwing up, not passing out." Questions were written on Doc's face. "Next time you have a craving, we'll monitor you." Doc regarded me. "I don't have any of your blood in reserves. While I have you here, meet me in the lab in about fifteen minutes. We'll need to set up a regimen because Orion will need your blood too. In the meantime, I'll have Dr. Martin do an exam on Layla. For now, stay put," he said to Layla in a tone that brooked no argument.

Layla pouted. "I really want a shower and to change into some decent clothes."

"Once you have a clean bill of health, you can," Doc said. "The good news is, Dr. Martin is still on-site." He collected the tray of vials and scurried out.

Layla swung her attention to the TV. "I can't believe what's happening. Your dad was right about Adam using the media. What are we going to do, Sam?"

That pain in her voice gutted me. But right now, I didn't want to focus on anything but her and me. I certainly didn't want to tell her about the council and that I might have to disappear without her and our kids.

I found the remote and turned off the TV. Then I dragged a rocker closer to the bed, dropped into it, and yawned.

"You look like crap, vampire," she said. "When was the last time you slept?"

I slid my ass to the edge of the rocker, leaned forward, and laid my head on a sliver of the mattress. "When you and I curled up in bed at nine last night."

She petted my head. "You should sleep. That's what the pullout couch in the room is for. Also, we won't have many quiet moments like this and not just because of our enemies but feedings and changing diapers in the middle of the night."

I was looking forward to dealing with that rather than our adversaries. "I love you, baby doll. We make beautiful babies together. Do you want more?" The last question came out of nowhere. What the fuck was I asking? I wouldn't risk Layla's life again. No fucking way. But I couldn't take the question back.

She grabbed a handful of my hair and yanked hard. "Are you high?"

"I'm high on you." My voice was trailing off, and my eyelids were heavy.

She knocked on my head as if she was trying to crack open my skull. "Sam Mason, are you serious?"

It took an enormous amount of effort to sit up, but when I did, she was glaring daggers at me.

I smirked. "Sounds to me you don't want more rug rats running around."

"I haven't thought about it." She twirled an imaginary circle around my face. "And don't for a second think those sexy dimples will sway me."

"Sexy, huh?" I waggled my eyebrows. "Sex sounds good." The word elicited images of her and me naked and tangled between the sheets.

She squirmed. "As much as I want to fuck your brains out or give you a blow job, that's not what we're discussing."

I growled, smelling her lust and cherry fragrance. The mixture was intoxicating, and my cock came alive. I was more than ready to devour her gorgeous body, something I hadn't done in what seemed like forever. Toward the end of her pregnancy, sex had been limited. Well, the rough, penetrative kind anyway. My huntress loved wild monkey sex. I chuckled at her reference as images assaulted me of our sweaty nights, both of us naked, her fondling her massive tits, me pumping my cock while I watched her play with herself. Oral had been the name of the game, which was hot as fuck. Still, my dick was dying for the tightness of her pussy, and the more I thought about ramming into her as hard and rough as she liked it, the more I was a second away from losing my load in my jeans.

I rubbed a spot on her inner thigh, my mind wandering as my fangs lowered.

Slapping her hand on mine, her breathing quickened, yet her expression was clinical. "The sex dungeon is closed right now."

I threw my head back and laughed, and it felt like a twenty-ton weight had been lifted off me.

She collapsed into a fit of giggles. The sound was music to my ears. After a beat, she shivered. "Now back to the topic of kids." The light in her eyes vanished.

Our relationship had grown so fast that we'd never talked about a family. In fact, I'd knocked her up during our very first roll in the hay. Honestly, I'd never expected her to have Vel-negative blood, the exact type for a human to get pregnant by a vampire. Yet here we were—mom and dad to four beautiful babies. If I'd known the ways Layla's life would be at risk while carrying inhuman babies, I would've thought twice about having children. But hindsight and all that.

I combed my fingers through my hair. "Baby doll, I'm sorry. The question came out of nowhere. Honestly, I would consider more kids in a fucking heartbeat. But it's dangerous for you." I tapped my chest. "You are the most important person ever. My heart stopped several times when I heard the nurse say you flatlined. I would die if you had to go through that a second time."

Her shoulders slumped. "You caught me off guard. But now that I'm thinking about it, I agree with you. It is dangerous, but we also can't bring more children into this world, not with the dangers facing us." She puffed out her cheeks. "There's something I need to tell you." She picked at a nail as a dark cloud formed over her. "I saw my mom when I died."

The door swung open, and my sister blew in like a powerful hurricane. "There you are, brother. I just talked to Sawyer." Jo regarded Layla as she sidled up to the other side of the bed. "Does Layla know?"

"Know what?" Layla asked, her smooth forehead wrinkling. "That Fred murdered my dad?"

Jo shook her head, astonishment etched in her silver eyes. "That you and Abbey are cousins, and if I'm right, first cousins once removed since your grandparents are Abbey's great-grandparents."

Layla sucked in air. "What?"

"Right, Sam?" Jo asked. "Isn't that what you heard? That's what Tripp told me."

I guessed Jordyn hadn't shared that news with Layla. But the potential relationship between Layla and Abbey shouldn't stress her out.

Doc poked his head in. "Sam, I've been waiting. Let's go."

I pushed to my feet. "Yes, if Fred Emery is correct, then Abbey and the Aberdeen sisters are related."

Layla's mouth was hanging open, her blue eyes bigger than I'd ever seen them.

Doc ambled in. "They're related?"

So much for giving blood.

Doc was an eager beaver to learn more as he settled at the foot of the bed.

I had no choice but to explain what Fred had told Tripp, Jordyn, and me. After this conversation, I was going to see my kids, then lock myself in the birthing suite and take advantage of the pullout couch. Otherwise, I wouldn't be worth a shit to fight another day.

17

LAYLA

I traipsed from my room to the infirmary's nursery around six that night, freshly showered, wearing a clean hospital gown and robe, and feeling physically great but emotionally spent. The day had been a whirlwind of shock, surprises, and life-changing events. I should have been thinking of what I needed to pack, but instead I couldn't shake thoughts of how I might be related to Abbey. If that were true, did that mean my sisters and I had magical abilities?

Abbey was a powerful ten-year-old human who could see into the future. She was also changing into a bloodsucker as she aged. She would be a full-fledged vampire when she reached her teenage years without needing to drink her vampire father's blood. In addition, she was prophesied to be the first female bloodsucker who would be able to conceive. No one understood the mystery of why Abbey would be able to bear children when she became a vampire. As it stood, female vampires couldn't get pregnant.

Regardless of Abbey's powers, Doc assumed my banshee scream and mind control came from the babies when they were inside me. Maybe they didn't. A million questions jumped around in my brain. Was my mom's sister, Vanessa, alive? Jo had said no. Abbey's maternal grandparents were presumably dead, or at least that was the story Abbey's mother Rachel had told before she'd died. But through Jo's research, it seemed Abbey's maternal grandfather might be alive.

I had my hand on the door to the nursery when a thought stopped me cold. I replayed the conversation with my mom.

"You can't leave me hanging like this. I need to know which of my children you speak of."

She pulled me in for a hug and whispered, "Find Kendra."

Did she mean Kendra knew about the prophecy and the child my mom was referring to? It was even more imperative to chat with Kendra, and not about my father, since she'd grown up with my mother. Kendra could tell me about my mom and her past and shed light on who she really was. More importantly, Kendra might know about the prophecy. If I recalled, though, she wasn't in the States and wouldn't be for a few weeks, according to her text.

A baby cried, severing my thoughts. It was close to feeding time. Normally, they would be in the birthing suite with me, but Sam was sleeping, and if anyone needed rest, it was him.

I ambled into the nursery, and the crying stopped. It took me a second to get my bearings as I focused on the four bassinets beneath warming lights along the left wall in a room filled with rockers, cabinets, drawers, sinks, a bathroom, and medical equipment. I then fixed my gaze on Jo, Jordyn, and Harley sitting in the rockers to my right. Jordyn and Jo were feeding Luna and Orion respectively.

Harley popped out of her seat, showing straight white teeth as her blue eyes swirled to black. "I'd never been more scared in my life than when I heard what happened in the OR." She pulled me in for a hug.

Her strawberry-blond hair smelled of vanilla beans, and suddenly I had a hankering for a vanilla latte.

I snickered as we broke apart. "Did you bathe in vanilla?"

"You could say that. Lotion and shampoo. It's my favorite

scent." She tittered, dipping her head at the empty rocker. "Come sit beside me."

I checked on my other daughters who were sleeping, itching to pick them up and squeeze them to me.

Jo, reading my mind, said, "Sit. You can hold your son. I have research to do." Jo rose slowly then handed Orion to me. "First thing tomorrow, Layla, you need to pack up as many things from the babies' room as you can. George ordered cribs, and they should be delivered to my house in Maine next week."

And so the running and escaping began. Not the way I wanted to start motherhood. My children needed stability. We had a beautiful apartment that we'd redecorated and an adorable nursery bathed in stuffed animals and musical crib mobiles. It was a place I could finally call home, something I hadn't had since my dad died two years ago.

Nevertheless, I eased into the rocker between Jordyn and Harley as I cradled Orion and continued feeding him. "Hey, little guy. Momma's here." His green eyes danced with delight as he sucked on the bottle of formula mixed with a small dose of blood.

My heart bloomed with such a deep sense of love that it almost hurt. My babies didn't need to be subjected to war. They needed a life free of strife to grow up unencumbered, to be kids, to climb into a tree house, play sports, play with dolls, or whatever else they would find interest in.

Staring at mini Sam, I silently vowed to him, *I will be your armor, your safe harbor in the storm we're walking into. I will die to protect you and your sisters.*

He continued to gaze at me, innocent and pure. Suddenly, that recurring dream flashed between us, and my heart skipped a beat. Orion's eyes penetrated through me as if he was pressing Play on the remote, and I was transported into the dream.

The fire died suddenly, and I was enveloped in a sea of darkness. As I blinked rapidly to adjust my vision, my breathing increased. As if someone had flipped a switch, the double white lines on the road beamed a vivid orange. Bright stars glistened in the inky-black sky, twinkling like tiny diamonds. A red ring circled the radiant moon that seemed ten times larger than I'd ever seen it.

"Over here," the young boy called.

I reoriented my vision to look ahead of me.

A boy about five years old surrounded by an iridescent glow held out his hand. "We need to go." Fear coated his small voice.

I was frozen to the heat of the pavement.

"Please," he begged. "She needs your help."

My limbs unlocked, and I jogged toward the little boy who had black hair and eyes so familiar I lost my breath.

"Who needs my help?" I asked as I reached the boy.

"My sister," he said with a slight lisp. "You're the only one who can help her."

"I don't understand. Why me?"

His green eyes were high beams in the dark of night. "Because you have the power." He tugged on my fingers. "We don't have much time."

"Who are you?"

"I'm your son," he said as if I was supposed to know that.

"Layla. Layla. Layla!" A chorus of voices called to me. Then hands were on my shoulders, and someone was shaking me. "Where did you go?" Jo's voice seeped into my ear canal.

I broke my connection with Orion and focused on Jo, who was standing like a giant before me. "Is something wrong?"

"You tell us," my sister said as she came into view beside Jo, empty-handed. She must've finished feeding Luna.

"Just thinking, and I'm suddenly tired." The adrenaline was slowly dissipating, and I was desperate to join Sam, not only to sleep but to feel his protective arms around me. I needed him to tell me everything would be okay, even if it wasn't true. I was beginning to feel as if my children were giving me signs, preparing me and alerting me of their powers and what was to come.

I prayed like a nun that dream wouldn't come true. But I swore Orion had been trying to warn me.

"You and Sam will need all the rest you can get," Jo said.

More than likely, he would be on the run without me. Yeah, I'd about blown my top when I'd heard how the Council of Elders wanted to use Sam as a scapegoat. However, Steven had a plan, but Sam didn't know the details. Whatever it was, I believed in Steven. I also understood that fleeing with a wife, who wasn't exactly in tip-top physical shape, and four tiny beings would slow him down and put us in danger.

The thirst to wipe out Intech was stronger than ever but nowhere near as fierce as the will to square off with Rianne. The bitch had thrown my children and me to the wolves, and I wouldn't be able to function until she was out of my life.

"Any news on Kendra?" I asked Jo.

In addition to Sawyer searching for Kendra, Jo had tried to call her but had no luck.

Jo was washing her hands at the sink at the back wall. "No. If you're right and she's out of the country, that might be why we're having trouble."

"We do have more important problems to deal with here than Kendra," I said.

The possible relationship between Abbey and me and my sisters was interesting, and I wanted to know more. Even the prophecy would have to take a back seat. Our safety was at the top of the list. We couldn't lose sight of our enemies either. Unless there was a connection between the prophecy and our adversaries. Somehow, I didn't think so. Besides, uncovering whether a child of mine would disrupt mankind would be like trying to find a needle in a haystack.

Jo ripped a paper towel from its silver holder on the counter. "Prophecy?" She spun on her cute black flats and angled her head. "Tell me more."

Jordyn, who was sitting next to me and had been super quiet, asked, "Did Mom tell you about a prophecy? I knew you were leaving something else out."

I snapped at my sister. "I'm sure you haven't told me some things." I couldn't quite put my finger on it, but there was more to

Jordyn's hatred for Fred. She'd used the word creep and Fred in a sentence many times. I had my own thoughts on the topic, but I didn't want to push her. In all fairness to her, we hadn't gotten past the shocking news that Fred Emery had admitted to murdering our father.

She shrank backward and lowered her gaze to her lap, where she was fidgeting with a fingernail.

"You saw your mom in a dream?" Harley asked. "Don't brush what she said off. In our world, discussions in dreams are messages not to be taken lightly."

I knew that, and I wasn't taking anything with a grain of salt. But I'd just learned of the prophecy, and the idea that a child of mine could change or shape humanity in a good or bad way hadn't yet sunk in.

Jo folded her arms over her lab coat. "Layla, it's important to lay out everything we're facing. We can't afford any more surprises." Her tone was matter-of-fact yet accusatory. She'd been wound tight since the press conference.

I pursed my lips. "I'm well aware, Jo," I fired back, not intending to snap, but I felt like she was attacking me for something I had no control over. "But cut me some slack, please. In a span of seventeen hours, I died three times, I gave birth, I saw my nutso sister enjoy her five minutes of fame, discovered Fred Emery murdered my father, and that I might be related to Abbey. That's more than I can swallow. So forgive me if I haven't told anyone about a prophecy."

Jo slipped her hands into the pockets of her lab coat, losing the anger carved into her face as she paced up and down the middle of the room. "I'm sorry. You're right. *You* more than anyone have been through hell." She paused for a breath. "Believe it or not, reading minds sucks the wind out of me because everything I learn comes with emotions that I feel as strongly as you do. That sets me on edge. I'm not upset with you, Layla. But I've been through this crap before, only this time, Edmund's war is child's play compared to the one we're about to fight."

Orion let go of the bottle's nipple, squirming as he started crying, severing the tension. Or maybe he was fussy because my muscles were tight and he could feel my emotions. If human babies could sense a mother's feelings, then a vampire newborn surely could more so with his heightened senses.

Harley held out her hand. "I'll hold that while you burp him."

I gave her the bottle, then adjusted him on my shoulder. "Shh. Momma's okay," I said, patting and rubbing his back. But he continued to cry. "Was Sam's blood mixed in with the formula?" I asked them.

After the jam-packed afternoon of planning and figuring out our next moves, Sam had managed to give blood.

"It is," Jordyn said. "I saw that nurse Beverly adding a teaspoon to the bottle."

Orion was becoming fussier.

"Maybe that wasn't enough," I said. "He probably needs more blood."

Jo lowered her fangs, closed the short distance between us, and grabbed my hand. Then she used her long canine to puncture the skin on my forefinger. "I think you're right."

I adjusted Orion in my arms, and the second he was sucking on my finger, he quieted. Oh my. I could only imagine that as he grew, he would require more and more of the sticky red stuff. Doc had mentioned Orion would need Sam's blood more than mine, which meant Sam would be tethered to a needle every day.

Silence zipped around the room.

Jo tangled her fingers, pinning silver eyes on me. "Again, I'm sorry for snapping at you. I'm worried about Abbey. With the mess we're in, it's not just about Sam's fate with the elders or your safety. We can't forget about Abbey. Who knows what Roman has in store for her? She's had visions of him taking her." She rubbed the back of her neck. "We need to regroup, strategize, and set priorities. The first one is moving Abbey, you, and my nieces and nephew to Maine. Then when you're physically ready, Layla, you'll need to begin working out. Jordyn too. This war might go on for months or, dare I say, years."

Her last line punched the wind out of me. But I was completely on board with everything she'd said.

I rocked Orion as he continued to suckle. I doubted he was getting much, but he had a hold on me that seemed to dare me to pull my finger out.

I moistened my dry lips with my tongue as a faint burn coated my throat. "Jo, there's not much to tell about the prophecy. My mom's message was gibberish and ambiguous. To sum it up, she told me two things. One, Sam and I play a key role in making sure humanity survives. Two, one of our children is prophesied to change the course of humankind with some type of ripple effect that supposedly will upset the balance of the world." I shrugged. "No clue which one, and I certainly don't know how. And while I would like to believe the outcome would be good, I didn't get that vibe from my mom."

Jo curled black strands of hair around her ear. "My dad's dreams as of late have shown him *you* are important in the war. Your mom intimated that very thing, which tells me we need to heed her warning about the prophecy too."

It wasn't as if I was discounting what my mom had told me. Again, priorities. One thing at a time—and one day as well.

"How do you suggest we decipher the prophecy?" I asked.

Jo exchanged a knowing look with Harley.

"When you saw your mother," Harley asked, crossing one leg over the other, her blue gaze searching my face, "did she have anyone with her, like an animal?"

I arched an eyebrow, dipping into my memory bank. "No, why?"

"My grandfather has a spirit animal—a panther," Jo said. "The animal has talked to me in my dreams, and now my dad is seeing the panther too."

"My dreams include a little boy who looks like Orion. No animals."

"What makes you think your dream has nothing to do with the prophecy? Maybe he's the prophecy," Jordyn chimed in.

A round of chills crawled down my arms, feeling like sharp talons scraping along my skin at Jordyn's statement. Orion had been in every one of my recurring dreams.

"She's right," Jo and Harley said in unison.

"Don't discount anything," Harley added.

I stiffened. "We're not going to figure out my mom's message from the dead anytime soon." I rose, removing my finger from Orion's mouth, and yawned. "Are the nurses on duty?" If they weren't, I would bring my kids into the birthing suite. I carried Orion to his bassinet and set him inside.

"They are," Jo said. "I gave them a reprieve. They're in the break room." Jo could fill in as a doctor or nurse. She pulled me in for a hug. "Again, I didn't mean to jump down your throat."

I returned the gesture. "I need you more than ever." I truly did. She was just as powerful as Sam or even more so.

After we broke apart, she said, "We'll get through this. Try to sleep. Tomorrow is a new day." Then she glided out.

"Layla, go," Harley said. "I'll stay the night in here."

"I will too," Jordyn said. "But first, can we chat? I'll walk you to your room."

Voices tittered in the hall, announcing two nurses as they sashayed in, smiling as if they had been telling each other secrets. The three nurses who had been in the operating room were nice and bubbly. All of them were vampires who worked at the Boston medical facility.

"Where's Wendy?" I asked.

Beverly, the redhead, checked on the babies. "She's not on until midnight."

Amy, brown haired and shorter than Beverly, crossed the room and punched the keys on a computer sitting on the counter. "She'll replace me."

Only two had been on duty, allowing the third nurse to rest. Not that I didn't trust the nurses. They had been vetted by Doc and Jo. But having Harley and Jordyn stay the night would just make me feel more comfortable.

Jordyn waited for me by the door.

"Can you add two teaspoons of Sam's blood to Orion's bottle instead of one?" I asked the nurses. "He seems to need more. I'll be in my birthing suite if you need me."

They both nodded as Harley struck up a conversation with them.

Once Jordyn and I were in the hallway, quietness followed us for several steps as Jordyn chewed on a nail.

"Spill, sis," I said.

"I want to wipe our slate clean. No more secrets on my part. It's been killing me not to tell you, but in my defense, Doc didn't want you stressed during your pregnancy." She traded one finger for the other and gnawed on the fresh one.

I gently tugged on her wrist. "Stop that, and just say what's on your mind."

She inhaled deeply. "Fred came on to me when I interviewed with Intech. Before you ask, no, he didn't violate me, but he would have if it weren't for his phone ringing in his office that day."

I ground my molars together as rage gripped my throat. Her actions and her hunger to seek revenge made more sense now.

She shuddered. "He told me I would be his."

I draped my arm around her. "Hey, he will never put his hands on you." No question in my mind that Fred Emery would face a slow and painful death. "You will have your revenge. I promise you that, Jordyn." Though I wasn't sure how.

Jordyn resumed chomping on a fingernail.

"Anything else bothering you?" I asked, knowing there was something else.

"I am worried about where we go from here," she said. "There are so many unanswered questions about who we really are. Who was Mom? And if we are related to Abbey, do we have latent powers that we don't know about? Sam said we couldn't be as strong as Abbey because our father wasn't a vampire. But since you have the Vel-negative blood type, that means we come from a line of witches."

"What are you afraid of? That you'll zip around the country on a broom?" I teased, trying to infuse some lightness into the conversation on our ever-changing lives.

She snickered. "Funny. I guess what I'm trying to say is, I hate the unknown. Can you imagine if Rianne had witch powers?"

Disaster came to mind, as did our evil grandmother. "Why do you think we haven't heard from Granny? Something is up. I can feel it. She would've been front and center during that press conference. Has she contacted you?" My sister had made a deal with our grandmother to spare me, but Jordyn never made it to Intech's West Virginia facility.

Jordyn lowered her gaze to the floor or perhaps her cute, red-painted toenails. "She has."

I shook the marbles out of my ears, glancing down one end of the hall and then the other. The act was more to collect my thoughts. "Did you talk to her? What did she say? When did she call you?"

She righted her head, her face ashen. "A week after the car accident. I didn't talk to her. She just left me a message that she was disappointed in me and that she would see you and me soon. That was it. I didn't call her back." She produced her phone from the pocket in her sundress and played the voice mail.

"Jordyn, this is your grandmother. I'm quite disappointed that you didn't honor our deal. As I told you, I am dying of an incurable blood cancer and would like to see my grandkids before it's too late. Also, I'm learning quite a bit about your mother's side of the family. And you and Layla might be able to save me. Your father would want you to." Her tone was even, but her narcissism made me nauseous.

I laughed. That was the only thing I could do. Or else I would be vomiting. "Granny is a piece of work." I yawned, gripping her shoulders. "I'm sorry you couldn't talk to me about any of this while I was carrying the quadruplets." While Sam had been over-the-top in protecting me from bad news or situations, I couldn't fault him or Doc's orders mandating that I avoid stress.

She brushed me off. "As Jo said, tomorrow is a new day."

I prayed it would be better than today. Right now, a bed and my hot, sexy vampire husband with massive protective arms were calling my name.

18

SAM

The Atlantic was peaceful on a bright, sunny afternoon, the waves crawling gently to the shore as if the sea was afraid to come in. The salt air trickled in through the glass accordion doors, the scent mixing with sweet, delectable cherries. My gaze bounced from outside to my naked, gorgeous, curvy, auburn-haired wife, who had her ass in the air as she bent over the couch.

Turning to look at me, she batted her long lashes, her cheeks rosy and her hair falling from her messy bun. "What are you waiting for, vampire?" She pushed her gorgeous ass into my rock-hard cock. "Something wrong?"

I jolted out of my reverie. "Just taking in the beauty of the scene outside and in."

"Well, my pussy is dying to feel that massive cock of yours inside me." Her tongue darted out to lick her lips.

I grinned, shaping her hip with one hand, and positioned my dick at her entrance with the other. "Massive, huh?"

"Beautiful," she said in her siren tone, widening her stance, lifting her butt higher in the air.

As if that was the answer I was looking for, I drove into her, swift and hard.

"Yes," she cried out. "Fuck me like you mean it."

I stilled, enjoying the feel of her tight walls wrapped around my shaft. "No other way, baby doll."

She pushed backward as I began a slow thrust forward, my eyes rolling back in my head. I never wanted to leave this spot or position. But I also wanted to take my time, to feel every thrust, hear her soft moans, and make this last for hours.

She clenched her walls, and my knees almost buckled as I let out a loud groan.

She giggled. "You know, vampire. How about I suck you off first?"

In a flash, I pulled out, lifted her up, and carried her over to the fireplace.

She laughed. "You want my lips around your——"

"Fuck yeah, but I want to taste you." I set her down. "On your back," I commanded as I dropped to my knees.

She obeyed, but her curious expression flickered in and out until lust brewed in the depths of her blue eyes. "Oh," she said, splayed out like a Roman goddess ready to be kissed by her king of gods. "Are we doing what I think——"

"My cock in your mouth and your pussy in mine," I said in a husky tone that didn't sound like me.

Her tits rose, her nipples poking out and her heart soaring. Her ball-squeezing smile almost made me come undone. I couldn't believe that this feisty, driven, and gorgeous woman was all mine—heart, body, soul—and that she was now my wife.

I was drunk on her beauty, her cherry fragrance, the anticipation of what we were about to do, the salt air spilling in and mixing with the aroma of sex and the fire crackling before us.

I positioned my dick over her hungry mouth. Before I could bury my face into her pussy, she flicked her tongue over my sensitive, wet tip, and I bucked. "Oh fuck, baby doll."

She giggled. "Eat, vampire. You're starving."

I was, and not only for her sweet juices but something equally orgasmic. My fangs shot out, and Layla spread her thighs wide open.

I licked a small area on her inner thigh, inhaled, then struck.

She whimpered, latching onto my cock, and froze for a mere second.

Her blood exploded on my tongue, sending me into the stratosphere, and even more so when she swallowed me whole, the head of my cock touching the back of her throat.

Motherfucker. The woman knew exactly how to play me.

While I took long pulls, she found a steady rhythm—sucking and licking. After I had my fill of blood, I retracted my fangs and kissed my way to the soaking folds of her cunt. She smelled of ecstasy and set my balls on fire as I suckled her swollen nub.

As we feasted on each other, moans and groans peppered the air, competing with the crackle of fire. The fragrant sex swirling around us made me high as a fucking kite. A high I never wanted to come down from, but when Layla played with my balls, that tingling in my lower back hit me out of nowhere. I was reaching that point of no return, and as much as I fucking loved her mouth, I had to feel her pussy walls gripping my shaft.

I flipped around in seconds before she could protest and drove inside her. "Legs over my shoulders," I bit out, holding back as hard as I fucking could.

Once she was splayed open, I fucked her rough and fast, just how she liked it.

She grabbed my hair and pulled my mouth to hers. "Fangs, vampire. I want to see them while you fuck me."

Who was I to disappoint?

She angled her neck. "Bite." Her tone was demanding.

Just as I sank my fangs into her, she clamped her teeth into my neck, breaking skin.

As I drank, fucking her, her love slid through my veins like warm butter, filling every cell in me. I was dizzy, high, and ready to explode.

She released me. "I can feel you so strongly when your blood is in me." Her voice was breathy. "Come with me, vampire."

I tucked away my fangs, licked my blood from her lips, and pounded into her like a madman.

"Yes, that's it, Sam. Harder," she said between breaths as I rocked and she rolled.

The sound of flesh slapping together, our moans peppering the air, and the crackling of fire was a well-orchestrated symphony of magic and mayhem.

Human and vampire. Fire and ice. Two beings twined together by fate, love, and an overwhelming desire to please each other.

My heart was punching my ribs. I was coated in sweat as I climbed higher with every thrust, breath, and groan, locking eyes with the most stunning creature I'd ever seen.

"Liquid silver," she panted out, reaching up and dragging a finger over one of my eyelids. "Your transformation to vampire sets my clit on fire."

As if that were my magic button, that tingle in my lower back struck fast and hard, wrapping around my waist. I threw my head back and roared my release while Layla shot up to a sitting position and screamed my name at the top of her lungs.

Fucking mind-blowing ecstasy as I rode out my orgasm, beaming at the beauty who I called my wife, partner, and soulmate.

She smiled from ear to ear, sweat dotting her forehead, her auburn hair damp and wild around her face. "Best sex yet."

I untangled myself from her when an intrusive ringing sound rudely entered my psyche, faint at first, and as I growled for the noise to stop, it grew louder as Layla's pretty face vanished.

I jolted awake. Disoriented, I rubbed my eyes, feeling like I'd just run a marathon. The sheets were drenched in sweat, and my crotch was wet. I swiped a hand over boxer briefs. Yep, I actually came from that dream. But fuck if it wasn't the best ever.

I glanced at my sleeping beauty, who had a smile on her face. I wondered if she'd experienced my erotic fantasy. I'd been the star of hers once before.

I leaned over the bed and snatched my phone from the top of my jeans.

"Sam."

Layla's sultry voice gave me goose bumps, and I turned to kiss her on the forehead. "Go back to sleep. I'm going to take a quick shower."

She snaked her hand under the sheet and found my wet boxer briefs that covered my semi-hard cock. "Did we just have sex?

Because I dreamt we were in a sixty-nine position." Her sleepy blue eyes were high beams in the darkened room.

A corner of my mouth turned upward, the blood rushing to my dick as her lust wafted into my nostrils. "I was curious if we were having the same one. Fucking hot, wasn't it?"

"For sure," she said. "I really wish we could replay that scene in real life."

My eyes were rolling back in my head as she rubbed my cock. "Oh, we will when you're ready. For fucking sure." I was ready to blow my load again.

"You know you're sticky," she said with a giggle.

"That's what you do to me even in my dreams," I said as another text message came in.

She sat up. "Who keeps texting you? Your dad?" She lost that seductive tone. "Is it a 911?"

Blowing out a frustrated breath, I opened up my message app.

Dad: *Son, I'm still knee-deep in meetings. We're waiting for the Secretary of the Navy to show up. I might be here for a few more days. We haven't talked about you yet. The human government is up in arms over the missing officials. But I'm still working on my plan in the background. I will message you later. Oh, and forgive me for not meeting my grandkids. But I will soon. Please tell Layla I'm sorry. I've ordered Webb to assign a guard to my grandchildren at all times. He should've posted one in the infirmary. And Conrad will be heading to Maine to help out. Give him a call and fill him in. I wasn't able to explain everything.*

I silently thanked the gods that the council's attention was diverted to the missing DOD officials, which would give me time to pack up Layla, ready my go bag, and spend time with my kids.

Me: *Thanks, Pops. I'll call Conrad and fill him in.*

Conrad, a scout who worked for my father, had for many years been assigned to watch the Aberdeens. He'd helped me when I flew to Montana for Layla.

"I like Conrad," Layla said as she laid her head on my arm and read with me. "And your dad shouldn't be sorry. He's trying to save your life, and that is a huge priority. I can't lose you, Sam."

I draped my arm around her and tugged her to me. "We can't lose each other, baby doll. But we might need to be apart for a while." That would gut me. Hell, I was already feeling like someone had carved out my insides with a serrated-edged blade.

She rubbed my bare chest. "It's going to suck the big one, but rest assured, I'm ready to fight. Well, once I get my body back in shape, of course."

"You'll have Conrad, George, Jo, and Harley. They have great skills. Jo will also help draw out any magical powers you might have."

She sat up. "You think we should be worried about anyone in our circle? I mean, the part about a guard in the infirmary raises the hackles on my neck."

We weren't immune to moles in our ranks. We'd had two during the Edmund war. "My dad is always extremely cautious." But I wasn't arguing. "I know trust is hard to come by, even when it comes to the closest people to us. I'm not about to say don't worry because I want you on your toes."

She let out a nervous laugh. "I will be. Remember Rianne."

I growled. "If you're up for it, want to go with me to our apartment? We'll check in on our kids first, but I would like to pack while it's quiet." I didn't anticipate any craziness at three that morning, but I hadn't twenty-four hours before either.

She swung her legs out of bed. "Hell yeah, I would love to change out of this hospital gown, and I need my phone."

"I'll duck into the shower quickly." I climbed off the uncomfortable pullout couch.

She skirted around the bed, throwing on her robe. "I'll meet you in the nursery."

Before she walked out, I blocked her, flattened my hands on her warm cheeks, and stared into her electric-blue eyes. "No matter what happens from here, know my life is a better place with you in it. You are the brightest star in my universe. I'm so in love with you, even more today than yesterday. We will survive what we're facing."

Her pulse kicked up as she shivered. "You're scaring me, and you know I don't get frightened easily, vampire."

I ghosted my lips over hers. "Forgive me. That's not my intention. I never want to go a day without seeing your beautiful face or telling you how much I love you. But we might be apart for some time."

She rose up on her toes and kissed me. "I'm the luckiest woman ever, and you're right. We will survive what's ahead. I have to believe that. Our children need us. We need each other. And the love we have for one another will only strengthen our powers."

I mashed my mouth to hers and kissed her hungrily and passionately.

My chest clenched at the notion that I might not see her and our children for a while. But if it kept them safe, nothing else mattered.

19

SAM

I snagged a bottle of blood from the fridge in my apartment, popped the top, and chugged. The aching in my gums diminished the more I drank, as did my bloodthirst. Hours of sleep, a hot-as-fuck dream, my hunger sated, four stunning children, and a ravishing auburn-haired goddess erased every fucking piece of bad shit that had happened in the last twenty-four hours. This time yesterday I'd been in hell. But no more. The next time I went to hell, I was taking my enemies with me—in particular, Rianne. That bitch was why my family had to run and was one of the reasons for Layla's tension. I would find a way to make Rianne suffer.

I skirted the kitchen island and wound my way over to the floor-to-ceiling window that spanned one wall. My apartment—or the penthouse, as my sister had dubbed the spacious open floor plan many years ago—had high ceilings with exposed white pipes and ductwork that blended in well with the walls, keeping that factory style of the former textile building.

Darkness crawled through the courtyard below, the stars twinkling in the night sky. A guard stood tall outside the prison across from me. Hawk was doing the same outside the infirmary's nursery.

I liked and trusted Hawk, the young SEAL team member proving to us he was ready for anything. He was respectful and didn't mouth off like our other new recruit Petty Officer Dawson. I appreciated Dawson's arrogance in certain situations, but he needed to learn where to direct his superiority.

Jordyn and Harley were also in the infirmary's nursery, helping Beverly and Wendy, the nurses on duty. Jordyn and Harley's presence gave me another reason to feel like I could breathe. Layla and I had several things to do, and in the quietness of the night and with our children fast asleep, we could begin packing.

Where I would bunker down if the council ruled against me or if my father didn't have a chance to enact his plan was a mystery. Sawyer had offered his childhood home. While I was grateful he'd been thinking of me, I couldn't put his parents in harm's way. They didn't need to take on my problems.

Sawyer had mentioned something about witches in his hometown, but even so, they couldn't protect me, although if they were seasoned witches, they might have a shielding spell or some witchy magic to throw off my scent.

My thoughts fizzled when I heard Layla sniffling. I chucked the bottle in the trash and dashed into the nursery.

Layla was sitting on the carpeted floor, legs curled under her and hugging a stuffed elephant, crying.

I crouched down. "Hey, baby doll. I'm here. What's this about?"

On the way to the apartment, Layla had been excited about heading up to Maine. She couldn't stop talking about the ocean and inhaling the salt air. The July weather was perfect for swimming in the surf, walking on the beach, and enjoying the sun. A pristine setting and environment for relaxing and healing while taking care of our little ones.

She giggled through tears. "I'm sorry. I'm a blubbering mess. I wanted a chance to use this room. I wanted Ellie, Luna, Rorie, and Orion to wake up with the elephants and be mesmerized by the cute musical crib mobiles."

I sat down and stretched out my legs on either side of her. "This room will still be here when we return. Besides, you love the ocean. And you can take the stuffed animals, the mobiles, and anything else except the cribs. Jo is having new ones delivered."

We planned for Harley to take the suitcases and boxes in her long-bed crew cab truck and leave before Layla, Jordyn, Abbey, Jo, and the babies. Actually, we were staggering departure times. That way we didn't look conspicuous. A caravan of vehicles leaving the base would draw attention given the masses outside our gates.

I was amazed how fast things were moving, and sitting on the floor in our nursery, I was beginning to feel emotional with Layla. I loved this apartment. Traipsing from one foster home to another for most of my life, I'd never lived in one place for more than two years. They hadn't been loving environments either.

She scooted between my legs. "What if the apartment is gone when we return?"

I wasn't about to tell her that wasn't possible, because the humans might be able to overrun the naval base. I didn't see that happening easily. Except for the human wives and children living on base, the populace was vampires.

I curled her hair behind her ear. "Whether or not the base is still standing when we return doesn't matter. What does is our family."

"I know. It's just the idea of moving again. My sisters and I haven't had a place to call home since our dad died." A waterfall of tears poured out of her.

"Wherever we are will be home," I said.

She played with the belt on her robe. "I get that. But the kids will need stability."

Sadly, we might be on the run for a long time. Maine was a great spot for the time being, but no one could stay hidden forever. Not with the media breathing down our necks.

"Everything is happening too fast, Sam. I feel like I'm falling into a rabbit hole with no way out. I mean, I know we're at war, and that bothers me, but not as much as the unknown does. How long will we be moving around? Can we live in peace when this is all over? Who was my mom? Her family? Who am I? What are our kids?" With each question came another tear.

I leaned away, my forehead creasing. "We know who *you* are. We know Orion is a vampire. The girls will show their powers soon enough." I had a feeling they carried the vampire gene, but maybe they needed my blood to activate it. After all, Doc had given Orion my blood to save his life. So he was the first to reveal who he was. "We're uncovering more about your mom's lineage."

"Yesterday, before Jo blew into the birthing suite, I tried to tell you something about my mom."

"You saw her when you died, right?" I remembered that, but it had gotten lost in the madness.

"My mom's message was about a prophecy involving one of our kids. She couldn't tell me who, but one of them will change the course of humanity and upset the balance of the world. What if just being born did that? Think about it. Adam's press conference happened after I gave birth, right?"

As far-fetched as her idea was, I didn't want to discount it. Fate and destiny had a way of playing out in weird ways. The birth of supernatural babies, which had only happened once in our history as far as we knew, could set off a chain of events.

She squeezed my thigh. "You think it's possible?"

I nodded. "Of course."

She slumped, pushing out a sigh. "I hope it's only that—being born. And I keep thinking of my recurring dream. You know the one where I see our son, and he says I have to help his sister? What if they are the prophecy? My mom couldn't tell me more." Her hands shook. "Maybe all four are."

I gently circled my fingers around her wrists. "Take a breath."

She inhaled deeply and blew it out.

I would guess that the prophecy was one of many opposing forces, but according to my father, prophecies weren't always cut and dry. The one about Abbey might have some loopholes. Her powers were certainly growing. But would she become the first female vampire to procreate?

"We should pack," I said. We weren't about to solve things anytime soon.

She caught my arm as I was about to stand up. "There's one more thing. After I pleaded with my mom to tell me which of our children she was talking about, she told me to find Kendra. I don't know if that means Kendra knows which child, but I got the feeling she knows about the prophecy."

"Maybe you should call her." I glanced at her phone on the floor next to a diaper bag.

"I did when we came in. But I got her voice mail."

"Keep trying," I said. "Later on, we'll talk to Sawyer when he's at his desk." It was the middle of the night, and even Sawyer had to sleep.

She jerked her gaze up to look at me and smiled. "I like that plan. You know…" Her eyes swirled with mischief as lust oozed off her.

I smirked as darkness flashed for a nanosecond—a sign my eyes had changed from green to silver. "You're not ready for him." I grabbed my growing erection through the fabric of my jeans.

She lowered her gaze, her tongue darting out to moisten her lips. "I'm always ready for your gorgeous cock." She dragged a nail over the bulge in my jeans. "I want to give you a blow job. We have time. I need a distraction, and we might not see each other for a while." She unbuckled my belt.

Fuck, I loved this woman. "But I can't please you."

She popped the button on my jeans. "Sex isn't always about me. I appreciate your attentiveness to my sexual needs, but shut up, lie back, and enjoy. I need to do this, vampire."

Who was I to say no to my wife? I hated that I couldn't be inside her. I hated that I couldn't touch her pussy, not until Doc gave us the go-ahead to resume normal activities. Maybe by then, we wouldn't be apart.

I kicked off my boots, and when I tore off my jeans, my cock sprang free.

She giggled. "I love when you're commando."

After I'd showered in the birthing suite, I had no other choice since I didn't have a change of clothes with me.

She stared at my rock-hard erection as if she was snapping picture after picture for her memory album. Maybe she was.

But I didn't even have a chance to take a breath before she dragged her tongue from base to tip then back down, moaning a sound that only made my dick granite.

Restraint, a voice in my head whispered. *Let her play. Don't pounce.*

That was my problem. Her blow jobs were epic but only drove my need to be inside her.

Motherfucker. My resolve was about to be tested.

She circled her fingers around my shaft, her lust-filled blue eyes nailing me to the floor as my heart punched my ribs. It seemed she was waiting for permission or was maybe teasing the fuck out of me.

"Suck me off, baby doll," I said in a husky tone,

As if that was the code to unlock her desire, she licked the head of my cock before diving in wild and free and becoming a madwoman, sucking and licking like never before.

But when the tip of my dick touched the back of her throat and she dragged a finger from my butthole to my balls then squeezed, I shot forward and roared my release.

She moaned as she sucked, gripping my shaft and swallowing every last bit of me. As soon as she let go of my dick, my mouth was on hers, my hands buried in her hair.

The kiss was salty, sloppy, and wet as our tongues fought for domination. I never wanted this moment to end. Because the minute we walked out of the apartment, nothing would ever be the same.

"How was that, vampire?" She gave me a seductive smile, her lips swollen and red.

"Best blow job ever," I said, searching her face. "I just wished it would've lasted longer." Then I frowned. "I'm hungry for your pussy and those massive tits."

She shuddered out an exasperated breath as she lifted her chin. "Touch these tits, and I'll rip off your balls. The healing potion is working but not on my tits. They're sensitive as fuck, and they will be until the milk dries up."

I raised my hands. "I need my balls." Chuckling, I stood then helped her to her feet.

An hour later, I'd taken another shower and was dressed in my black uniform complete with weapons. I'd also packed one duffel bag of clothes and one with extra weapons and ammunition that I had locked up in my bedroom closet.

I grabbed another empty duffel to fill with items from my safe in the pantry before checking the nursery. Scattered about the floor were several piles that included stacks of unopened diapers, car seats, clothes, stuffed animals, bottles, and everything else possible for four newborns.

Layla seemed to be on a mission, but she wasn't in any of the bedrooms or the bathrooms. Instead, she was sitting on the couch in the family room, flipping through TV channels with a mug in her hand.

It took me a beat to smell the caffeine as I dropped my duffel on the kitchen counter. "Are you the Energizer Bunny?" I grabbed a mug of Joe myself.

"It wasn't difficult to organize the baby stuff," she said, flashing her big blues my way. "Nor was throwing on clothes, which by the way, feels amazing even though I can't fit into my pre-pregnancy clothes yet. But this sundress is perfect for now."

The simple powder-blue fabric draping down to just below her knee brought out the color of her eyes perfectly.

"You look fabulous." I took a sip of black coffee and almost choked.

She laughed. "Sorry. I know it's bitter."

I dumped the crap in the sink. "That's not bitter. Did you use the entire bag of coffee beans?"

"I like it strong," she said. "If we had whiskey or bourbon, I would add a shot to it."

"That shit will grow hairs on your chest."

Again, she was laughing, a sound that warmed my heart.

I ducked into the pantry at the far end of the kitchen and moved a package of paper towels to my right on the top shelf. My dad had two safes built into the walls. One was in the master bedroom and the other was the very one I was unlocking. Once the safe was open, I pulled out an envelope of cash I kept for emergencies, three burner phones, and two daggers that I'd forgotten were in the safe.

When I emerged from the pantry, Layla came over and refilled her cup then did a double take. "Is that my dagger? I wondered where it was." She snatched it from me, lighting up like the Fourth of July.

The dagger looked like it belonged in a museum. The letter A was carved into the black leather handle, but it wasn't just a plain letter. Two lions made up its sides, and a double-edged blade connected them.

"I kept it in the safe. I have a leg holster for it in my duffel in the bedroom." No sooner than I had said the last word, I heard my name on TV.

Layla and I turned our attention to the screen.

As I watched a replay of me stopping Carly's car, the blood in my veins turned to dust. I couldn't catch a break.

She regarded me with an *oh-shit* expression, but in a cool, calm, and collected tone, she said, "At least you look hot, vampire. I always love to see you exercise your elemental powers, and on a dark road, that blue light you whip from your hands is fucking cool."

I had to laugh. If I didn't, I would shatter the windows in my apartment. Regardless, if the council members had any inclination to spare me, they wouldn't anymore. I hoped like hell my old man was either putting his plan into place or convincing the ancient elders to focus their attention on the bigger issue at hand—Intech and the public outcry. My ass behind bars or dead wouldn't change the public's perception or satisfy anyone except our enemies. Even at that, Rianne would be quite disappointed she wouldn't have a chance to best me.

20

LAYLA

S am and I were in an interrogation room in the command center behind Sawyer's cubicle, waiting on the techie vampire. He'd gotten tied up with a computer server issue.

As I sat there, I scanned the bare-bones space that contained a table and four chairs and nothing more. This room brought back memories of the day Tripp and Sam had questioned Wyman, the former CIA agent who'd gone by the alias Dowell.

Dowell had hired my sisters and me to capture Sam. But regardless of his name, he'd met my father at the Deer and Elk in Montana. I flipped through the conversation from that day, and something Wyman had mentioned about my dad now made perfect sense.

"Your father didn't want anyone to know he was working with me. His brothers didn't believe in keeping vampires alive, and he had to be careful. But he was lured by the money. He thought he could use it to start a better life than hunting vampires. He wanted that for you and your sisters."

My dad, Wayne Aberdeen, had made a similar deal with Fred Emery—feed Fred living and breathing bloodsuckers in exchange for money. Although the deal with Wyman was for one vampire—

153

Sam Mason. Still, my chest tightened. My dad had died because of my sisters and me. Not directly, of course. But he fought to make a better life for us.

I was so flipping pissed at him though. He should've talked to me. He should've included Jordyn, Rianne, and me in his deals. We were a family. We hunted together. We killed together. We could've helped him. But my dad was a proud man. A patriarch through and through—a protector, a great husband, and a wonderful father who would give anyone the shirt off his back if need be.

After my mom passed, he didn't want us hunting anymore. He desperately tried to talk us out of the family business. "Life is precious," he'd said. "You have to find what makes you happy and do that. Go to college or join the military. I'll find the money to help you."

We hadn't been poor. My father's day job working with my uncle Jack in the horse and cattle business kept a roof over our heads and food on the table. But it wasn't enough to send three kids to college.

Sam blew in my ear. "Baby doll, your phone is vibrating."

Goose bumps blanketed me, bringing me back from my trip down memory lane. I picked my cell up from the table. "Oh, it's Jordyn."

Jordyn: *I'm going home to sleep. Harley left at four this morning since she had to work. Abbey and Jo are here for baby duty. Wendy and Amy are on duty. I'll check in with you later.*

Me: *Thank you. As soon as I'm done talking to Sawyer, I'll be up there.*

Sam and I had checked on our little ones before we came here, and they were sleeping soundly. I'd planned on relieving Jordyn then, but she was insistent that I talk to Sawyer. She was just as anxious to find Kendra as I was.

"I'll be up there as soon as my meeting is over," he said, reading over my shoulder. Then he returned his attention to the headline news on his cell and growled.

"Another video of you?" I asked.

Sam had been in a bad mood since we'd seen that video of him stopping Carly's car on TV.

"No. Listen to this," he said. "The first vampire-related deaths. Five bodies were found in an alleyway in downtown Fall River drained of their blood. An eyewitness tells us two men with fangs were seen following the victims out of a nightclub.'" He pushed out an exasperated breath. "And so it begins."

As the hours and minutes ticked by, the planet was becoming darker and darker. But the depressing news went by the wayside for the moment when a deep male voice trickled in, and Sam jerked his head toward the open door.

"Stay put," the man said to someone before his hulking body filled the doorway.

Literally, since the broad and massively tall vampire with wavy blond hair, eyes the color of a deep cherry-stained wood, and tatted arms barely fit through the opening.

"Look what the cat dragged in," Sam said, his ogre mood lifted. "How the hell are you, Kraft?"

It took me a second to figure out where I'd seen him before. Kraft had been the one guarding Wyman the day Tripp and Sam interrogated him.

Kraft moved deeper inside the room. "Fucking peachy, man. You know it's a shitstorm out there. People are chanting 'Free Layla,' or they want to talk to her." He rounded his gaze on me.

"Maybe I should talk to the press." My mouth and brain weren't on the same page. I had no idea where that thought came from.

"The fuck you will," Sam rushed out, his tone dropping to a growl.

I ruminated on the idea for a beat. "Why not? I can show them I'm fine. I wasn't compelled. Think about it. If we could rally more humans who believe you guys aren't monsters and are helping humanity, maybe *we* can control the narrative. Fight fire with fire, as Adam said."

"Not happening." Sam's tone was lethal. "The council will surely lock me up and throw away the key."

"If they can catch you," Kraft said. "Dude, you know the team has your back. Fuck the council rules. They went out the window after that press conference."

From the expression on Sam's face, I assumed he had his thinking cap on. "It's not the right time. And I know the way we operate now will change. But if anyone talks to the press, it should be me, and only if the SEAL team and my dad agree."

"No," I bit out. "We do it together." The idea was taking shape until another thought blindsided me. "What if we *showed* humans what happens if they sign up for Adam's experiments? We have two people on base who are products of the serum. Carly and Noah. Think about it. The crowds are growing, and until we give them something to prove genetic engineering won't work, Adam Emery has the upper hand."

Kraft and Sam swapped a *that's-not-a-bad-idea* look.

Then Sam's expression turned sour. "It all sounds good, but my dad pointed out that every move on our part needs to be thought out with precision since Adam has the public's attention. If we did a show-and-tell news segment, it could blow back on us. Humans might think we were the ones who changed Carly and Noah. I doubt the public fully understands the meaning behind the fact that we were born, not made. Matthew made mention of that in his speech, but my guess is, people were shocked at Matthew's vampire features, and they haven't yet grasped the true meaning of what he said. But I'll present the idea in the meeting."

I pouted. "I can see your points."

"On another note, there's a Jack Aberdeen here to see you, Layla," Kraft said.

I guessed my uncle was the person Kraft had ordered to stay put. I was surprised Jack listened to him and hadn't stormed in, yelling at Kraft to fuck off.

"Jack," Kraft called. "You can come in now."

My uncle Jack came around the doorjamb in zombie mode. His face was ashen. His blue-gray eyes were dull and filled with tears.

I glanced at Sam for no reason other than to collect my thoughts. I was 100 percent sure Jack had seen his son Noah.

The team who'd been assigned to watch Intech's West Virginia facility had returned to base with my cousin at around five that morning.

I hadn't known the SEALs had Noah until Sam told me earlier in the apartment. He'd been bound by his top secret clearance and SEAL business to keep Noah's condition under wraps, and only those on a need-to-know basis were privy to the information.

But Steven had felt it was time Noah's family knew his plight, which wasn't good. My cousin was feral, according to Sam. Humans like Noah, who didn't have any vampire DNA or markers, supposedly didn't live long after a gene-altering injection. In fact, the serum, depending on the potency, eventually would attack the body's main organs like the heart and brain, which was what had happened to Blake Turner, Patrick Mason's first victim.

My uncle shuffled to the chair across from Sam and me, running his hands through his red hair.

"You've seen Noah," I said softly. That was the only reason Jack wasn't his usual boastful self.

I hadn't seen my cousin since the day in the West Virginia mountains when I learned he'd been injected with the serum. It had been a horrific sight then. Given Jack's state of mind, Noah had to look even worse now.

I rose and went over to sit beside Jack. "Uncle Jack, did you see Noah?" My gaze flicked to Sam then Kraft.

Kraft nodded with a dour expression. "We just came from the prison."

I wrapped an arm around my uncle. I could empathize with him. Rianne might end up like Noah, and that would gut me even though I was furious with her and had a strong desire to murder her.

My uncle shuddered. "His features are…" He shook. "Noah's face is covered in hair, he has red eyes, and he's been changed into an animal. A fucking animal. What is wrong with Adam Emery and Carly? To think I accepted that woman into our family."

My jaw came unhinged. "Hair on his face," I mumbled to myself despite Sam preparing me on what to expect.

Sam studied my uncle. "Jack, your heart is beating extremely fast. Take a breath."

Jack popped up and kicked the chair backward. "Take a breath," he yelled. "Have you seen my son?" He fisted his hands, then paced an area between the wall and the head of the table.

My pulse quickened as I felt sorrow, pain, and anger. Not at Jack but at the situation as well as at Adam, Carly, Rianne, Harriet, and everyone who was on this kick to genetically change humans. It was fucked up on a level that couldn't even be measured.

Sam watched Jack, seemingly concerned.

Jack paced like a madman. "I want to talk to your resident doctor. There has to be a way to reverse the process. There just has to be."

A great idea, but I would guess highly unlikely. "Dr. Vieira and Jo should work on a way to do just that," I said more to myself than to him.

Sam nodded, still keeping his eyes on my uncle. "We'll call Dr. Vieira, but first I need you to have a seat and breathe, Jack."

My uncle was turning red as he wore a hole in the floor.

"Kraft, see if Doc is available," Sam said.

"Copy that." Kraft stalked out.

"Uncle Jack, can I get you some water?" My heart was breaking by the second as I thought about my aunt Tabitha, who'd lost her eldest son recently to a car accident. If Jack was freaking out, Aunt Tab would collapse on the spot if she saw Noah.

My uncle bared his teeth. "I'm fine. Good thing my wife didn't come with me. She wouldn't be able to handle this." He growled through a heavy breath. "I will go to hell for saying this, but I want to murder my fucking mother." He came to an abrupt halt and slapped his hands on the table. "And your sister Rianne. I always knew she had a screw loose."

Sam flew to his feet. "Jack, I'm going to say this one more time. You have to calm down. Your heart rate is off the charts."

"Uncle Jack, please," I said, sitting up straighter. "You know heart attacks run in the family." The last thing we needed was for him to croak like my uncle Ray had.

Jack inhaled deeply, exhaled, then glanced at me before he whirled around and drove his fist through the wall.

I flinched, stifling a gasp.

Sam was at Jack's side in a second, grasping his arm. "Man, I get it."

Jack jerked out of Sam's hold, breathing fire at my hubby. "Do you, vampire? How the fuck would you know how I feel? You don't have a human son who's been changed into something far worse than anything I've ever seen."

Sam backed away. "You're right, Jack. I don't have a human son. But right now, I'm concerned about you."

A maniacal sound came out of my uncle as he again slapped his hands on the table and shouted, "Fuuuck!" Then, before Sam could catch him, my uncle's chin hit the table as he collapsed on the floor.

My pulse beat so loud and hard that the room spun when I ran to my uncle and dropped to my knees. "Jack." I tapped on his face as blood oozed from the gash underneath his chin. I felt for a pulse, my own soaring, beating erratically.

Sam lifted Jack without any struggle. "I'll take him to the infirmary."

"He doesn't have a pulse," I cried.

Kraft came in, his eyes wide.

"Alert Doc," Sam said to Kraft as he hurried out.

I was right on Sam's heels, tears spilling as I prayed for my uncle's life.

21

SAM

I stood at Murphy's desk while his long fingers flew over the keys. The tech guy was one of Sawyer's expert hackers. But I didn't need anything hacked.

I'd left Layla in the infirmary with her uncle while I attended the strategy meeting. I had a few minutes before it started, and I wanted to see Noah with my own eyes. It was easier and faster to bring up the camera feed in Noah's cell than it would be for me to visit him, which I'd never intended to do. But after Jack reacted so strongly to the change in his son, I was intrigued. I also wanted to see what Carly's serum did to a person the longer it had been in his system.

"Is that human man who collapsed going to be okay?" Murphy asked.

"I think so. Jack was breathing when I brought him to the infirmary." That was the good news. The bad news was Jack's blood pressure was through the roof. Doc was taking measures to lower it and start him on fluids.

Murphy's dark eyes swept upward from his monitor as he turned it toward me. "Here you go, man. This dude is fucked, if you ask me."

I leaned in close as if I needed glasses. "He looks like a—"

"A circus show?" Murphy interjected.

Noah's face was covered in hair, his red eyes were bulging, his brow bone protruded outward, his ears were pointy, and he was lying on his back, staring at the ceiling. I could see why Jack had flipped out.

I hadn't expected Carly's SS2 mixture to mimic my uncle Patrick's. But for fuck's sake, compared to Blake Turner, Noah was far worse off.

"Murphy, can you bring up Carly Aberdeen's cell, the woman who was brought in yesterday morning?"

Noah had the serum in his system longer than Carly, but I wanted to see if she was exhibiting any new features. Because she hadn't had hair on her face when I'd seen her yesterday morning.

Five keystrokes later, Carly was on-screen. Squinting, I had to lean in toward the monitor. She didn't resemble Noah, but she was flopping around on her bed as if she was having a seizure. Then a red light went off in her cell before the guards rushed in.

"It looks like she's seizing," Murphy said.

"Can you find out from the master-at-arms what's going on?" I asked.

The guards hauled her out while Murphy got on the phone. The prison had a small medical office but not an infirmary.

Sawyer waltzed up with a folder in hand. "I heard you say Jack will be okay."

"He should. But now Carly is seizing. This serum is not good."

Sawyer leaned around Murphy's cubicle into the next one. "Veronica, can you bring up the feed on Intech in Chicago?"

The *tap, tap, tap* of keys resounded, then the large wall screen above us displayed lines of people outside Intech.

"I doubt every one of those humans have any supernatural ancestors," Sawyer said. "They're there for the one hundred thousand dollars."

The question I had was—who was whipping up a new batch?

Roman? In addition, Dane and I hadn't been at Intech long enough for Carly to extract a ton of our DNA. Though Adam had Matthew and two shifters. I was assuming Ross Gray and Tucker Whyte were being held by Adam. Still, my uncle's notes outlined that I was the key—my DNA was needed for genetic engineering.

"It will be interesting to see what comes out of the experiments," I said. "Because Matthew was born in a lab, I doubt his DNA will work."

"In a way, that could be good for us," Sawyer added. "As they fail and try again, it will give us time to strategize and build our plan to attack."

He had a point, but it didn't give me a warm and fuzzy.

"On another topic"—Sawyer waved the folder in his hand —"we couldn't find much on Kendra Talon or Layla's mother, Meredith Drake. Except we do know that Kendra grew up in Shelby, Montana. It's a small town in the northern part of the state about thirty miles from the Canadian border. That's it."

I leaned against the edge of the cubicle while Murphy chatted with the master-at-arms. "Layla has left Kendra a voice message and a text."

Sawyer dragged a hand through his light-brown hair. "Talking directly to the source is best. Also, I want to apologize that my team couldn't intercept that reporter's video. We found a bug in our servers that took top priority."

I straightened. "Are we compromised?"

Sawyer swiped a finger over his eye, seemingly tired. "No, we caught it in time."

"We'll probably have many more attempts, given the chaos we're in," I said. "Everyone and their brother will try to get a glimpse of us or info anyway. Don't be surprised if the human military or CIA is trying as we speak."

"The Special Forces unit has offered up their tech gal. I'm showing her the ropes after our meeting. Speaking of which, I need to gather my iPad and head into the war room." Sawyer sped off to his cubicle.

Murphy set the receiver on the phone's base. "Sam, the guards are taking Carly to the infirmary. They confirmed she's having a seizure."

Maybe her body couldn't handle the serum.

I gripped his shoulder. "Thanks for your help."

"Anytime, man," he said.

The Aberdeens were falling one by one, and my first thought was why couldn't Rianne? Carly had started the bullshit, but I would rather see Rianne fighting for her life than her cousin-in-law. And Jack and I would never be friends, but he didn't need to suffer because of his mother's stupidity, or Rianne's, for that matter.

I massaged my neck as I wound my way out of the command center and into the war room that was buzzing with voices, high and low, as stories were told and introductions were made. Viking II, Special Forces, and my SEAL brothers were mingling in groups or sitting in seats.

My gaze bounced around, and I didn't see Ben until he called my name.

He came toward me, looking haggard and scraggly—thick beard, long reddish-brown hair in need of a wash, and black uniform crusted with mud near his ankles. Not surprised. Living in the woods for months had that effect. Missions could sometimes be brutal on the body.

"It's great to see you, man," Ben said as we exchanged a bro hug.

"Same. I don't think I've ever seen you with more than stubble on your face or long hair."

Ben Jackson, half human and half vampire, had a baby face and always wore a military haircut.

He pulled on his beard. "This fucker is coming off after the meeting. I haven't had time to do much since we rolled in." He sized me up. "You're officially a father. My mind is blown, man. It feels like yesterday when we were playing baseball in high school and ogling girls. Now you're married." He frowned. "I wished I could've been there."

"Me too. It was a beautiful ceremony. At some point, we'll celebrate." It might be eons, but when we did, it would be great to have a big blowout party.

Ben slid to my side and turned to face the room. "My father has been calling me nonstop. I was able to placate him after the hospital incident when your mug showed up on TV. But since Emery's fucking announcement, my dad has left me twenty voice mails."

I cringed. Poor Mr. Jackson. When Jo and I first turned, Ben's dad had been relentless in trying to report my father to the authorities for child neglect. He'd suspected something wasn't right with us, but he couldn't put his finger on it. It hadn't helped that Ben had been in and out of the hospital because of Edmund Rain. Travis Jackson blamed my father for everything bad that had happened to Ben since Jo and I became vampires.

But Ben couldn't bring himself to tell his dad about him or us, and my old man had ordered Ben not to anyway. For the last five years, Mr. Jackson thought he was going crazy. I felt bad for Ben's dad and had a soft spot for him. He'd gone out of his way to help Jo and me when we were humans. Hell, I owed him for saving me from jail and keeping Jo and me from another foster home.

"It's time you're truthful with your dad," I said. "If anyone deserves the truth, it's him, Ben."

He blew out air through his nose. "I know, and I'm not sure I can break the news that his son isn't human anymore. I'm afraid he'll stroke out. And he's beside himself from seeing you on TV. He's asking if Jo is like you. I haven't answered him. He adores you guys, and I know it's killing him."

"Dude, don't ignore him. You know what happened the last time you did. Your dad has friends in high places. We can't afford more attention on us." Not only was Mr. Jackson's best bud chief of police, he was also friends with other city officials. "I would help you, but the way things are headed—"

"You have enough shit to deal with, man," Ben said. "I just need to grow some balls and talk to my father. But I won't until Webb gives me the thumbs-up. I am desperate to flush out my family history, and I need my dad's help. There's a reason I'm a hybrid. Your uncle's serum worked on me, which tells me there's some otherworldly shit in my DNA. Thank fuck I don't look like Noah."

"Amen, bro." I nodded at Olivia, who was talking to Sergeant Rebekah Whyte, as I scanned the room. "No word on where Tucker Whyte and Ross Gray are?"

"Nope," he said. "But two nights ago, an Intech guard by the name of Barnes walked into our camp."

I titled my head at Ben. "He's Carly's guard. I remember the name. Carly called him when she, Layla, and I were running out of Intech. He was supposed to show us the way out that night. What did he want?"

Ben toyed with his beard. "He was disoriented and mumbling, 'They're all dead.' We thought he was drunk until he started to convulse and flop around like a fish out of water. Then the dude died right on the spot."

I reared back. "Seizure? Because Carly was just rushed up to the infirmary from one."

"Rebekah thinks it was a toxin. Anyway, right before Barnes showed up, the team on duty watching Intech had radioed in that something wasn't right. The West Virginia facility had gone dark. Next thing, the place was on fire."

I zeroed in on the toxin theory until Webb strutted in.

"Take your seats, everyone. We have a ton to talk about," he said and climbed down the stairs from the entrance at the top of the theater-style room.

Ben and I sat at the end of the first row.

Once everyone in the room was seated, Tripp, Sawyer, and Webb huddled below the movie screen.

I quickly searched faces, looking for Dane Gray. I was about to ask Ben where he was when I did a double take.

Petty Officer Kodiak Snow, the blond, green-eyed vampire, nodded my way from his seat beside Olivia in the second row at the opposite end from me.

She stabbed a thumb at our SEAL brother and smiled. Olivia and Kodiak were tight. Anytime we had to split into small groups during a mission, Olivia and Kodiak were a team. He'd joined our ranks before I'd become a SEAL.

Webb cleared his throat, causing me to return my attention to the front.

My brother-in-law stood tall as his blue gaze swept the room. "I want to start by saying thank you to the Army Special Forces Unit for joining us. They'll be part of our team for the foreseeable future. We've also reached out to other military units to join us as we navigate through an unprecedented time in our supernatural history. It will take more than just the soldiers in this room to combat the issues before us." He rolled back his shoulders, his features stoic. "We're not about to solve any of our issues today." He glanced at Sawyer, who in turn tapped on the iPad, and a slide popped up on the movie screen, depicting a scene of a large crowd picketing with signs.

One read Kill Sam Mason. Another read We're on Your Side, Sam. The list went on with "Free Layla" and "Hunters unite. We need to eradicate these predators."

My blood boiled as I gritted my teeth. Every vampire on the planet would be hunted. I wouldn't be surprised if Jack Aberdeen reopened his vampire hunting business.

"The fear is real," Ben uttered. "Hopefully, I won't see my dad picketing."

Voices buzzed until Webb held up his hand to quiet us. "Soldiers, this is the crowd outside our gates, and it's growing by the hour. The master-at-arms command is maintaining the security around our perimeter, but we need more bodies to patrol the compound. We also have families living on base who are ready to move out."

The group of picketers had multiplied since I'd last checked the camera feed. Before long, we wouldn't be able to stop a stampede from coming through the gates.

"Sir," Rebekah said as she raised her hand. The she-wolf stood to attention as if she was addressing her superior officer. "Before we came in, we got word from our captain that one of our sister units is on their way here. ETA should be 1300 hours."

"Thanks, Sergeant," Webb said to her. "We also have the National Guard on their way, and they'll be escorting the families to safer locations."

My pulse was banging in my ears as I stared at the image on-screen. If we were overrun, no one would be able to leave. A boulder dropped into the pit of my stomach. Layla needed to leave as soon as possible.

"Commander London." A woman stood up in the third row. "I'm Sergeant Vivianne Young, weapons officer. If you haven't already, I suggest you reach out to the Marine Special Forces. They have a small secret tactical squad of witches called the Midnight Raiders. I'm sure they can help barricade this base so no one can get through."

Ben leaned in. "Viv was telling me about them the other night. They sound badass. They can make this place invisible. The Air Force also has a team of witches who control the weather. Similar to you, man."

His excitement about the witches did nothing to energize me. My mind was glued to Layla and figuring out how fast I could pack Harley's truck and the other vehicles and drive her and the babies out of here.

"Thank you, Sergeant Young," Webb said. "We have contacted them, but they have yet to respond. In the meantime—"

Sirens blasted in the room, followed by an announcement.

"All personnel report to your stations. Intruders have compromised the compound. I repeat. Intruders have compromised the compound."

Well, fuck me sideways.

22

SAM

Webb and Tripp barked orders left and right.

Rebekah's golden-yellow eyes glowed amber as her wolf rose to the surface. "It's best if we shift. We're faster that way. My team and I will split up and scour the woods and along each side of the naval base. We'll have it locked down in no time."

My battle station was the roof, but I was worried about Layla. With the sirens blaring, she was probably freaking out and thinking the mob was coming for her. Or she might think the intruder was her sister.

I called her, but she wasn't answering.

My phone buzzed with a text. It took me a beat to register the 911.

Dad: *911. Five guardians left Boston five minutes ago. Get out now! Lie low, and I'll be in touch. Still working on my plan that didn't go over well. If you're captured, I might be able to break you out, but let's not take that chance.*

For fucking sure.

Webb hurried over. "Did you get the 911? Your father alerted me just in case you missed it."

The pandemonium was making me dizzy and nauseous. What

was up? Or what was down? The lines between the two were blurring. I hadn't even found a place to lie low. But I couldn't leave without saying goodbye to Layla.

I stood frozen for a beat.

Come on, asshole. Get your ass in gear.

Webb got in my face. "Sam."

His hot breath snapped me out of my haze, and I ran as if my ass were on fire. In a roundabout way, it was. It pissed me the fuck off that the universe was crashing down around me and I couldn't do a fucking thing about it.

I blew by a giant man in the hallway who was coming out of the restroom. It didn't crystallize who he was until I reached the stairwell.

"Whoa!" Dane Gray yelled at my back. "What's with the sirens? Are we under attack?"

Ignoring the alpha shifter, I shoved open the door, flying up the stairs at vampire speed. I plowed into the infirmary and checked Jack's room. Layla had been with her uncle when I left for the meeting. No sign of my wife, but Jack was out cold with an IV in his arm.

If she wasn't here, then I figured she had to be in nursery—until I remembered Carly had been brought in. Layla had been dying to talk to Carly.

Doc came out of the next room with blood vials in his hands and reared back. "Slow down, Sam. Are we under attack?"

"Seems so." I didn't have time to explain. "Where's Layla?"

"She's in the nursery." We were under siege, and it didn't faze Doc one bit. Not surprising. Doctors and medics had to stay calm and focused when attending to patients during battles.

I quickly glanced at a comatose Carly, full of questions that didn't matter at that moment.

I was almost flying through doors and down halls, and as soon as I entered the birthing suites, the sirens stopped.

Thank fuck.

Hawk snapped to attention outside the nursery as I approached.

"Is Layla in jeopardy? Do I need to rush her and your kids somewhere?" His green eyes turned a fathomless black.

"Not yet. But I don't want you to leave this spot. Do you hear me?" My tone was harsh and commanding.

"Yes, sir," he said emphatically.

I tried to regulate my breathing as I entered the nursery. Nurse Beverly, with her red hair and pink scrubs, was sitting on a stool in front of the computer while my beautiful wife walked around the room with Orion in her arms, humming to him.

"He doesn't like loud noises," Layla said, batting her eyelashes at me.

"I know how he feels," I said.

She must've seen the dire expression on my face because she said, "The guardians? Are they here? Is that why the sirens went off?"

Dread settled over me like a hot vat of oil, scalding, searing, and burning. "I have to leave. They're on their way. I calculate an hour and a half at most unless they're stopped in morning rush hour through Boston."

"Then what are you doing here?" she asked. She appeared to be calm, as was her tone of voice, but her pulse was beating as fast or faster than mine.

"I couldn't leave without telling you."

Beverly hopped off the stool. "I'll give you two some alone time. Layla, just yell if you need me. I'll be in the break room." She glided out.

My daughters were wide-awake. "That siren could wake the dead," I said as a painful lump grew in my throat. I was a second away from shedding tears. This would be the last time I got to see my kids in who knew how long.

For fuck's sake, they were just born, and here I was, bolting faster than a bullet train. But pain, vengeance, and fury lanced through my skin, boiling my blood, and it dried up my tears. This wasn't the time to brood or show any weakness. It was a time to prepare and plan how I would destroy Adam, Roman, and Rianne. Because they were to blame for my own kind hunting me and taking me away from my family.

I lifted Rorie into my arms, holding her head as I did. "Hey, sweet girl. I love you." Fuck, buckets of tears were on the verge of pouring out of me.

Layla blinked away tears. "We'll be fine, Sam. You need to go."

I rocked on my feet as I held my daughter. "I know, but I don't want to leave."

Layla closed the distance between us. "You have to. Do as your father says. He'll fix this."

"I can have us all packed and out of here in thirty minutes." I was sounding desperate and weak.

"Sam, we talked about this," Layla said. "The babies and I will only slow you down. Now, did you ask Dane if you could hide out with his pack?"

During our time in the apartment, she and I had discussed many things, like the prophecy and my fate with the council, and a question had come up. Where would I hide if the council decided to unleash the guardians? She'd suggested Dane. But the shifter and I weren't exactly friends. And I didn't know how I felt about hanging out with a pack of shifters. Their dog stench alone might be more than I could handle.

"No, I haven't had time. But I just saw him as I was running up here. Don't worry, baby doll. I'll find a spot." I also had camping gear. Anyone would have a difficult time finding me in the mountains, which wasn't a bad idea. I could find a spot in Maine, and that way I would be close to Layla.

"I am worried about you," she said, flashing her big blues at me.

I kissed Rorie on the head and returned her to the bassinet. I had bent over to kiss my other two daughters when heavy footsteps sounded in the hall, and Layla's heartbeat shot from sixty to one hundred twenty beats per minute. I would be lying if I said mine hadn't done the same. Maybe the guardians had left Boston an hour before my father had been told. If they were here, I wouldn't go without a fight.

Hawk blocked the doorway. "Sorry, but you're not allowed in."

Dane's white hair stood out just enough over his head. The shifter was an inch or taller than Hawk. "Is that so, bloodsucker?"

Hawk stepped into Dane's personal space. "Leave, or I'll throw you out."

Dane guffawed his deep belly laugh, loud and irritating.

I had to hand it to Hawk. His courage and aggressiveness to protect Layla was just what I wanted to see.

"Hawk, let him through," I ordered.

Neither of them moved.

"Hawk," I said in an iron-cold tenor.

The new recruit SEAL stepped aside.

"You got yourself a good one here." Dane stabbed a thumb at Hawk.

"What do you want, mutt?" I asked, though my piss-poor mood wasn't directed at him. He just happened to be in my line of fire.

Layla handed me Orion. "Say goodbye to your son."

As soon as Orion was cradled against me, I felt a spark of energy electrocute me. I beamed at my son. "Well, now. Your magic is strong."

Layla marched up to Dane, who didn't make any effort to move.

"I can feel their magic from here," he said. "Powerful."

The prophecy came to mind. But I quickly banished the thought. I needed to get the fuck out of here. Time was ticking away.

"Dane, we have a favor to ask you," Layla said. "Sam is being hunted by the guardian force. He needs a place to hide."

Dane belted out a laugh. "Your vampire laws are fucked-up." He glanced over Layla's head at me. "Aren't you powerful? You can handle your own kind."

"I could hand myself over and be done with it. But that isn't happening. Believe it or not, my government wants to use me as a scapegoat. And I'm not staying to fight. Those fuckers will light my ass up like a towering inferno." Truth.

Layla fastened her hands on her hips. "We're wasting time. Look, Dane. You see that boy Sam is holding? And the girls in the bassinets. They need their father. If these guardians capture him, I'm afraid we'll never see Sam again." Her shoulder rose along with her voice on every breath between sentences. "As my husband said, he could be used as a scapegoat or rot in prison. Also, let's not forget, Intech wants shifter DNA just as much as vampire DNA. Your pack and every shifter pack are at risk. And don't get me started on the media. Supernaturals need to unite. Yes or no, Dane?"

"Fine," Dane acquiesced. "But you'll have to convince my pack of the reason we should open our compound to a vampire. If you stay, bloodsucker, you'll be pitching a tent. Otherwise, I hope you have a plan B."

The mountains north of my sister's house in Maine was the only spot I had in mind, and that would work for the short-term until I could figure out a longer-term solution.

For now, I would put on my Mason charm and persuade the wolves that they should hide me. I had my work cut out for me. Shifters were freaky about their territory, and it didn't help that they hated my kind. I didn't have any love for them either, but we did have to unite as a team if we wanted to coexist with humanity.

"This should be fun," I said sarcastically even though I was appreciative.

"Good. Then it's settled." Layla returned to my side, took Orion, and set him in his bassinet. "Now get your vampire ass out of here."

"The queen has spoken," I teased, pulling her to me, basking in her cherry fragrance. "I love you, baby doll."

She craned her neck up at me, tears pooling in her ball-squeezing blue eyes. "This separation isn't permanent. And don't you irritate Dane's pack. Play nice." She rose up on her toes and kissed me. "You are my sun, moon, and stars, Sam Mason. I'll see you in my dreams." She giggled on the last line.

I whispered in her ear. "I'll let you come up with the next fantasy." I gave her one last short kiss then ran out as fast as I could. If I didn't, I would never leave.

23

LAYLA

Late July in Maine was absolutely wonderful. The days were warm and the nights cool. I'd been here for two solid weeks. My entourage and I left the base the day after Sam and I said goodbye in the nursery. Since then, Sam and I had managed to video chat twice through a secure connection, keeping our time brief but long enough to catch up and for him to see his babies. Sawyer had assured us we wouldn't be compromised, but I didn't trust fate, which had a way of fucking with Sam and me.

I stared out the passenger window at the Atlantic to my right. George, Webb's longtime friend who took care of the Maine house, was driving. Jo was in the passenger's seat in front of me, and Conrad sat beside me.

I'd met the former scout in Montana months ago when Sam had shown up unexpectedly at my uncle Jack's ranch. For years, Conrad had been assigned by the vampire government to watch the Aberdeen family and report on our hunting activities. Now, the black-haired vampire was assigned as my bodyguard.

While my babies were napping, we were on our way to look at a house that had recently been listed on the market. Aunt Jordyn,

Aunt Harley, and Cousin Abbey were babysitting along with five vampire sheriff deputies plus one shifter. Sergeant Rebekah Whyte had joined my security detail the night before. She'd offered to replace Harley, who had to return to base tomorrow to resume her role as Webb's assistant.

I hated that Harley had to leave, but I was happy Rebekah was here. Vampires had sharp senses, but Rebekah could scent danger faster and better than bloodsuckers—in my opinion anyway. She was also a medic, and having her and Jo's skills made me feel even more comfortable in the event something happened to the babies or any of us.

Jo peeked around the seat, her silver eyes sparkling in the morning light. "Are you doing okay?"

I nodded. "I'm good."

When Jordyn heard George telling Jo about the house for sale, my sister encouraged me to take a look, mainly to cheer me up. Postpartum had been hitting me hard. I hated to admit that I, Layla Aberdeen Mason, tough as nails, could be susceptible to mood swings, crying spells, anxiety, and difficulty sleeping. But I had to call a spade a spade.

The beautiful scenery, the soothing sounds of the ocean, and working out on the beach in the early-morning hours was a prescription to ease my anxiety, but it wasn't enough to wipe out postpartum depression altogether.

Watching the news hadn't helped my mood, so Jordyn, Jo, and Harley had put the kibosh on my TV time.

Humans across the country were becoming restless. Some demanded answers. Others wanted to hear from me, and a large majority was desperate to eradicate vampires. The latter was a huge problem. The hunters were coming out of the woodwork, which was the cause of the threat the day Sam had gotten his 911. Three men dressed in armor and protective gear had scaled the electrified fence only to be captured by vampires and shifters. Yep, the Special Forces unit had shifted. As stupid as those men were, they hadn't been harmed, but they had been compelled to forget they'd seen a wolf the size of a full-grown lion and men with fangs.

I was itching to fight, mainly to finally go head-to-head with my sister Rianne. I wanted to fuck with her just like she was fucking with me. The saying fight fire with fire was cliché, but I yearned to do just that—stand at a podium and tell the country how my sister had been brainwashed by Adam Emery. Show humans that I was alive and well and tell them how my family was distraught over Rianne's decision to shed her humanity.

But returning fire in a public manner wouldn't solve the larger problem, and with our luck, anything I said, any show-and-tell we did, could have a negative effect on us and the supernatural community. Sam might be right when he mentioned that if we presented Carly and Noah to the world, humans might think that they had been bitten by vampires.

Besides, battles weren't won with words. Yet we had to find a way to control the narrative. We had to show the nation that Intech was killing humans, not engineering them into otherworldly creatures—at least not any who would live long enough to see their next birthday. How would we do that? I didn't have the answer.

As much as I wanted to join the fray, I wasn't ready—physically or emotionally. Though I was working out and growing stronger by the day. My goal was to be in better shape than before I'd gotten pregnant, not only to fight but to have the strength to protect my kids.

George turned into the driveway of the sprawling slate-blue house with gable dormers, skylights, a two-car garage, and shrubs and plants that needed some tender loving care.

As I moved to get out of the SUV, Conrad swung out his arm. "Wait here. George and I will check things out."

I doubted our enemies were waiting for us inside or anywhere on the property—or even in town, for that matter. For two solid weeks, there hadn't been any signs of suspicious activity or strangers in town. But we couldn't let our guard down.

I leaned on the armrest separating my seat from Conrad's. "Have you heard from Webb this morning?" I asked Jo.

We received daily updates from either Webb or Tripp about base activities or council business, if they were allowed to tell us. What we did know so far is that Steven Mason hadn't come through yet on calling the guardians off Sam. I wasn't tuned in to vampire politics, but apparently their government had not only five elders presiding over their kind but other top officials and heads of state who needed convincing to wake up to the new age. More importantly, Steven was trying to prevent a division among his kind, which would only lead to war that would end in bloodshed and anarchy. In the meantime, the hunt was still in high gear for my husband.

"I have," she said. "Aside from a small crowd still picketing, Webb told me they've had the base under control since they captured the intruders. It also helped that we leaked to the press that Sam was seen at a rest stop, heading toward Chicago."

Webb and team told the guardians that Sam had been sent to Chicago on a SEAL team fact-finding mission to gather intel. To support that story, I'd suggested we tell the media the same. Some in the news had reported they'd seen Sam going into Intech.

All of us had a great laugh over that headline.

Fun times.

George waved at us before he unlocked the front door. The local real estate agent had given George the key to show us the place since she couldn't join us. The century-old vampire knew every person in town. If they had a local mayor, George would win hands down.

Conrad stood at the end of the driveway, scanning the road.

Once out of the vehicle, I inhaled the salt air. I could see Sam and me living here. I could picture myself walking with the kids along the winding path jutting out from the side of the house and down to the sandy beach below. I angled my face toward the cumulus clouds skating across the deep-blue sky, a canopy hanging over the peaceful Atlantic in the distance. I wasn't here to buy, but I could see my family living here.

"Layla," Jo called. "You gotta see the inside."

George's brown eyes shimmered with excitement as I entered. "This place would fit your family perfectly. Six bedrooms, four baths, and plenty of storage. Although I think the kitchen needs some work." He sounded like a real estate agent.

The world outside faded as I stood in the grand foyer that boasted a crystal chandelier and a spiral cherrywood staircase. I felt as though I'd stepped into a fairy tale, even more so when I walked into the vast great room that melded with the kitchen and dining rooms.

Jo's house was beautiful, but this one was ten times better, larger, and would fit my family to a T. I could see a life of happiness through the three sliding glass doors that overlooked the ocean. I could picture a Christmas tree in the corner by the fireplace with a slew of presents underneath for the kids to open. I could almost feel the love and happiness as we gathered as a family on Christmas morning, or any time for that matter.

I twirled around, absorbing more of the details—the crown molding throughout gave the space an added touch of richness along with the myriad of windows, including two skylights. The built-in bookcases on each side of the fireplace would be home to family pictures and children's books. The kitchen was a decent size but definitely needed some upgrades.

"I think I might buy this place." Jo tittered.

I would myself if Sam and I were ready. But could we afford the million-dollar property? Sam had money, but I didn't. My pride made me want to contribute, but I didn't see myself working outside the home with four children to raise.

Jo opened the middle sliding glass door. "Come out here, Layla."

I followed her outside to the tiled patio of red clay and gray stone with an outdoor kitchen and lounge area. The house could be a shack, and I would fork over the money just for the view.

In the distance, sailboats tacked along the ocean's surface, a picture-perfect backdrop that would entice anyone to buy on the spot.

Tears threatened as I thought about Sam, wishing he was here. Any little thing set off my mood swings as of late. Damned hormones.

"Layla, look at this." She stabbed a finger skyward at a hexagon-shaped windowed gable dormer that reminded me of a castle, as the roof pitched to a point.

I quickly squeezed my eyes shut, stamping down the tears. "Wow." I could envision my girls in that room, dressing up as princesses, having tea parties, and entertaining Sam and me for hours on end.

The waterworks opened up in full force. *Fuck me.* Would we ever be able to live without someone chasing us, fighting, war, and bloodshed?

Her silver eyes probed me, soft yet wary. "Breathe," Jo said. "Maybe this was a bad idea."

"No, it wasn't. I'll be fine." I cried through a laugh. "I'm just flipping pissed and sad that we can't plan for the future."

I wanted my children to have a quiet upbringing and the opportunity to just be kids. I didn't want them to live in seclusion like Abbey. The poor ten-year-old didn't have friends because Webb and Jo kept her hidden. I couldn't blame them. I was afraid I would be in the exact same boat.

A gentle breeze ruffled Jo's hair, and she moved wispy strands from her face. "Why not? You could buy this house now, and it will be here for when you need to get away. Just like Webb and I use ours."

I sat on a cushioned wicker chair. "You're right." I puffed out my cheeks. "I'm overwhelmed. I can't believe how my life has changed in such a short span of time. I married a vampire. I gave birth to quadruplets. I'm separated from my husband. He can't see his children. He's wanted by the guardian force. We're about to fight a war I'm not sure we can win, and there's a lingering prophecy about one of my babies." There was more, of course—Intech, the public frenzy, and my crazy family members.

Luckily, my uncle was going to be okay. Jack had worked himself into a nervous breakdown after seeing Noah's transformation. Then there was my cousin-in-law Carly Aberdeen. She'd had a seizure and suffered a stroke, according to Dr. Vieira. She wasn't able to talk or write anything down to tell us what had happened to her.

Jo fixated on me with a faraway look in her eyes. I couldn't tell if she was trying to snoop inside my head or was deep in thought.

If it was the former, she couldn't read my mind. I'd taken the mind-blocking potion. I loved my sister-in-law and was envious of her talents, but anytime she was reading me, I felt violated. There were memories and thoughts I wanted to keep private along with the intimacy between Sam and me.

I understood why Sam got irritated whenever Jo was reading his mind. Plus, it was exhausting having to consciously erect a mental shield when I was with her. I'd complained to Sam about this, and he'd given me his stash. I was elated that the bitter-tasting concoction took effect instantly. It was definitely a freeing moment to finally have my thoughts to myself.

I waved a hand in front of her. "Jo, did I say something to upset you?" I had been a mood buster lately.

Her long lashes swept over her cheeks as she blinked. "You reminded me of when my foster dad stabbed me."

My features twisted and scrunched in every direction. "How does that incident connect with what I just vomited up?"

She snickered. "In a way, I've been in your shoes. That night I ended up in the hospital with stitches in my face"—she traced a faint outline of the scar on her cheek—"my life changed by the minute. Men with fangs chased Sam and me, I had to turn vampire to save my brother, and I met my father for the first time. I couldn't tell you how many times I was kidnapped and used as a lab rat or killed enemies. I never had a chance to fully breathe until Edmund Rain was dead. The point is, Layla"—she regarded me with a weak smile—"we *will* take down our enemies. But it won't happen overnight. So in between, you need to daydream and fill your well with happiness. The more you do, the more your dreams will come true." Her confidence was erasing my moodiness.

"As for the prophecy," she said. "I'm hoping Kendra can shed some light when we finally connect with her or at least locate your mother's family tree that my uncle has in his data collection. If the people on that tree are alive, we can surely find the answers we're both looking for."

I hadn't had a chance to respond or weigh in when a prickly feeling spread through my thighs as if it was a warning of sorts. Odd. I'd never felt the tingling sensation as if I'd touched a live electrical wire in my thighs before. I'd only ever had a similar feeling in my stomach, right before a banshee scream.

As I rubbed my legs, I spotted Conrad rushing up to George, who was standing by the dining table and reading from his phone. Suddenly, Conrad shouted my name.

Razors of fear cut into my skin as I hurried inside. "What's wrong?"

"We need to go. A guardian is on his way to the house," Conrad said.

Ah, fuck. So much for daydreaming.

After a nail-biting car ride that felt like an hour but was only ten minutes, I was sprinting into the house behind Conrad and George. I wasn't sure why I was nervous. Sam wasn't on the premises. Or maybe he was, and I didn't know it.

A tall, dark-haired imposing vampire was standing in front of the kitchen island while Jordyn, Rebekah, and Abbey sat on a couch near the fireplace staring at the guardian.

The air crackled with tension.

Rebekah rose, setting her golden-yellow gaze on me. "The

babies are sleeping," she said as if she was trying to ease my anxiety. "This is Norman Collier, a guardian for the council. He's here to ask about Sam."

Jo came in behind me and went over to sit by Abbey as Jo stared at the guardian, no doubt trying to read his mind.

Mr. Collier straightened as he handed Conrad his badge. "I have orders to check out the house and town for Sam Mason."

"What makes you think Sam is here?" I asked, even though I was sure the council was covering their bases. If the tables were turned, I would scope out the area if I knew where my perp's family was.

Collier's dark eyes were hollow, his mouth tight, and a muscle jumped along his jaw as he stared right through me. "I don't think anything. I'm only following orders."

I shivered as the hairs on the back of my neck rose.

"Why are you alone?" Jo asked. "The guardians normally travel in groups."

He studied her with a calculating glare.

My intuition sprang free with a vibe that made me nauseous. I wouldn't want to be caught on a dark street alone with him. Then again, as an officer of vampire law, he'd probably perfected his don't-fuck-with-me attitude.

"We're spread thin at the moment," Collier said. "Look, I just need to check the house, then I'll be out of here."

George cleared his throat. "I'll show you around." He waved his hands toward the hallway leading into where the nursery and bedrooms were. "We'll start here."

I rushed out and into the nursery ahead of George. I didn't want any strangers near my babies, especially not without me present.

My heart was in my throat, and I wasn't sure why. Maybe I was overly paranoid. Maybe my postpartum hormones were the cause of my paranoia.

Rorie was the only one awake, so I picked her up and sat in the rocker. "Hey, baby girl. How's my goddess of sunrise?"

She squirmed in my arms, her mahogany eyes dancing with delight.

Instantly, my racing pulse settled until Norman came in. I watched him intently as he opened the closet door before he ambled over to the cribs.

Like Sam was in a crib.

He studied my children for far too long with a clinical expression.

The hairs on my arms stiffened.

After a long beat, he swung his blank expression my way then left the room.

Something was off about him, but I couldn't quite pinpoint what.

Nevertheless, I had to call Sam.

24

SAM

I was yanking the hair from my skull. I'd wanted to jump in my Jeep so many times in the last two weeks and head to Maine. I could be there in nine hours from the Catskills. But I couldn't risk it. I'd even thought about trekking to Chicago and blowing up Intech. After all, the nation thought I was in the Windy City, but I doubted the guardians would have fallen for that ploy. Still, with vampire law enforcement in every state, I had to be careful.

To make matters worse, Sawyer's team had been surfing our dark web as well as the human one, and only hours ago, they'd found an ad offering a million dollars to anyone, vampire or human, who brought me in dead or alive. A fucking contract was out on my head.

Layla's worst nightmare had come to fruition.

Maybe I would be better off in the hands of the guardians—unless they were behind the ad. I wouldn't be surprised. If so, my father hadn't said anything. I didn't expect to talk to him. Webb hadn't heard from my dad in the last three days, which wasn't that unusual. Sometimes meetings with our government officials and elders and even with our human counterparts could go on for a week without any communication with the outside world.

I had to trust that my old man was diligently working his plan and prayed something would give in my favor soon. I couldn't stay cooped up with shifters for much longer. I was a soldier, and the itch to fight was growing stronger by the day. I wasn't made to take orders from wolves or work in a kitchen.

I wasn't complaining. They had reluctantly welcomed me into their lair—even though they were afraid that my presence would bring war and death.

That certainly was possible, but my response had been, "All supernaturals are in jeopardy, and we have to pool our powers and resources to fight together. If we are to announce ourselves to the world, then we have to do it with a united front. We can't allow people like Adam Emery to use us for his own sick benefit."

After I'd given that speech, the wolves voted, and while some believed I was the crux of the problems before us, the majority agreed with me. Maybe because their beta, Dane's brother Ross, was missing and assumed to have been kidnapped by Roman Brown.

While life went on, I was chopping wood for the umpteenth time. In order to stay, I had to contribute. Fine by me. Swinging the ax allowed me to release pent-up energy and gave me a chance to think. It was also my silent enemy. The more I got lost in my thoughts, the moodier, broodier, and angrier I became. I was desperate to see my family, hold my kids, and touch and kiss my wife. And because of Adam Emery, I couldn't do any of that. If the wolves blamed me for the public frenzy, then I blamed Adam, Roman, and Rianne. They were the culprits and complicit in outing us to the world.

I growled as I set the ax next to a pile of logs, wiped the sweat from my face and chest, and snagged the bottle of water from the ground beside me.

The temperature was dropping as the sun slid down behind the massively tall trees that were interspersed in and around log cabins, a community center, a weapons-and-equipment building, and the main hub of activity—an L-shaped log structure that was home to offices, a medical wing, and a tech center.

In addition to chopping wood, I'd been tasked with kitchen and janitor duties—washing dishes, pots, and pans, emptying trash, and mopping the soiled floor of their chow hall every night. By the end of my shift, I had a newfound respect for my fellow vampires who were assigned to do the same at my mess hall on base. But I'd never laughed at them like the mutts did every night at my expense. My feelings weren't hurt. I was grateful they'd agreed to hide me, no matter how abrasive their hospitality. Even my accommodations were lacking. I'd thought Dane had been kidding when he'd said I had to pitch a tent, but nope. My humble abode was a cot and a camp light—nothing I wasn't used to as a soldier. Hell, I would sleep on a bed of snakes if it meant I wouldn't be the council's scapegoat. My family needed me alive, not dead or burned to ash.

I downed the bottle of water and resumed chopping wood. On one swing of the ax, I envisioned Adam's head. I couldn't wait to level Intech and burn the skyscraper to the ground once and for all. I had no idea what Webb and Tripp were planning for Adam Emery, but whatever it was, Adam was mine. The asshole would be hanging by his toes from his skyscraper before it imploded.

On my next swing, I pictured Roman's head. The next Rianne's. I repeated the process, and when the blade met wood, the tension lifted, and a sense of freedom engulfed me until I was interrupted.

A teenage boy, broad and tall, jogged up, his curly brown mane whipping around in the wind. "Bloodsucker, Cooper needs to see you ASAP." Before I could ask why, he fled as if I was about to sink my fangs into him.

The shifters on the compound knew my name, but bloodsucker was how the majority addressed me. *Whatever.*

Nodding, I hoofed it from the equipment area where they stored the wood to the tech center on the other side of the property. My stomach fisted into a big fucking knot. ASAP meant urgent, and that was never good. Only hours before, I'd been summoned when Tripp called to tell me about the contract on my head.

What the fuck was happening now? My immediate thoughts always revolved around Layla and my kids. Maybe someone had found my family to use them to draw me out.

Anxiety clawed through my nerves, scraping and cutting. I was a bomb ready to detonate. The two weeks of quietness had to come to a screeching halt.

With a dip of my chin, I acknowledged some folks heading toward the community center as I passed by. I recognized a few since I worked alongside them in the chow hall.

"Sam," a middle-aged lady named Greta called. The petite brunette was the pack's chef and in charge of the kitchen staff. The nice she-wolf had a sharp tongue and a big bite, and even the alpha didn't cross her. "Don't be late. Tonight's movie night, and we'll have a big turnout for dinner."

I saluted her. "Yes, ma'am." Another night of sweat and hard work.

I swore Dane had probably assigned my chores just to laugh his ass off at me, which he did when he saw me garbed in an apron, a hairnet, and yellow rubber gloves. *Fucker.*

I hadn't forgotten he owed me a sparring session. We'd planned one months ago when he'd been our guest on base, but that never happened once he learned his brother Ross had gone missing.

Maybe it was time to loosen up and beat the shit out of each other. Dane was a ticking time bomb like me. If it wasn't for his brother, Cooper, convincing Dane not to do something stupid or reminding him of the chip in his head, Dane and I would probably be in Chicago. His anger and aggression matched my own, and at this point, we were feeding off each other to the point that we could convince each other to do something idiotic.

Regardless of the mounting tension, Dane was sure Ross was

imprisoned at Intech in Chicago and was not a pile of bones at Intech's West Virginia facility that had been gutted from a fire. Dane's wolf senses told him Ross was alive. As the alpha, Dane had some otherworldly connection to his pack members.

If Ross was alive, he was most likely strapped to a table in a glass room in the basement at Intech like Dane and I had been. After the fire I'd set at the Chicago location, Adam had months to remodel the lab.

I breezed into the L-shaped log building, slipping on my T-shirt and beelining it to the last office on the left.

Cooper Gray, technical guru and Dane's younger brother, monitored and maintained communications for the pack. No calls came in or went out without him knowing.

He was shaking his shaggy brown head of hair as he looked at his computer screen. "Sam is doing fine. We're keeping him busy. Remind me to send you a pic of him in a hairnet."

The sweet laughter coming through the speakers melted my black heart, and I skirted the gray metal desk in two seconds flat. "Layla, is everything okay?" My nerves perked up. I loved that I was looking at her pretty face and hearing her siren voice, but our next scheduled video call wasn't until the end of the week.

Her blue eyes shifted back and forth as she gnawed on her bottom lip.

I was having trouble reading her emotions. "Layla," I said in a shrouded tone that didn't sound like me. My fucking stomach was pitching and rolling. "What happened?"

I could feel Cooper's apprehension.

Layla's chest lifted. "A guardian showed up here late in the morning, looking for you." She sounded more perplexed than worried.

It had been only a matter of time before they trekked up to Maine. What surprised me, though, was that only one had shown up instead of five. "They must've split up."

Cooper rose. "I'll alert the enforcers." He excused himself.

I sat in his chair and rolled it closer to the desk as I gazed at my wife. Her sun-kissed skin brought out the freckles around her nose. Her auburn hair had been twisted in a loose braid and pulled over one shoulder, and those eyes were so damn blue, it took my breath away. The beach environment definitely suited her.

"Do we have a name of this guardian?" Not that I knew every vampire working on the force. He could very well be one who'd gone rogue for the million dollars on my head.

"Norman Collier," she said. "There was something off about him that I can't pinpoint. He had the credentials showing he's a guardian for the vampire government. Even Conrad said the badge was legit. I didn't recognize him, but I was only questioned by two out of the five who showed up on base. No one else here recognized him either. Anyway, Conrad is trying to contact your father to verify the guardian's credentials, but he's not having any luck reaching Steven."

We weren't worried yet, although the thought had crossed my mind that the council could've thrown my father in the brig. Maybe the ancient elders had instituted their own coup d'état. If so, we might be fucked.

"Was Jo able to read his mind?" A guardian lived on a mind-blocking drug similar to the one Alia Costner whipped up in her kitchen. If Jo couldn't get into his head, then that might be proof he was legit. However, we were finding that Jo's secret weapon wasn't so secret anymore, given how people were finding a way to block her.

She worried her bottom lip. "No. I'm the only one who is suspicious of him. Even Abbey didn't get a bad vibe."

I picked up a pen. "If he was working for Roman, you wouldn't be there, nor would Abbey or our children." I pressed the pen's cap down over and over again, the clicking sound helping me think. "No signs of others with him?" I hated to drop the bad news about the contract on my head, and I'd told Tripp not to share that with anyone. I wanted to tell Layla myself.

"No. Stan and his deputies George and Conrad scoured the town. The deputies even followed Collier until he got on the highway toward Boston." She played with the end of her braid. "I'm probably overly paranoid. My hormones are out of control, Sam."

"Baby doll, hormones or not, I want you to have your radar on at all times. I'll have a chat with Dane. You and the babies might be better off here." Especially with the new development.

"Maybe, but it's not a good time. If we are being watched, I'll only lead them to you. Rebekah came up last night because Harley has to return to work, so we have shifter skills."

Rebekah's shifter and military background brought an added level of comfort, but supernaturals weren't impenetrable. Wolfsbane was their kryptonite as cobalt was ours. I didn't even want to think about a toxin like Edmund Rain had used as a weapon on us. Ben had mentioned that a toxin might've caused the deaths of Intech's human guards who had stayed behind at the now burned-down West Virginia facility.

Her tongue licked out to run along her bottom lip. "I miss you terribly, vampire. You look sweaty and dirty. Are you still chopping wood?" Laughter rolled from her luscious lips.

"Every day. The wolves are preparing for winter. I also have to report for kitchen duty shortly."

"Cooper says you look funny in a hairnet." She was holding in a laugh.

I rolled my eyes. "Just think, baby doll. Me naked except for a hairnet and rubber gloves."

She burst into laughter. "You might have to model that for me."

"Your wish is my command. Well, when the time is right." I had to shuck the images of us naked that were playing out like a porn movie in my head. "How are my children?"

She glanced over her shoulder briefly. "They've just been fed and are napping. Hold on." She rose, then took the computer over to the cribs and moved it so the camera was panning over my sweet babies. "Can you see them?"

"I can." My voice cracked as emotions clogged my throat.

Four innocent souls sound asleep. I was ready to bawl my eyes out. I should be there with them. I should be protecting them.

"Call me crazy, but they look bigger, and their hair grew in more." Or was I seeing things? Rorie and Ellie had more reddish-brown hair than I remembered.

Layla giggled. "They're gaining weight. It's still too early to tell if their growth will follow the same pattern now that they're born." She turned the screen back toward her and was on the move until she sat down again.

"How are your morning workouts? Any signs of magical powers? And my blood isn't having a negative impact on you, is it?"

"You ask me the same questions each time we chat." She stood up. "Is anyone around you?"

I shook my head. "I'm alone."

She lifted her sundress and twirled around in her yellow lace bra and panties. "How do you think my workouts are going?" She ran her hands down her curves, shaping her waist, then her stomach as she stuck out her massive tits.

I swallowed thickly, biting back a growl as lust curled around my cock. Her thighs were toned, her stomach had flattened but not by much yet, and her arms were well-defined. But her physical features would always be beautiful no matter if she was skinny, fat, or pregnant. I was more concerned about her strength and her ability to fight and protect herself and the kids.

I adjusted my dick just the same despite my priorities as she lowered her sundress, covering her beauty.

She returned to her seat with a flirty smile. "What say you, husband?"

I whisked a hand through my hair. "You're gorgeous, and I'm proud of you. You'll be in fighting shape before long." I leaned over the desk toward the screen. "You know what I'm dying to do?"

She felt her breasts. "You want these."

My wife knew me well. I swallowed down my lust. "Bingo."

Her sweet laughter slid over my skin, sinking in and drugging me into a deeper lustful state. "They don't hurt anymore. I'm ready for you, vampire."

My cock was painfully hard, and I had blue balls for sure. "Back to my blood. I'm assuming it isn't making you pass out or sick?" I had to change the subject. Otherwise, I would blow my load in my jeans.

"At first, I felt queasy, but I haven't passed out like I did in the infirmary. Doc called yesterday to check on things, and I asked if he had the results from the mislabeled vials. Remember the one I drank that I thought was yours? Anyway, with Carly and my uncle Jack in the infirmary and the craziness on base, he hasn't been able to deal with much else. Before you ask, Carly still can't speak. Doc says she's improving little by little though. Whatever is in the serum is not good. I'm just thankful the amount Rianne injected me with when I was her prisoner wasn't enough to do any damage to me or the babies."

Thank fuck. But Layla had vampire and witch DNA in her family history, and Carly and Noah didn't—at least not that we knew.

"We'll find out soon enough how the serum works on the hundreds of people lining up for the one hundred thousand dollars," I muttered.

"I'm happy my uncle will be okay." She rubbed her eyebrow, and her ruby engagement ring glinted in the light filtering in from the windows above the cribs.

"I see the ruby fits now."

She glanced at her ring, beaming. "It does, but it's still a little snug. Oh, not to change the subject, but please thank Dr. Hammond for pulling your blood and sending it on a regular basis."

"I do every day when I show up in medical," I said as Cooper came in.

He twirled his finger in the air, gesturing to me to wrap up my conversation.

"Baby doll, Cooper is giving me the time's-up signal. But I have some bad news. Earlier today, Sawyer's team found an ad on the black web."

"Let me guess," she said. "There's a contract out for you." Anger twisted her features.

I nodded. "A million dollars."

Her nostrils flared. "I knew something like this would happen." She puffed out her cheeks. "Don't worry about me. I'm well protected, but Maine might not be safe for long."

"I should've brought you with me to begin with."

"We can't dwell on should-haves and hindsight, Sam," she said. "At the time, I would've only slowed you down. And aside from that guardian, we haven't seen any media, strangers lurking, or dare I say Adam or my sister. I believe they still think I'm on base."

I prayed like a motherfucker that they kept thinking Layla was behind our fortress.

Cooper gave me another signal.

"Baby doll, I have to go. I'll talk to Dane and his pack. I love you. Kiss the babies for me."

She touched her heart. "Love you too."

As soon as I ended the video call, I growled, ready to flip the desk over. "I hate this."

Cooper leaned against the doorjamb, his blue eyes appraising. "No signs of strangers within a ten-mile radius, unless we want to add bears to the list."

I pushed to my feet, my stomach still in one huge fucking knot. "Where's Dane?"

Cooper blocked me. "Dude, before you walk out of here, you need to calm down. You reek of anger. It's bad enough that both you and Dane have every wolf on edge. You, especially."

"Then maybe it's time for Dane and me to punch the crap out of each other."

He cocked an eyebrow. "The pack would enjoy that."

Chopping wood didn't give me the same adrenaline rush as hearing or feeling bones crack. Besides, there was only so much wood I could chop. But first I had to talk to Dane about my family coming here.

25

LAYLA

The rhythmic slide of the waves along the shore kept time with my breathing as I ran on the beach. The cool breeze did nothing to douse the sweat sliding down my temples, neck, and back.

Conrad jogged behind me. Since he couldn't be in the gym, he took advantage of my morning workouts. I slowed to a fast walk as I approached Jo's house to my right. The sea stretched out to seemingly touch the sun as the bright orange ball drifted higher on the horizon to my left.

I felt as though I was living in an alternate reality—a beautiful one, if I was only talking about the scenery. I wasn't. Life was moving forward, but I felt stuck in limbo with the same routine as if I were in that movie *Groundhog Day*. The repetitiveness of each day was the same—work out, feed babies, change diapers, contend with sleepless nights, worry my head off, and then start over again the next day, hoping another grenade didn't drop in my lap.

It was alarming that Sam was being hunted. The million-dollar bounty had to be from Adam Emery. The council couldn't be that desperate to make an example out of one of their own. Unless my grandmother was funding the project. To my knowledge, she did have that kind of money, but I was really only guessing. After all, she was an investor in Adam's project, and she was yearning to cure her blood cancer. But in that case, she would want Sam alive, not dead.

I screamed, but it wasn't my banshee coming out to play. I was bottled up with so many emotions that it was difficult to process any of them. In one breath, I was happier than I'd ever been thanks to my children, and in the next, I was distraught and furious, feeling constricted and strangled to the point I couldn't breathe sometimes.

My gloom-and-doom mood wasn't perking up, although talking to Sam three days ago had helped, even though he had shared bad news. It was hell without him. A wife needed her husband. I needed intimacy, the feel of him next to me at night, the smell of him whenever he was close to me, his lopsided grin, those sexy dimples, and fuck, his kids might not know who he was if our separation went on for a few months.

Then there was Norman Collier, who I believed wasn't really a guardian. Maybe it had been the way the vampire had been staring at me, or the way he was cataloging every detail of the house, or how he stared at my children for far too long with no emotion on his face. Most people lit up when they saw babies. They didn't look at them as if studying them for some science project.

I wasn't all knowing and a clairvoyant, but my intuition was prodding me that something had happened to Steven. Webb hadn't heard from him in six days, and Conrad tried to reach Steven three days ago. Jo had explained how his elder meetings could keep him behind closed doors for a week. Maybe so, given the state of the country. But if he was planning to overthrow the council, he needed to hurry up.

To make the mystery more bewildering, Alia Costner had informed Webb that she hadn't seen her father, Victor, in about a week, which aligned with the same time frame since Webb had last heard from Steven. She also had left him several voice mails. I felt bad for Alia. Her son was in the hands of Adam Emery and Roman

Brown. She'd been beside herself, according to Jo. I couldn't blame Alia. I would be freaking the fuck out if any of my children had been taken. But I agreed with the majority. Matthew Costner hadn't appeared to be in any kind of duress when he'd spoken at the press conference.

Nevertheless, his grandfather Victor Costner was a prominent vampire among the Council of Elders. They respected Victor and often asked him to help out with precarious or top secret projects. I'd learned recently that Victor and Steven didn't always see eye to eye on things, and Victor had thrown Steven under the bus a few times with the council before Steven had become an elder.

Speculation among the SEALs was that Victor might be helping the council get rid of Steven. Just what we needed. More problems, more enemies. But I hadn't trekked off to Maine because of the guardians, or even my sister and grandmother, but rather the dangerous atmosphere surrounding the naval base. With idiots trying to overrun the military installation, it wasn't safe. In fact, every family had been moved to a more protected location.

I stopped in front of Jo's house where the dry sand met the wet, kicked off my running shoes, and walked into the surf. The water was cold but refreshing against my heated legs.

Conrad ran up and joined me, only he didn't take off his shoes. "Great run. Five miles this morning. You're doing better."

I chuckled. "If you call having to slow down to a walk better, then okay." I could do three miles without stopping, but the last two I'd struggled and had to fast walk several times.

"You'll get there," he said, bending over and splashing water on his arms.

"What do you think today will bring?" I asked rhetorically.

Conrad didn't have the foresight to see future events. I'd had visions since I'd met Sam but none since giving birth. Dr. Vieira attributed my powers to being pregnant with inhuman babies. But now that I wasn't, I kept wondering if I would have magical abilities. So far, I still had my banshee scream. Did that mean I would continue to have visions and the mind control I'd experienced when I'd carried my babies? Or as Jordyn had mentioned, did my sisters and I have latent magical abilities we weren't aware of because of our mother's supernatural heritage?

"Earlier this morning, I finally connected with a guardian who is team Steven," he said. "Jonah hasn't been able to reach Steven either. But when he drove into the parking garage at the vampire administration building this morning, Steven's car was there. I don't think there's anything to worry about."

I held my stomach as acid swished around inside it. "Maybe not, but my intuition tells me otherwise."

"Jonah is investigating. He'll ping me when he finds something out," Conrad said. "I suspect Steven is probably polling people to see who's with him and who's not."

"You mean Steven is building his army?" I asked.

He smoothed a hand over his crop of windblown black hair. "I suspect he is. Each state has a police force of vampires along with scouts. Sort of like the guardians are cops, and scouts are detectives. Anyway, the vampire population has to work as a team if we want to deal with humans' knowledge of our existence and change with the times." He splashed more water on his arms. "Steven has always been well-liked in our community. Some of us believe he should be our leader. The days of council rule are over. They've done their job in keeping us hidden for centuries. We're living in a new age."

"Whatever he's doing, he needs to make it happen quickly. We need to take down Intech—not Sam because of some stupid elder who has a hard-on for using my husband as a scapegoat."

He chuckled. "We have many missiles coming at us. That's for sure. But Steven will come through. He needs his son at his side if we're going to win any war."

I needed my husband by me if I didn't want to go insane.

"Changing the topic, did Jonah confirm if a Norman Collier was a guardian?" I asked.

He dragged knuckles over his close-shaven beard. "He did say there was a guardian on staff by that name. Tall, dark hair, and dark eyes, like the man who came here."

I didn't know if I should be relieved or not.

Suddenly, out of nowhere, an ominous, powerful, and unrelenting feeling wrapped around my thighs, burning and stinging. What the fuck? It was similar to the feeling I'd gotten when looking at that house for sale, only stronger and deeper.

Something bad was about to happen. I could feel it in my bones and taste it on my tongue.

26

SAM

The scent of dew and pine mixed together in the morning air provided a welcome relief from the wolves' dog scent that was burned into my nostrils. I was on my way to see Dane. Why the alpha had requested my presence in his office at such an early hour was beyond me.

The wolf didn't sleep much. I'd often found him sitting on his porch at two in the morning when I hadn't been able to keep my eyes closed for more than an hour at a time. My nervous energy had reached new heights since I found out there was a contract out on my head.

I was so looking forward to the festivities that night. Word about a boxing match between the pack's alpha and a vampire zipped around the compound like white lightning. For the last three days, I'd heard bragging and arguing about who would win. Money was changing hands, and wolves were eager and hungry to watch a fight rather than a movie. I'd been surprised that some shifters were rooting for a vampire.

I was quite excited myself. My boring routine and chores were becoming old and drab. I hadn't had time to visit their gym either.

Above all that, I was sick over the fact that I wasn't with my family and my kids were growing up without me.

I pulled open the door of the L-shaped admin building and strutted down a wide hall, the stench of dog saturating the air. I would've thought I would be used to the disgusting smell by now, but I wasn't. I passed Cooper's empty office, then banked right toward Dane's.

As of last night, Dane hadn't yet spoken to his pack about taking in my family. He'd been tied up in video meetings with other packs about the same crap vampires were dealing with—humans knowing about their existence. No one had an answer or a plan other than it was time to confirm humanity's fears and curiosity and deal with the consequences as they hit us. But that was coming from the alphas who Dane knew and not the supernatural bigwigs in charge of each of the secret groups within the armed forces. In my opinion, whether we confirmed or denied, either choice had its own demons, and whatever we did plan, it wouldn't happen overnight.

I knocked on the open door as I entered the spacious room where two walls of windows met in the corner with a view overlooking a dense forest of massive trees.

Dane glanced up from his computer screen, rolled his chair back, stood, and circled around his wooden desk, clutching the back of his neck. "Have a seat." He pressed his lips into a thin line, nodding at the black leather couch in front of him.

"Why do I get the feeling you're about to scold me?" I almost added *mutt* at the end of the sentence, but I would save the barbs for our fight tonight. Besides, I didn't want to shit where I ate, so to speak. I could be an arrogant fuck, and Dane and I weren't best buds, but he and his pack had opened their gates for me.

He leaned against his desk, crossing his legs at the ankles. "Just sit, bloodsucker."

I gritted my teeth and obeyed only because I'd been standing and swinging an ax for the last two hours. "Talk." I snarled the word. "Your errand boy made it sound like your message was urgent. Is someone here to chop off my head for the million-dollar prize?" My voice was thick with sarcasm.

"My pack could use that kind of money," he fired at me.

I growled, showing fangs. Anyone on the compound could turn on me, and that notion felt like a cobalt stake through the heart. Not that I hadn't thought about that since I'd learned of the contract three days ago. Sleeping with one eye open was my reality. But hearing the alpha saying shit like that out loud and to my face gave me reason to pause.

Maybe I wasn't safe here.

Motherfucker.

"Chill, bloodsucker," he said. "I'm not stupid. We need each other."

"What about your pack? They could leak to some hunter where I am. People do crazy shit for that kind of money," I said, my anger simmering under the surface.

He whisked a large paw through his white hair. "If anyone here does, we'll know about it. Cooper monitors all calls in and out."

I'd spaced out on that tidbit. "Why am I here?"

"The pack has agreed your family can stay here, but we don't have an empty cabin. But Greta has offered her home. She's a lone wolf and would love the company."

Greta, my boss and chef, had lost her mate three years ago to a hunting accident. A human shot him dead while he'd been in wolf form.

I retracted my fangs. "I'll ask again. Will any of the wolves leak anything to the press or anyone?"

His features darkened. "Look, Sam. My pack doesn't want to go to war with anyone. We've been off the grid for years. But the important thing to know is, if any pack member leaks anything to someone outside this compound, they know I will deal with them personally. We have no room, especially with the tides turning, for fuckups or greed." He delivered that speech with authority and stoicism, reminding me of Webb. "I want to apologize for the barb.

We've had a tumultuous relationship, but I wouldn't put your wife and kids in harm's way."

The fact that he called me by my first name instead of bloodsucker told me he was serious. "I appreciate all that, man. I feel like we should hug."

He threw me the middle finger, and we both laughed.

"Also, there's someone here to see you." He eyed the door.

I followed his line of sight as Tripp's voice trickled in.

My jaw came unhinged as my lieutenant and best bud stalked in alongside Cooper. Tripp had a backpack over his shoulder and was wearing casual clothes like some mountain man—jeans, hiking boots, T-shirt beneath an unbuttoned plaid shirt jacket. His sandy-blond hair was tied at the nape, and he was sporting a beard.

"The fuck are you doing here?" I asked, hugging the crap out of him.

I couldn't even begin to conjure up theories. We had so much to deal with that what was up or down was becoming one big blur. But Layla was always on my mind, although if anything had happened to my wife, he would've called immediately.

"Layla's okay," he said, feeling my anxiety. "What I have to tell you needs to be said in person."

As if Cooper knew my next question, he said, "We just got wind an hour ago that Tripp was on his way."

Tripp unhooked his backpack and set it on the floor. "I had to be careful I wasn't followed, and I wanted to keep the communication down to a minimum. Not so much because of our government but other enemy forces."

"As in Intech or whoever is forking over the million dollars for my vamp ass?" I asked. It had occurred to me that the CIA, FBI, DOJ, or any other human government entity could be behind the contract. Those groups had the means and the money.

Tripp bobbed his head, acknowledging my question, but he didn't have to. Unless some rich entrepreneur fuck wanted me. That was a possibility.

Then something dark and gut-wrenching hit me. "Please tell me my old man isn't dead." Dread froze me into a sheet of ice as I held steadfast, holding my breath.

"Not at all." Tripp pulled out a bottle of blood from his bag.

The sigh that escaped me rattled the windows and shook the desk.

Dane straightened. "Cooper and I will leave you two alone."

"It's best if you and Cooper hear what I have to say," Tripp said as he unscrewed the cap.

Cooper closed the door and sat on the couch while Dane dropped into his desk chair.

I couldn't sit still. My nerves were on edge, and my stomach felt like I'd drunk a cup of acid. I found a spot near the windows and stood there. Whatever Tripp was about to share was big, but if he was including the shifters in the conversation, then the topic had to revolve around something other than our government. The shifters didn't give a rat's ass about our laws or the guardians hunting me.

Tripp eased onto the cushion next to Cooper while drinking blood, and as he did, his bronze eyes brightened. "Steven Mason is about to overthrow our government from the top down."

"Fuck yeah," I said, my voice hitching as elation washed away the nerves. "About damn time." I understood the need for laws, but several had to be revised and updated to change with the times.

"But," Tripp continued, regarding me, "we might have a second enemy to fight. The elders, the guardians, and those in Eternal Affairs, who all help govern our laws, are not about to go quietly. Some might not agree with your father's belief that we need to let the world know we exist and show humans the good we have done and can do."

"That will be a tall order," Dane chimed in. "And not an easy task either." He rested his forearms on his desk. "What does an overthrow of your government have to do with shifters?"

"For starters, I'm here to ask if we can use your compound as a safe harbor and secondary command center." Tripp stared at Dane.

"The base as it stands has been locked down. The Special Forces shifters, along with our master-at-arms command, have the perimeter and the crowd under control. The military families have been moved to a safer location. I'm asking for your help taking in casualties and using Cooper's skills to help Sawyer."

Dane and Cooper exchanged a silent message as if they were mind-speaking. I had no clue if they could do that or not.

Their silence allowed Tripp to plead more of his case. "As I was coming in, I heard you agree to take in Layla and the kids. I would like to ask if Webb and Jo's daughter, Abbey, and Alia Costner can stay here as well."

"You mean the mother of that traitor who showed the world he was a vampire at the press conference?" Cooper asked.

"That traitor," Tripp said, "is in fact on our side."

My jaw hit the floor. "Since when?"

Matthew had given us the impression that he was happy to be part of Adam's team and experiments, which didn't add up since he'd been kidnapped by Roman's men. But maybe Matthew was more cunning than I'd given him credit for. Maybe he'd convinced Roman and Adam he wanted to play ball with them, so to speak. But Roman and Adam weren't the types to be easily convinced.

Tripp dug his elbows into his knees. "I don't know the specifics, but Matthew sent two messages three days apart to a secure server on Victor's estate. How? I don't know. According to Wyman, Victor's computer expert, Matthew detailed three things. One, he's fine, and we shouldn't think he's sided with Adam. Two, the experiments are failing. Three, there are two shifters working with him to free the others."

Dane jerked back so hard he and his chair almost fell into the window behind him. "Does that mean Ross is alive?"

Cooper froze, fixating on his brother.

Tripp shrugged. "Not sure, but Matthew was taken around the same time Ross went missing."

Cooper popped to his feet and paced. "When do we leave for Chicago?"

The air crackled with tension as both wolves were ready to bolt out and rescue their brother.

Dane scraped a hand along his jaw. "Cooper, relax. We can't go off half-cocked, even though I'm ready to." Then he swung his hard gaze at Tripp. "I sense you have more to say."

Cooper sat on the arm of the couch, features tight, hands fisted in his lap.

Tripp rose, dumped the empty bottle of blood in his backpack, then nailed a stern look on each of us. "Between the knowledge of our existence and the war with Intech, the supernatural community needs to work together. This isn't just about vampires or Steven overthrowing our government. Shifters, witches, and all types of supernaturals are at stake, both on a worldwide scale and because of people like Adam Emery. He won't be the only one who will study us or want to build an army. And let's not forget the hunters who are already showing themselves. Or the contract on Sam's head. Our survival is the war we're now fighting."

"You sound like him," Cooper said as he pointed a finger at me. "He gave a similar speech to our pack."

"Which is why my father is stepping up, no matter the consequences," I uttered. "If we allow the ancient asshole elders to lead us, vampires are fucked."

Tripp gave me a nod. "Exactly. Soon enough the elders, guardians, and those vampires not on board with us will either realize Steven is right and join us, or they'll perish. There's no room for rogue vampires."

I leaned against the cool window, which was a welcome relief to the sweat on my back. "Does that mean I'm free from the guardians?" I sure as hell wasn't safe from hunters.

Tripp straddled the other arm of the couch. "You're not out of the woods just yet. As we speak, Steven has called for a vote from the scouts and guardians nationwide. He's also preparing to round up those in Boston who do not stand with us. But I suspect that if your father is successful, those elders against him will use you to piss him off and will follow through on bringing you in."

I bit my lip. "I'm damned either way. There's no need for me to hide from the guardians anymore."

"Which is another reason why I'm here," Tripp said. "Sam and I are heading to Maine."

Fuck yeah! Best news ever. "You said she was okay. So what's the plan?"

"To pack up Layla and the kids and bring them here." Tripp regarded Dane. "That's okay, right?"

"Yes," Dane said. "And you can include Abbey and Alia. But as far as using our place as a second command center and us joining your fight, Cooper and I have to discuss that with our pack. We *are* desperate to find Ross, but like you, we need to be strategic. I'll have an answer for you by morning."

I was itching to see my feisty huntress and our children, but I had to ask Tripp the obvious question. "Can't Conrad, Jo, Rebekah, and Stan's men escort everyone here?"

"Conrad is needed in Boston, Stan's men have to protect their town, and Rebekah is only one wolf," Tripp said. "Also, Jo and Abbey are on their way to meet Webb and Alia in Boston. Jo will pick up Alia, then return to Maine while Webb helps your father."

"No argument from me," I said. "I just needed to understand the plan. I'll pack my things."

I was out the door before Tripp could stop me, and as I wound through the compound, butterflies were going wild in my stomach. The nine-hour drive would be long, but knowing I would have my arms around my wife and be kissing my babies by dinnertime tonight would be worth every confining hour, minute, and second in the car.

27

LAYLA

By lunchtime, I was ready for a nap alongside my little ones, who were snoozing away in their baby rockers by the fireplace while I lay on the couch. My run that morning and my talk with Conrad had wiped me out. Not to mention diaper changes, feedings, and cleaning up my bedroom. I was sleeping in the nursery with my children, and my room was a disaster. I'd always been a neat person, but that went out the window with quadruplets.

Jo and Abbey had left about five hours ago. They should be in Boston by now, picking up Alia Costner, who had ridden with Webb. Jo's husband had a meeting with the council. Otherwise, Webb would've driven up to the house.

When I probed Jo for more information on Webb's meeting, her response had been, "I can't say anything. But all will be revealed soon enough." She'd seemed relaxed, which told me Steven was working his magic. My gut had failed me on Steven. I'd thought something happened to him, but I guessed it hadn't.

I suspected Alia was coming to stay with us because she needed protection. She hadn't heard from her father, her son was in the hands of Adam, and since she carried the vampire gene but had never turned, she could be targeted as a guinea pig for her DNA or experimented on to confirm if the serum worked on a person with her vampire lineage.

The ocean outside the glass accordion doors appeared calm. The skies were crystal clear and bright blue, and the salt air floated inside. It would be a perfect day for the beach if it wasn't for Rorie. She was warm to the touch. Even after Rebekah examined her and confirmed Rorie's vitals were normal and she didn't have a fever, I didn't want to leave the house. As a first-time mom, I was paranoid and anxious. It didn't help that my hormones were acting up. But Rebekah assured me nothing was wrong with Rorie.

Truth be told, I was tired. Exercising in the mornings, taking care of four littles, missing Sam terribly, and worrying were physically and emotionally draining.

I closed my eyes, sleep a second away from taking me under when my phone vibrated, dancing on the coffee table with a low buzzing sound.

Damn it. With the babies sleeping, I'd switched my cell to vibrate. But the vibration against the table was loud enough to disturb them —or at least Orion with his sensitive vamp hearing. A quick glance confirmed otherwise. Thank God. I'd just gotten them down for their naps.

Jordyn's name came across the screen. My sister and Rebekah had gone into town to pick up lunch at Trina's, and I suspected Trina was out of elderberry pie. She always ran out and couldn't make the delicious dessert fast enough, especially with Jordyn and me buying it on a daily basis.

"Is Trina out of pie?" I asked as I answered.

"Not at all," the female voice on the other end said.

I was on my feet in less than a second, my pulse lighting up like the Fourth of July, the steady *boom, boom, boom* ramming against my skin. I opened my mouth to speak, but my tongue was stuck to the roof of my mouth. The room spun into a wild vortex, and before I could take one step, large hands were around me, guiding me to sit down.

I blinked, and Conrad's hazel eyes swirled to black.

"Layla!" Rianne's voice shouted through the cell.

I managed to hang up with shaky hands. I needed to collect my thoughts as questions fired left and right. How did she get Jordyn's phone? If she had it, that meant Rianne was in town and with Jordyn. But how did Rianne know where I was? And oh my God, was Jordyn okay?

Or maybe I was having a nightmare.

"Breathe," Conrad said as he sat beside me. "I heard your heart go from sixty to a hundred and ten in seconds. Who was that?"

The phone vibrated again in my lap.

Conrad glanced at the screen as Jordyn's name flashed on it.

"I can't answer," I said. "Not yet." I inhaled a trembling, aching breath into my lungs.

"I've been around Jordyn long enough to know her voice, and that person I heard wasn't Jordyn," Conrad said.

The vibration finally stopped, only to start up again.

That time Conrad answered. "What?" His tone was lethal as his fangs elongated.

"Put my sister on." Rianne's voice was loud enough for me to hear.

Conrad's vampire-black eyes widened as he ended the call.

I still couldn't speak as shock rolled through me. My brain hurt trying to figure out how she knew where I was.

Even Conrad looked confounded. "That was Rianne." He knew Jordyn's voice well, but he had to know Rianne's too. He'd been the scout who had watched the Aberdeen family for years.

Suddenly, déjà vu hit me. The last time Rianne and I had been on the phone together was in Montana while Conrad and I sat in his car in the Deer and Elk parking lot. That day had changed the trajectory of my relationship with her when she had officially jumped to the dark side.

Adrenaline powered through me, clearing the dizziness but not my confusion as to what the fuck she was doing in Maine. "I need to go. Rianne has Jordyn. She must be at the diner."

Conrad's large frame blocked me from moving. "Not so fast."

I pushed him, but the muscled, toned vampire didn't budge.

"Rianne will not give up. If I keep ignoring her, she'll come to the house." She couldn't be here with my children. She could never know I had more than one. If my grandmother found out, she would burn the planet to get her evil hands on them.

"I'll call Rebekah," he said, whipping out his phone.

Where *was* the she-wolf? Surely she could handle Rianne, who was human—or at least my sister had admitted as much at the press conference, although that had been three weeks ago. She might be a monster now.

Rianne called again. That time I held up my hand to Conrad. "I got this." Fear for Jordyn wormed its way into my skin, digging in like a tick into a dog. "Where are you?" I asked Rianne as I answered.

"Waiting on you at this shabby diner. Holding Jordyn and, oh, about six or seven others hostage." Disgust bled through the line. "If you're not here in five minutes, then Jordyn and your wolf will be injected with our spanking new serum." She emphasized the word spanking. "Do you know what happens when a wolf has the serum in their system? It's a unique transformation to watch as they suffer a slow death."

Conrad was listening intently.

I rolled my shoulders back. "The serum kills everyone subjected to it." Maybe not Ben or Matthew, but they were a product of Patrick Mason's genetic-altering concoction, and he hadn't mixed vampire DNA with shifter DNA like Carly had. "Why are you here?" I had an inkling.

"First, sis," Rianne said, "I want you to come down to the diner. I know the town is full of vampires. But none of you will hurt me. If you try anything, I have a reporter with me and a cameraman who is videotaping everything. I'm sure my death broadcast on national television will incite more violence and anger. People are rooting for me, Layla."

I stuck my finger in my mouth to mime gagging, but she couldn't see me. I hadn't seen the news in several days. As hard as it was, I hadn't read the headlines on my phone either.

"You're telling me it's just you and a couple of journalists in town. They're your bodyguards?" I refrained from unleashing a condescending laugh so that I didn't disturb my babies.

Rianne's demented chortle pierced my eardrum. "I can handle myself, but the reporter is an added benefit. You see, I know vampires worldwide are cringing that the public knows about them. Just think what will happen if the news stations converge on this small town. I also hear the vampire government is hunting Sam, and there is a contract out on his head. Are you just beside yourself, sister? Wouldn't it be fun to see a slew of hunters like our family chasing down Sam? I've even suggested to a few of my fast friends that vampires look great strung up over a firepit."

"Reporters don't scare me, and neither do hunters. You should know that."

"Layla." She said my name with that tone I was accustomed to hearing whenever she rolled her eyes. "You should be afraid of this reporter. Because if I give him the signal, he'll call the human cops. And last I checked, you were still human, which means if I press charges, they can lock you up."

Conrad was shaking his head as if he was trying to say she was a piece of work.

Rianne Aberdeen was an unpleasant person, but she was also smart, and her psychological warfare was reaching new heights. She'd fucked with the minds of a few of her high school classmates when they had gotten on her bad side. She definitely had a bullying personality that had literally bitten her in the ass while hunting vampires when one had literally sunk his fangs into her ass one time.

I snorted at the memory.

"You think this is funny," she snarled.

I hung up on her again. No more talk. It was time to take off the gloves. When we faced off in West Virginia, I was pregnant and couldn't bash her head into a wall.

Excitement exploded in my belly as I called for George.

"You are not going down there," Conrad said. "The sheriff will take care of her."

I plastered on a tight expression. "No. Rianne is mine to deal with."

Footsteps clamored down the hall from the back bedrooms before George came in, freshly showered and dressed in casual attire. "What's going on?"

"Rianne is at the diner, holding Jordyn and everybody else who was there hostage," I said. "I need you to watch the babies, please."

George's dark eyebrows disappeared into his thick hairline. "Sure. But do you think it's wise to engage Rianne? I heard everything she said."

Gotta love vamp hearing.

"If I don't go, Rianne will hurt Jordyn. I'm not sure what happened to Rebekah."

Conrad was on his phone. "Rebekah isn't answering."

So much for her astute shifter skills.

While my sister was intelligent, it was her ego that drove her actions. Her bravado had gotten her into trouble many times before. But I wasn't willing to risk Jordyn's life by not taking Rianne seriously. She had changed since she joined my grandmother and Adam. In several ways her behavior was beginning to remind me of Roman Brown and the head games he liked to play with Sam. Regardless, I wasn't foolish enough to believe Rianne didn't have something up her sleeve.

The reporter was a ploy. He had to be.

"We need to confirm she's here alone and doesn't have an army of Intech goons with her," I said, as if I was coming up with an excuse not to go. But I had to be smart. I had too much to lose. She could be using Jordyn to draw me out for several other reasons—like my grandmother, for one.

George and Conrad talked about a plan while I changed into fighting clothes and collected my daggers. I had no problem stabbing Rianne to save Jordyn's life.

28

LAYLA

As Conrad drove down the mountain road, we could see the sleepy town in the distance as the coastline blipped by to our left. Wispy clouds skated across the sky, intermittently blocking the sun, and whitecaps broke over the ocean's surface.

I bounced my foot and adjusted the air conditioner vents on the dashboard in front of me. Sweat coated my skin, my heart didn't know whether to beat rapidly or stop abruptly, and nausea was churning inside me like a fast-moving tornado.

Other than the occasional tourist stopping at the diner as they passed through town, the area was clear of any enemy vampires or strange humans who didn't belong. The sheriff and his men had done a thorough sweep alongside the residents.

I picked at a nail, my mind spinning and my nerves rocking and rolling as I dipped into a memory of the stormy day when I'd been locked in a room at Intech and squared off with Rianne. I replayed bits and pieces of our provoking and tense conversation.

"In whose universe do you think we can become an exact replica of someone like Sam? We might have similarities to the bloodsuckers in our genetic makeup, but we don't carry the gene," I said.

Rianne mashed her lips into a thin line. "You're not the scientist here."

I could only speak for myself, but I didn't carry the gene, according to the tests run by Dr. Vieira. I wasn't sure about Rianne or even Jordyn. As siblings, we shared about 50 percent of the same genetic coding. And just because I had the right blood type to get pregnant by a vampire, that didn't mean Rianne and Jordyn did. Truth be told, Rianne and Jordyn had more traits from our mother —brown hair and eyes and the same shaped nose. As for me, I resembled my dad with auburn hair, blue eyes, and freckles. If I was a gambler like my uncle Ray had been, I would bet Jordyn and Rianne probably had more of the vampire DNA markers than I did.

"Once you go down that route, there's no turning back. You'll never be human again. Are you sure that's what you want?" I asked in an even tone.

She stuck out her chin, that defiant side of her rearing its ugly head. "I've never wanted anything more. Think about it, sis. Immortality. Powers to control the weather." She waved her hand at the window. "The ability to compel some-one. The list goes on. But the best part? I would have the power and strength to fight Sam on an even playing field."

I rolled my eyes. "Why do you hate Sam so much?"

Revulsion swam in the deep depths of her brown eyes. "Hate is too weak a word to describe how I feel about that asshole vampire." Disgust was stamped on every word. "He doesn't deserve you. You're too good for someone like him." Her voice softened. "That day he compelled me into a vegetative state, I vowed I would kill him. Then, after I found out you slept with him, I knew I'd lost you, and that only confirmed what I needed to do."

I could feel my eyebrows squishing together. "But you came around after he saved your life from the explosion at our rental house. If I remember correctly, you even threw yourself at Sam and thanked him." My voice hitched.

"None of that changes the way I feel about him. But if we're laying our cards out on the table, then here's the truth." She flashed a softer look my way. "I loved you once, Layla. I would've died for you. You, me, and Jordyn could've changed the world. But you and Jordyn and your desire to live with and fuck vampires is wrong. Jordyn's excitement to work alongside the Vampire Navy SEALs was revolting. While you were sick, she wouldn't shut up about them.

She kept talking about Sam like he was a god and saying how you were in love with him. And when Noah overheard Jordyn one day, he went nuts. So I told him everything. Noah didn't brainwash me. Granny isn't doing that either. I am my own person. You and Jordyn go against everything the Aberdeen name stands for. It's just wrong for you to love a vampire." Her face had turned red.

The more we argued, the more a nagging pain in my chest intensified. "If you had known Mom's family history while she was alive, would you have murdered her?"

She stuck out her chin. "But she isn't alive."

I blew out a breath, hoping to ease the chest pain. "That's not an answer."

"Here's one for you," she said. "As long as you're with that bloodsucker, you'll never be my sister. And you can't have that baby. The world doesn't need another Mason. They have too much power and arrogance, and I'm going to stop that."

I was stuck on "you can't have that baby."

"You want to kill an innocent unborn child? Because it's Sam's?" I flew at her and got in her face. "Over my dead body." I would become the Queen of Death if she or anyone dared to try.

She practically pressed her nose into mine. "Save your energy, sister. You and I will have our chance in the ring. But first, you're going to witness my rebirth. I want you to see a phoenix rising from the ashes. It's time the Aberdeens ruled humanity. It's time to show the vast population of bloodsuckers that they can't kill humans for sport or hunger. Either they bow down to us or we eat them for breakfast. Once my rebirth is complete, I'll watch yours. Afterward, we'll be sisters again, fighting side by side."

"Layla, did you hear what I said?" Conrad's deep baritone voice jarred me back from hell.

I quivered. "Rianne isn't human."

"What?" He slowed, veering the SUV into a gravel lot across from the diner.

Ding. Ding. Ding.

"That's why she's here. She wants to show me she isn't human anymore. And she has the serum with her that has my name and

Jordyn's on it. She thinks that's the only way we can be sisters again."

A muscle ticked furiously in his jaw. "I'm turning around. There's no way I'm allowing you to go into that diner. If she injects you with the serum, you're as good as dead."

My nostrils flared as I lasered a narrowed gaze on the handsome vampire. "Look, I can handle Rianne. I have to save Jordyn. And if I know Rianne, there's another reason she's here. If her goal is to also kidnap me, she would've brought Intech goons and not just the journalists. Maybe she wants my help. I suspect Carly came to us in need of assistance. Rianne can be too proud to ask for anything. And she certainly isn't the type to admit when she's wrong."

"She's sick," Conrad said.

"No argument from me. But the other question is how did she know where I was?"

"I'm sure Adam and Roman have their spies, but we can't rule out a mole within the SEAL organization either." He wheeled out of the gravel lot, crossed the road, and parked in a space near the edge of the road. "You have five minutes to talk her down, then I'm coming in."

"Fair enough." I climbed out of the SUV, wiped my sweaty hands on my skinny black jeans, adjusted the dagger strapped to my leg, and felt for the other weapon at the small of my back.

My stomach fluttered with nerves, my heart was beating quite fast, and sweat glided down my spine. I hadn't physically fought in… I couldn't remember when. The night my sisters and I commandeered a vampire nightclub, intending to capture Sam, we'd used drug-filled darts. I didn't consider that a fight. Nor had it been a brawl when Noah and Rianne had Sam strung up over a firepit on that stormy day in Montana. The most I'd done that day had been tackling Rianne and throwing a rock at Noah. Not exactly a fight. Nevertheless, it was time to discharge some nervous energy.

Several townsfolk, men and women, exited their vehicles. Some had guns. Some had swords, and others had axes. I stood up taller, knowing I had my own small army. I felt like a Viking about to go into battle to save my kingdom. That alone gave me a much-needed dose of courage.

The group surrounded me like a swarm of bees as the sheriff pushed his way through the circle, setting dark eyes on me. I'd finally met the tall, skinny vampire when we'd first arrived. I'd never had the chance the other two times Sam and I had stayed at Jo and Webb's house.

Stan peered down at me from his six-foot height, the shiny silver badge on his chest glinting in the afternoon light. "Are you sure you want to do this?"

"One hundred percent," I volleyed back. "How many patrons are inside?" I sounded like I was a cop. I'd almost signed up for the police academy.

"To my knowledge," Stan said, "there are ten in total, and that includes the media and your sister Rianne."

"The building was built to withstand enemy vampires," a brunette woman said. "If your sister realizes it, we might not save anyone."

I silently laughed. Of course it was. "What does that mean?"

"The windows and doors are bulletproof. If an emergency button is engaged during an attack, then cobalt shields drop down to cover windows, walls, doors—everything," Stan explained. "Oh, and she has a dart gun. One of my deputies got shot when he went inside. He's sleeping it off in the cruiser."

I gnawed on my bottom lip. "Good to know."

Conrad finally joined the group and handed me my phone. "Rianne called. I also tried to get ahold of Webb. But he's not answering."

We agreed not to alert Sam. For starters, he would leave the shifter compound and expose himself. It was too dangerous for him. Webb and Tripp held the power to send reinforcements anyway.

I plowed through the crowd, calling Rianne on my phone to let her know I was coming in. I would be lying if I said I wasn't nervous, because my stomach was in a tight-fisted knot.

"Five minutes," Conrad reminded me as he walked me to the entrance.

I waved him off. It was showtime.

29

LAYLA

A thick layer of grease burned the hairs in my nostrils when I entered the restaurant. It took my eyes a few seconds to adjust from the sunlight to the dimly lit space. Before I could track movement, a blinding light was shining in my face.

Squinting, I raised one hand to shield my eyes and the other to grab the dagger on my leg. Since I couldn't see, I sharpened my other senses, and a laugh broke out in my head.

You're not a vampire. You don't have acute hearing.

Maybe not, but adrenaline was a beautiful thing in times of flight or fight, and I still had my banshee scream. I hadn't yet gotten around to testing to see if I could still control someone with my mind or had any other new magical abilities, like Sam and I had talked about.

"Bob, cut the lights," Rianne ordered the cameraman, her haughty voice grating on my nerves as if someone was clawing at me with sharp nails. "You'll have a chance to film the Aberdeen sisters."

I held steady, the leather handle of my family heirloom feeling

223

like it had belonged in my hand for eons, and I primed myself to launch it at a moment's notice.

I quickly assessed the room. To my right was Bob, husky and broad, alongside a familiar-looking reporter dressed to accept the Pulitzer in a black tailored pinstripe suit. To my left was a family—father, mother, and young son, who had fear written over their pale faces. Directly ahead of me, Rebekah, Trina, and the cook were out cold and laid out flat on their stomachs in the aisle that separated the counter and stools from the main dining room. Then, in the middle of the restaurant, Jordyn was tied to a chair at a table, blazing mad. As my attention finally landed on Rianne, who was standing on top of the table next to our sister, I choked out a laugh. I shouldn't find any of this funny, but I couldn't help myself.

Rianne was holding a dart gun, head shaved—as in stubs of hair poking straight up—dressed in black from head to toe and wearing a bulletproof vest with wires sticking out of a pocket.

Before my pulse went haywire, I studied the vest for C-4, but I didn't see a bomb.

"Are you taking a play out of Roman's bag of tricks?" I asked, my feet glued to the wood floor by the door.

The blood cartel lord, though he might not be running the blood trade anymore, had commanded his troops from the top of an SUV during my first battle encounter with him.

She sneered, aiming her weapon at me. "Roman is a fucking putz."

One eyebrow went up and the other down as I cocked my neck. "Trouble in paradise, sis?" I didn't need a response. It was clear she hated Roman. "What's with the wires on your vest? You plan on becoming a martyr?"

Rianne smirked proudly. "I have a camera, so I can tape your reactions of our meeting."

"She's sick in the head, Layla," Jordyn grunted, and then she growled, struggling against her restraints in the chair.

Rianne kicked Jordyn in the jaw. "Shut the fuck up."

Anger, blazing hot, burned through my veins, causing me to grab the dagger on my back. "Come on, Rianne. Lose the dart gun and face me like a warrior. Stop screwing around." I had children who needed their momma, and I didn't have time for much more childish antics.

Jordyn shrieked, turning red. "If it's the last thing I do, I will rip your guts out." She spat at Rianne.

"You couldn't scare a bear, sister," Rianne said to Jordyn. "You know I'm the better fighter."

"Then do as Layla says. Shuck the gun," Jordyn urged. "I'll fight you."

Jordyn could hold her own, but out of the three of us, Jordyn came in third with her fighting skills. But that was up until we arrived in Maine, after which Jordyn had been a machine, running six miles without breaking a sweat. Every muscle on her was toned, her attitude and mood were better than I'd ever seen, and she was anxious to learn Krav Maga.

"The humans have no stake in our fight. Let them go," I said in a scolding tone I'd used many times to reprimand Rianne when she was a kid. My heart broke for the family as the young boy who was about Abbey's age shook in his mother's arms. "Do you want the nation to see you're a monster? Aren't you trying to show humans you're the victim? I'm sure Bob would be happy to turn on his camera."

She swung her weapon at Bob, who seemed eager to pop on the trusty piece of equipment he held on his broad shoulders. "He knows better."

Bob didn't react, but his partner did. "Rianne, the plan was to film you and your sisters. Not harm innocents," the reporter said.

As soon as he spoke, I remembered him. His name was Tim Cox. He'd interviewed Roman outside Intech in Chicago.

"I suggest you say what you came to say, Rianne," I said. "It won't be long before these three wake up or the townsfolk storm in." Conrad had given me five minutes. "Right now, I'm the only reason you're still breathing." I waved at the humans. "Come on. She won't hurt you. The most she can do is knock you out."

Rianne roared like a lion, diverting my attention from the family to her. My eyes bugged out of their sockets as I dropped into a fit of laughter. Why I thought her transformation from human to monster was funny, I wasn't sure. But the stupidity of her to think she could become a creature like Sam, who was born with the right DNA to turn vampire, was comical and sad.

Her cheekbones and forehead extended outward. Her nails were sharp and long, curling toward her fingertips. Her brown eyes were a deep red just like our cousin Noah's. It was crystal fucking clear to me that having vampires in our family history wasn't a shoo-in to becoming immortal.

The family screamed as they scurried out.

Jordyn tried her best to shuffle away in her chair, her eyes saucers, her face ashen.

Bob turned on his camera. The reporter held up his phone as if he, too, was filming the freak show. But the freak show was turning down a dark road, and I had to stop it.

Rianne dropped her dart gun, pulled out a syringe from her vest pocket, then hopped off the table and moved toward Jordyn.

Fear erupted within me like a volcano, spewing hot lava through me as I ran toward her, dodging tables. "Rianne!" I shouted. "It's me you want. Don't you want me to change with you? That's the reason you came here, isn't it?" I was 1,000 percent certain I was right.

Rianne whipped her grotesque features my way, those fangs murderously long and dripping with saliva.

What in the fucknation was happening to people? Why would any human think they could become immortal? I understood how those who were dying of an incurable disease would take a chance. My grandmother came to mind. But mere mortals who were healthy and vibrant like Rianne were stupid. I took back what I'd said about her intelligence. Then again, her ego had blinded her decisions, as had her desire to exact revenge against Sam.

"I wanted to wait for the perfect moment to reveal myself while the nation watched the three of us transform." She snarled at Bob. "It's your fault. You ruined everything." She stomped in his direction.

I tossed one dagger across the room to Jordyn, which landed near her chair, then shouted, "Rianne! I'm right here." I stood behind a table along the aisle, not far from Bob.

The reporter grabbed Bob's arm. "It's time for us to leave. I didn't sign up to become a monster freak."

They left in a flash.

Jordyn banged the wood chair against the counter, trying to break free while my deranged sister set her bloodred gaze on me.

I wound around the table and stepped into the aisle. Now she was at one end with the windows overlooking the ocean behind her, and I was at the other with the entrance slightly behind me and to my left.

I opened my arms, a dagger secured in my right hand, heart punching my ribs. I'd never imagined I would face off with either of my sisters, yet here I was, ready to kill Rianne. But if her transformation followed the same path as Noah's, I might not need to end her life.

With the long needle pointed at me, she stalked in my direction, stomping her feet, fangs overlapping her lips. "I told you at Intech that day, we would be sisters again." Sweat coated her face as if she suddenly had a fever.

"And I told you it would never happen," I volleyed back. "Have you seen yourself in the mirror? How do you think you resemble someone like Sam?"

She growled like a wolf in the wild. "Where is he?"

My lips curled into a sarcastic grin as I marched toward her, passing a booth along the wall. "This isn't Sam's fight." My husband would flip the fuck out if he knew I was confronting Rianne, even though he wanted me by his side when we went into battle.

"Layla, don't engage," Jordyn yelled.

I had to stop Rianne. I wasn't exactly sure how, given her talons and fangs. Those could do more damage than the blade in my hand, although maybe cobalt affected a lab-made monster like it did vampires.

I charged Rianne, dropped to the floor as if I was sliding into second base, and kicked her legs out from under her.

The needle flew in one direction as she fell face-first with a resounding thud.

I hopped to my feet and pivoted, dagger at the ready.

Rianne rose like a phoenix out of the ashes, arms outstretched, talons lethally long, then spun around to face me. "Good move. But you can't kill me." She darted over to the door and locked it. "In case we're interrupted."

I would've liked to argue that she couldn't keep vampires out, but the brunette's words rang in my ears. *The building was built to withstand enemy vampires. If your sister realizes it, we might not save anyone.*

I was going with the assumption that Rianne did realize it, and Jordyn and I were screwed. Conrad wouldn't be able to get in.

There had to be an emergency exit in the kitchen. The sliding glass door behind me was a way out, and I could easily leave, but not without Jordyn, who was struggling with her restraints.

I was about to help Jordyn when Rianne stalked into the aisle directly ahead of me.

Think, girl. Act now. Catch her off guard. She has claws and fangs. You can't compete with that.

"All exits are locked," Rianne bragged. "I heard the cook saying the building could withstand enemy fire."

As she marched in my direction, I flung the dagger, and as it soared through the air, Rianne came to an abrupt halt, grinning as if she had a secret. When the knife pierced her throat, her lips split into a bloodthirsty smirk.

My pulse shot through the roof, even more so when she removed the weapon and licked the tip of the blade.

Fuck me.

I caught a glimpse of Jordyn on my right, now free, bending down to retrieve the blade I'd thrown to her.

Rianne charged me, claws primed to scratch out my eyes, canines gleaming from her upper gums.

I crouched down, shoving my head into her stomach as I latched on to her legs, and right before I lifted her, her talons scored my back. Pain lanced through me, infusing me with more adrenaline as I shrieked before throwing her behind me. I whirled around as she popped to her feet.

"You don't stand a chance, Layla," Rianne boasted.

Jordyn charged her with the dagger. "My turn." My younger sister yearned to inflict pain on her.

Rianne snorted. "Give me all you got, sis," she said rather proudly to Jordyn.

I grabbed a chair and rushed toward Rianne and swung at her head. The impact did nothing other than make her growl, giving Jordyn a window to flee.

"Get out of here, Jordyn," I shouted.

Before Jordyn could move, Rianne had her by the throat, lifting her and pinning her to the counter. "I wanted Layla to be first, but I'll settle for you."

I jumped onto the table and dove at Rianne, and when I was midair, she swung out her free arm, backhanding me. Her powerful strength sent me flying through the air. My back hit a booth, taking the brunt of the impact before my head followed suit. Every ounce of air left me, and I lost the ability to breathe as I landed on the floor. My lungs burned as I tried to get air in them but failed. I punched my chest, my mouth agape, inhaling. The ceiling spun above me, my head ready to explode.

Don't you dare pass out, girl. Get up. You're strong, resilient.

How the fuck could I stand? I couldn't breathe.

I took a deep breath, and a smidge of air filled my lungs. On another inhale, more air. I repeated this process as I got on all fours and pushed myself upright. I staggered, catching the booth's table, orienting my vision at my two sisters.

Rianne pulled a syringe from her vest pocket.

Fear squeezed my chest, but anger neutralized it, allowing me to gulp in as much oxygen as I could. I shouted, but nothing came out.

I grabbed a sugar jar off the table and threw it at Rianne. The fucking thing missed but distracted her enough to bare her fangs at me.

I picked up the saltshaker and launched it at her. Then the pepper and a dirty dish that had a half-eaten burger on it. I kept launching anything I could get my hands on. Some items hit her, and others didn't. But my actions were enough to distract her from using the syringe.

She threw Jordyn into the window as if our sister was a piece of trash. Jordyn slumped like a rag doll before she crumpled to the floor.

Fury pumped through my veins, spiking my adrenaline enough to clear my mind. From where I stood, I looked for but didn't see the dart gun. It wouldn't kill her, but it might slow her down.

Rianne came toward me, hunger in her red eyes, needle ready to inject me. "It's always been you I wanted."

"Why?" I inched backward. "To hurt Sam?" That had been one of her reasons.

"That, and I want you and me to be sisters again, Layla," Rianne's voice was deep and didn't sound like her as she stomped in my direction with a predatory ferocity.

"Not Jordyn?" I asked, dodging a table like a drunken sailor.

She shrugged. "She'll be next."

My head throbbed, my pulse pounded, and my lungs were on fire but not as much as they had been. As I kept my sights on Rianne, I inched around furniture, trying to look for the dart gun on the floor, and I stepped on something before losing my balance. I fell on top of Rebekah, who was still passed out. I was about to try to wake her when I spotted the gun.

Someone banged on the door and kept pounding. Was it Conrad?

I had crawled on all fours under a table when Rianne lifted it and tossed the wooden piece of furniture to the side as if it weighed nothing.

I would be lying if I said I wasn't afraid of Rianne, because the terror was real. But even more terrifying was the long fucking needle filled with the serum. I wanted to spend eternity with Sam and our kids but not as a beast.

Try your mind control, woman, or scream.

Unfortunately my banshee scream didn't work on immortals. But was Rianne truly immortal?

The gun was within arm's reach, so I scampered like an animal running from a predator, and just when my hand landed on the gun, Rianne literally kicked my ass. I fell on the dart gun.

Her maniacal laugh cut through me like shards of glass.

I rolled over to face her, lifting my upper torso while I felt for the dart gun behind me.

She loomed over me and crouched down. "It's quite freeing to be like this. You'll suffer for about twelve hours, but when the serum begins to work its magic, the pain will subside."

I laughed nervously. "You're sick." Barbs and retorts wouldn't hurt her, but I had nothing left in my arsenal.

Or maybe I did. I studied her as I envisioned her using the needle on herself. If I had mind control, now would be a good time for it to surface. But the more I glared and imagined her injecting herself, nothing happened other than her cocking her head.

"You're trying to use mind control," she said, snorting. "It's not working. Is it?"

Then two things happened at once. She stuck the needle in my leg at the exact moment that I grabbed the gun, and just as she was about to push the plunger, I pulled the trigger, once, twice, three times in rapid succession.

Darts embedded in her neck as she rocked from one side to the other.

My heart banged against my sternum as I scooted away from her as fast as I could, praying I didn't have any serum in me as I yanked the needle from my leg.

Rianne finally fell to the floor before her eyes rolled back in her head.

Using the booth's bench, I pushed myself up and set the needle on the table, then rushed over to Jordyn. "Sis, wake up." I tapped her face. "Hey." I checked for a pulse and sighed when I found one.

Then I lost my breath. I hadn't seen Rianne use the syringe on Jordyn, but maybe she had.

Jordyn's eyes fluttered open. "You're alive." She touched the back of her head. "It feels like someone whacked me with a sledgehammer."

"Did Rianne inject the serum in you?"

"She was about to when you interrupted, then she threw me." She clutched her chest. "I don't ever want that shit in me either."

Relief steadied my nerves. "We have to stop Adam."

My mom's message blared like a bullhorn in my head.

"The world needs you. You and Sam are instrumental in making sure humanity survives."

It was time to regroup and start training. Daggers weren't going to cut it, and I had just the weapon in mind.

30

LAYLA

By six that night, only four hours after the showdown ended with Rianne, I was pacing in the sheriff's station, waiting for Rianne to wake up. I needed answers like I needed water. I doubted she would give me any, but I had to ask. I had to know how she found me and where my grandmother was hiding. I wasn't naïve enough to believe that Adam didn't have spies, like Conrad had mentioned. They could've followed me. But if they had, Rianne wouldn't have waited three weeks to make her appearance. We had a mole in our close-knit circle. I was almost sure of it. On top of that, my sister had something up her sleeve other than her thwarted show-and-tell transformation on national television. I couldn't quite put my finger on what yet.

I stomped in one direction, biting my thumbnail, then switched to my forefinger. What was taking Stan so long? He'd been on the phone since Conrad and I arrived thirty minutes ago.

Conrad sat on a bench in the small lobby, his hazel eyes tracking my every step. "You're going to drive yourself crazy."

I bobbed my head. "I'm way past that."

He crossed one black-panted leg over the other. "Rianne probably isn't awake. You shot a good amount of drugs into her."

I gnawed on my lip. "Then we'll just have to wake her. I'm not leaving here without answers. I also want to talk to the reporter."

Tim Cox, the news correspondent who had interviewed Roman on TV, was being detained in a cell along with his cameraman.

I hadn't had a chance to talk to anyone. After I'd finally unlocked the diner's door, it had been a whirlwind of law enforcement, town residents, and paramedics. I didn't want to leave Rianne's side, afraid she would somehow break free if she woke up. But Stan assured me the jail cell could withstand immortal beings.

I was still dumbfounded at Rianne. The past two times I'd been in her presence, she'd bragged about changing, excited to give up her humanity. But part of me hadn't thought she would actually go through with it. Even when I'd seen her on TV, she'd said she was human. She'd pretty much signed her own death warrant unless our family history with vampires and witches served to keep her alive or from becoming feral. Time would tell.

Conrad smoothed a hand over his black hair. "I would like to hear what Tim Cox has to say myself."

Cox had to know more about my sister. Hell, he probably had details of Adam's operation or rumors thereof. Reporters were determined to get at the heart of a story, and one who revealed that vampires existed probably had an award-winning piece of news.

I ambled over to the glass-encased counter, where a lovely dark-haired woman with kind brown eyes sat at a desk to answer phones and type. "Grace, any idea how long Stan might be on his call?"

She frowned. "It's hard to say. After what happened today, he might be a while."

I rubbed my lips together, wondering who he was talking to about the incident. Steven came to mind. After all, my father-in-law was trying to overthrow the council. "Thank you."

Grace smiled warmly. "How are you feeling?"

I returned a polite grin. "Pretty good." Except the knot in my stomach, the anger in my veins, and the bile in my throat.

Jordyn and I'd been taken to the town's medical clinic, which was a quarter mile north from the sheriff's station. The paramedic had been afraid we might have concussions, but after an exam, neither Jordyn nor I had any symptoms. We were, however, bruised, and I had several scratches on my back from Rianne's talons that were healing nicely thanks to the elixir Doc had prescribed for my surgical wounds.

"And your sister?" she asked.

"A little shaken up, but she's fine," I said. "She's home babysitting."

As vampire hunters, Jordyn and I had seen and dealt with bloodsuckers, so nothing really shook us. But seeing our sister as a monster was a blow to the gut and would take some time to process.

She propped her chin on the back of her hand as she dug her elbow into the desk. "How are those sweet babies?"

I smiled from ear to ear. "Doing well, eating like horses, and I swear they've grown overnight."

She was about to say something when her phone rang. "Sorry," she said, picking up the receiver.

I tuned her out as I sat next to Conrad. "Did you reach Webb?"

After I'd gotten home from the hospital, I called Cooper Gray, but he hadn't answered. The shifter was my go-to person for contacting Sam. I had tried Sam's burner phone and his regular one, and I struck out.

"I finally talked to Jo," Conrad said. "She wanted to rush back, but I told her we had things under control. Webb has been in meetings, which was why he'd been unreachable. But Jo, Abbey, and Alia will return in the morning. Then we'll regroup."

The small town of Dewsbury, Maine wasn't the spot to lie low anymore, particularly if Tim Cox ran with his story of what had happened while he'd been in the diner. I was relieved he hadn't witnessed Rianne sling Jordyn and me around the restaurant.

Mainly because if anyone saw the strength Rianne had, every human on the planet might want that capability.

I tangled my fingers together in my lap. "Did Jo say anything about her dad's plan?"

"Nothing except he's behind closed doors."

I bounced my foot, hoping Steven would force the elders to call off the guardians. One fewer problem to deal with. Then I could have my husband back. We had a ton to do to prepare for the road ahead. More importantly, this was a critical time for a father to bond with his son and daughters.

I massaged a knot in my neck, then my shoulder. I would feel the soreness more tomorrow, but nothing two Advil wouldn't help. "I'm going to step out for some air." If I sat too long, I might not be able to move, and the station was rather confining and stuffy. I could also use a walk on the beach, but that would have to wait, although there was a park across from the station.

Conrad was about to follow me out when his phone rang. He raised an eyebrow at me. "Don't go far."

He was still on high alert, and I couldn't blame him. If Rianne knew where I was, then I would think my grandmother, or even Adam and Roman, did as well.

"You can watch me through the glass door."

Nodding, he answered his call.

Once I was sniffing the salt air, I looked around the immediate area. Aside from the park across the street, there wasn't much for a quarter mile. I leaned against Stan's cruiser, eyeing Conrad, who was standing inside watching me as he talked.

The vampire scout was attached to my hip, it seemed. But I wasn't complaining. I liked having him as my bodyguard. He reminded me of Lane, who'd died protecting me. I felt sorrow and guilt for what had happened to him. I didn't want anyone dying because of me. But like Lane, Conrad was a wealth of knowledge. Conrad was fascinated with how bridges were built, had a love for old western movies, and was a history buff.

I angled my face toward the waning blue sky as a light breeze played with my hair. I closed my eyes and prayed we would catch a break.

Having Rianne in custody was a huge win, in my book. But I wouldn't be able to sleep until I knew how Rianne found out where I was, and I wanted to know the whereabouts of my evil grandmother. Harriet Aberdeen's last words to me had been, *"Layla, if I were you, I would protect that baby at all costs."*

She was the one I had to worry about, and since Rianne had found me, my grandmother had to know where I was. Conrad was right. We had to regroup, which meant we had to find another hiding place. Sam had mentioned he would ask Dane if I could stay at the shifter compound. I doubted Dane would say no, although I might have to state my case to his pack, which was fine by me.

The loud rumble of an engine, tires crunching over gravel, and the screeching of brakes had my eyes open and my dagger in my hand.

Before I could track movement, Conrad was outside as the passenger emerged from the black SUV.

I did a double take, confusion mingling with happiness. My heart thundered as my mind scrambled to figure out why my gorgeous husband was in Maine. Steven must've called off the cavalry.

But while I was over the moon, my hot-as-sin vampire with his black hair unbound and free about his massive shoulders was anything but elated. It was clear that the worry steeped in his green eyes was a direct result of Rianne. Jo must've told him.

I lifted my hands. "I'm fine, husband," I felt compelled to say.

He stalked toward me with a sense of purpose, no doubt dying to wrap his arms around me. Instead, he sized me up from head to toe, his features tight, his lips pursed, and his carotid artery pulsing to beat the band.

I gave him a flirty smile, hoping it would help loosen his tight muscles. But nope. His nostrils were flaring, and his green eyes swirled to liquid silver.

I reached up and flattened a hand on his stubbled jaw. "Sam, I'm not hurt."

Quick as a whip, his hands were around me, tugging me to him. He buried his nose in my hair. "I've been a fucking freak with worry for ten minutes."

The second our bodies were touching, everything was right in the world despite the chaos around us, and I sighed, relieved I had my husband in my arms.

"We were operating on radio silence," Tripp said to Conrad behind Sam and me. "I just turned on my phone, and Webb's message was short. Rianne was here, and Layla was fine. I tried to call him, but he's helping Steven. We didn't have any luck reaching Jo."

"She doesn't know much," Conrad said. "I only gave her the good parts. Layla wanted to talk to Sam before we shared the details."

Sam edged away, then took my dagger from me. He smirked that dimpled grin that made me weak in the knees, and as his gaze took a hike up and down my body, desire and intent pooled in his green eyes.

Now that the tension had eased, my pulse shot into the stratosphere, my excitement reaching new heights. A ball of love and uncontained lust rushed through my veins—fast, hot, hard, spinning, and out of control. My husband was home. It felt like forever since I'd snuggled up to him, when in fact, it had been three weeks since he and I had shared the pullout couch in the birthing suite on the night we'd shared an intimate and mind-blowing sexy dream. More importantly, he would see his babies, hug them, help feed them, and bond with them.

I flattened my hands on his toned chest and felt his heart beating furiously. "Are you free? Please say yes." But I would take one night if that was the case.

"For the time being," he said.

Someone knocked on the glass door.

I peeked around Sam to find Stan waving us in.

I grabbed Sam's hand. "Come on, vampire. Rianne must be awake. Time for some answers. Then I'm all yours."

31

LAYLA

I was a ball of nerves as Stan escorted me down into the basement. The farther I followed him, the more sweat beaded on my skin. When we reached the bottom, I was breathing heavily, and my insides were churning. For fuck's sake. Rianne was my sister. The woman I'd loved since we were practically walking. Yet my heart was shattering, knowing she would never be human again. The pretty brunette with big brown eyes, long hair, and a laugh that was contagious. The sister who'd climbed trees, rode horses, and ogled boys in high school with Jordyn and me.

There wasn't any question that I was livid with her, despised what she'd become, hurt that she'd chosen my grandmother, and confused at her extreme hatred for Sam. Above all else, she had broken the bond of sisterhood. As much as it pained me to say this, I hoped she survived. I hoped she was truly immortal—could shift from monster to human and back at her will—and not feral like Noah, whose time on earth was probably limited.

The basement was clean and not the musty and dirty kind that gave me the creeps and nightmares about creatures lurking in the dark.

Bright lights turned on overhead automatically when we walked by a wall monitor with a keyboard on a desk below it.

Stan came to an abrupt halt, spun around, and regarded me with stern brown eyes. "Layla, here's what will happen. When I give the order, Rianne's cell door will slide open. There will be two-foot-thick bulletproof glass separating you from your sister. Behind that glass is steel bars as an added layer of protection, which means she won't be able to get out. There are cameras in her cell and on the ceilings in the hallway. There's also a speaker on the wall adjacent to her cell door. I'll be at this desk, watching you from this screen. Any questions?"

I shook my head. "Sam is watching, right?"

I didn't want him to join me, only because Rianne would focus on him, and I might not get the answers I was looking for. Still, knowing he was observing from afar made me feel as if he was protecting me. I also knew he would be down in a flash if anything happened. But from the security measures Stan had just described, I doubted I would need saving.

"If you don't want him to, I can shut off the cameras upstairs."

I swished saliva around in my mouth to erase the dryness. "It's okay. I just don't want Rianne to know he's here. She might not talk."

"He won't be able to respond to what he hears. He doesn't have access to a microphone." He flipped a switch on the wall just inside the block of cells.

I followed him, and with each step I took, I felt as though I was a dead man walking. *Thump, thump, thump* went my heart while the *click, click, click* of my shoes echoed as we passed three jail cells. Since I'd had blood on my clothes from the fight, I'd changed out of my skinny jeans and into a simple sundress I wore with mesh tan flats.

Stan got on the radio tacked to his shoulder. "Mike, open four, please."

As the thick metal door slid open, my thoughts scrambled over where to begin, if I could even speak. The convo between Jordyn and me before I'd left for the sheriff's station played out on repeat.

"You won't get answers," Jordyn said with her hands on her hips and a scowl on her face. "You know she's stubborn. She probably hates who she is now but will never admit it."

"You're right," I replied. "But we have to try. She's here for more than her five minutes of fame on TV. Or to change us into freaks. Come with me."

Jordyn's face turned red. "No. She made her bed. She can croak for all I care."

My emotions had been up and down—hatred, love, frustration, fury, sorrow, pity, and many more since Rianne had broken our sisterly bond. None of that had changed. I still had a strong urge to somehow save her from herself. Yet I couldn't. Not anymore.

Stan placed a gentle hand on my shoulder. "Good luck."

Stepping in front of the glass, I inhaled and exhaled a quiet breath. My heart was beating like rapid fire on a battlefield. I suddenly wanted Sam by my side, to hold my hand and to tell me how fearless I was. Because at the moment, I didn't feel brave. I wasn't sure why. Maybe it was her creature-like features that messed with my psyche. Or maybe it was the close call when she'd stuck the needle in my leg. I'd gotten lucky twice after the first time she'd tried to change me at Intech when she hooked me up to an IV bag full of the serum. Thank God not enough of it had gone into my system before I'd woken up and yanked out the needle, although I had no idea what had been in the IV bag until Carly had told me after the fact. Nevertheless, Rianne was persistent, and if she got out of here, she would continue to come at me to try to change me. Deep down, the old cliché that three times was a charm had me on edge.

Rianne was sitting on the floor, leaning against the back wall with her legs stretched out, canines gleaming, bloodred eyes glaring, and she was picking at a claw, an actual two-inch talon, as though she was bored and waiting on something.

I folded my arms over my chest. "Can't you—" The first word

came out, but the second sounded garbled. I cleared my throat and tried again. "Can't you change?"

"I like the way I am," she said in a casual tone.

Growing up, she'd been unassuming, not the type to worry about her appearance except when she'd gone to parties in high school. Before she left the house, she'd always made sure her makeup had been done to perfection. Though Jordyn, Rianne, and I didn't wear makeup that often. The vampires we hunted didn't give a shit about how we looked. Most of the time, we'd worn face paint to camouflage ourselves while hunting.

"Bullshit," I said. "You can't tell me you like your forehead protruding outward or those long nails or your canines. Aren't you supposed to shift like vampires and wolves?"

If she followed the same trajectory as Noah, she would grow hair on her face. I shivered at the thought that my sister's features could be permanent.

"Stop caring about me, Layla," she said, not looking at me. "And if you're here to knock some sense into me like you always do, that ship has sailed."

I snorted. "You're right. Been there, done that, and got the goddamn T-shirt." My tone dropped an octave. "I'll cut to the chase. How did you know where I was?"

She laughed. "Like I'm going to tell you my secrets." She rolled her eyes. "Puh…lease. You know I won't tell you shit."

Ire overtook my fear. "Where's Granny?"

"I heard you had four babies. Is that true?" she asked, ignoring my question.

I schooled my features. "It seems your information is lacking." *Liar.*

She studied me with calculating intent. "I don't think so."

My mother always knew when I was lying. I had a bad habit of pulling on my earlobe or twitching my shoulders. But I wasn't doing either. My hands were tucked underneath my arms, and I was stiff as a board as I glared at her.

Studies showed that when they lied, the majority of people tended to look away. Jordyn usually did that very thing while fibbing. Rianne, on the other hand, would scratch the side of her nose. But when our parents had pointed out how they knew when we lied, the three of us began to be more conscious of our tells.

We definitely had someone on the inside feeding her information. Either that or the SEAL compound was bugged. Or maybe not. Aunt Tabitha and Uncle Jack knew I was having quadruplets, and if my grandmother had spoken to Aunt Tab or Uncle Jack, they could've told Rianne. I wouldn't assume intentionally.

Regardless, before long the entire fucking world would know I had quadruplets. Then the crazies would come out of the woodwork, especially Harriet Aberdeen, vying to get their hands on my children's DNA. Maybe that was the prophecy. Maybe the way my child could upset the balance of mankind was by his or her DNA being used.

Rianne's psychotic laugh zapped my thoughts. "The fact that you look like a deer in the headlights confirms what I was told. I didn't believe you had four vampire spawns. But it's true. Isn't it?"

I rolled my shoulders back, hoping I wasn't showing any emotion. "What's true is, I was thinking about something Mom told me the other day."

She perked up. "Mom? Have you lost your mind?"

"Nope. I saw Mom when I died," I said. "She's quite disappointed in you." The dying part was true, at least.

Rianne was riveted as she stared at me.

I inched closer to the glass barricade. "You see, sister, Mom told me how you're going to die." Whoa! The lie was coming out, and I was beginning to believe my words. "She gave me insight into our future. Yours in particular." A wild laugh broke out in my head. *Keep going, girl. You're on a roll.* Good news for me—Rianne was intrigued.

She narrowed her eyes. "I know what my future holds, and so do you. That little girl Abbey saw me killing you."

I stopped the cold chill from racking my body. "Do you want to kill me? Your own flesh and blood?"

"As long as you're with that vampire fucker, you deserve to die, and so do your spawns."

I took another step toward the glass. "Then why haven't you killed me yet? You've had plenty of chances, Rianne. And who are you kidding? You don't want me dead. You want me to change like you and become sisters again. That was what you told me at the diner. Remember?"

She was on her feet in a flash, standing before me with her ugly clawed fingers wrapped around the steel bars. "What I want, Layla, is Sam Mason's head as a trophy on my wall. What I want is for you to come to *your* senses. We hunt bloodsuckers. We're not vampire lovers. They've murdered our family and innocent humans for centuries. Wake the fuck up, *sister*."

I mashed my lips together, my eyes slits. "You're the one who has blinders on. You think giving up your humanity is the answer to wiping out vampires? You're the one who needs to wake the fuck up. Don't you still want to join the military?" Too late for the human armed forces, but the supernaturals had their own military. Rebekah and her Special Forces unit came to mind. "You could kill criminal supernatural types, and don't put Sam into that category. You know as well as I do, the Vampire Navy SEALs help protect humanity. Think about it, sis. You could fly jets and helicopters." She'd always wanted to fly planes. "It's not too late." Though it actually might be, depending on how she fared from the serum.

She stared at me with an angry expression. "You think they'll take me?" she asked in a bitter and sarcastic tone.

"Ben Jackson, the hybrid, is a SEAL," I said.

She laughed. "Nice try, sis. Steven Mason and his asshole vamps wouldn't even consider me for their military."

I couldn't argue that point, and I wouldn't convince her of anything right now. But I had planted the seed. Maybe she would come around. "What will you do when Granny dies from her blood cancer?"

"Who said she would die?"

I raised an eyebrow. "Did she take the serum too? And where is she? Why isn't she with you?"

She retracted her talons. "An enemy never shares her strategy, Layla. You, of all people, should know that." She went over to a cot, which was the only piece of furniture in the room, and lay down as if dismissing me.

My mind worked overtime, piecing together a few things. "You found me through an informant, and you came here to inject Jordyn and me with the serum while the nation watched. Adam and Roman didn't send you here. Granny did. For what? To take my child? Confirm I had four? Or is Granny dead, and you're working for yourself?"

"Adam and Roman are assholes. Just like Carly. She got what was coming to her."

"You injected Carly?" My voice pitched higher.

She folded her hands behind her head. "That bitch helped Sam. She deserved to be punished."

"But taking the serum isn't punishment. You think it's the Holy Grail for immortality."

"For Carly it isn't. She doesn't want to be immortal." Her evil laugh made the hairs on my arms stand to attention. "Now she is."

A part of me felt sorry for Carly. "Do you know that for sure or even where Carly is?" I wasn't about to tell her if she didn't know.

"I don't care about that bitch," Rianne said with disgust.

I tapped my finger on my lips as I connected the dots. "But she is the scientist, and she was trying to help those with incurable diseases like Granny."

She shrugged. "Not anymore."

The lightbulb suddenly shone like the sun on a hot summer day. "Adam kicked you and Granny out of his circle because of what you did to Carly."

Adam and Carly were tight. He knew her motives and she his. Plus, Carly had told my grandmother that Adam was only tolerating Harriet because of her money and that my grandmother was supposed to keep Rianne from pulling stunts. I would bet my life that Adam sent them packing.

"You're also here because Granny is livid with you. She's not part of Adam's team anymore, which means she has no access to find an immortal cure for her blood cancer. And you're trying to make up for your indiscretions, hoping to show Granny you're worthy, which means you came here to snag my child for her."

Our grandmother's words strangled my throat. *But now that you're carrying Sam's baby, I don't need him.*

She sat up, glowering at me. "You think you have it all figured out. Don't you?" She guffawed. "You have no clue."

"Maybe not," I volleyed back. "But one thing I know for sure is you won't be leaving this cell."

She let out an evil laugh as if to negate my statement. "I'm done talking." She resumed lying down.

I'd gotten more from her than I'd expected, and she wasn't going anywhere. I could always come back tomorrow if I had more questions, but I doubted she would give me anything more than she already had.

I started to walk away.

"Layla," Rianne said. "Be careful who you trust."

"Thanks for the warning," I said as I left.

If a mole existed among our ranks, I was sure the SEALs would flush out that person. For now, I had babies and a husband waiting for me. I wanted to spend as much time with them as possible because the way our lives were headed, I was afraid I wouldn't have very many opportunities, especially if fate decided to fuck with Sam and me even more.

<h1 style="text-align:center">32</h1>

<h2 style="text-align:center">SAM</h2>

The moon was big and bright, drowning out the canopy of stars. Low tide gave way to a wide carpet of wet sand as Layla and I sat on a blanket in front of the stairs leading up to the house.

Sleep was a thing of the past, and knowing Rianne was in town set my nerves on fire. Layla couldn't relax, and Rorie was unusually fussy. She didn't have a fever. She had drunk her full bottle of formula a couple of hours ago, and she had no symptoms of colic, at least from Rebekah's medical expertise. I was siding with Rebekah for the simple fact that once Layla picked Rorie up, she'd stopped crying, which pierced a hole in my heart because I'd tried to calm my daughter down. I'd even given her a drop of my blood, thinking that might have been what she'd needed. But no such luck. I felt like a failure as a father. She should know who I was, but I hadn't been around for three weeks.

At the moment, Rorie was snuggled against Layla's chest in one of those baby wraps, and my gorgeous, feisty huntress was rubbing gentle circles on Rorie's back while seated between my legs.

"Penny for your thoughts," Layla whispered on the wind.

I kissed her ear, staring out at the water. The moon's rays glinted off the ocean's serene surface, giving the water a glassy look. "I love you, baby doll. More and more each day. My heart stopped when I heard Rianne was in town. But Conrad said you did great."

I'd never been more afraid in my life than when I'd found out Rianne was in Maine. How the fuck did she know where to find Layla? It was crystal fucking clear that we had a mole among us. Tripp had Sawyer checking the command center. After all, Sawyer mentioned we had a breach in our security system that he'd caught quickly. But maybe not in time. We couldn't rule out anyone, even our closest confidants. Hell, for all we knew it could also be one of Stan's men.

"Not really," she said. "I got lucky. I need weapons training. I want a sword. When dealing with creatures like Noah and Rianne, it will take more than a dagger to kill them. I feel like we're about to go to war with zombies, and the only way for them to die is to cut off their heads."

I inhaled her cherry scent, an aroma that had a way of relaxing me. "We have plenty of swords in our weapons room on base. I know just the one that would fit you."

She turned her head slightly so her cheek and mine were touching. "I know you'll worry your handsome head off about me. And I'm not saying you shouldn't. But I would like to remind you that we're in this together. We fight for what we believe in and those we love. Does that last line sound familiar?" She giggled.

I dragged my lips to her earlobe and nibbled. "I remember my marriage proposal. Would you like to hear it again?"

She flashed her big blues up at me with a dick-jerking smile. "I'm listening."

I kissed her neck as goose bumps pebbled on her skin. "Layla Aberdeen, would you be my sidekick, the woman who will keep me sane, a partner who will stand by my side and fight for what we believe in and those we love? Above all else, will you love my arrogant ass no matter what?"

She sighed and quivered. "To the day I take my last breath, Sam Mason."

I was dying to lay her out on the blanket, strip her naked, and show her how much I fucking loved her. But sex wasn't on the agenda, at least not tonight.

As if she was in my head, she said, "I'm dying to feel your naked body pressed into mine and feel you inside me. It's been too long, vampire."

I groaned. "Kind of hard at the moment. But we'll find time." For fucking sure. Intimacy was important for both of us.

"Not to ruin the mood," she said, "but we need to find my grandmother. I can't stop thinking about my talk with Rianne."

She didn't ruin the mood. She obliterated it.

Her whacked-out sister had stolen most of the show since we'd left the sheriff's station several hours ago. Frankly, I was tired of dealing with Rianne. The woman had to die, but maybe she would because of the serum. Highly unlikely, in my book. Only because I wasn't that lucky.

I had, however, gotten an official reprieve for the next week. While the votes were coming in, the guardians had been ordered to stand down. At least I had one fewer group on my ass. The human hunters might be another story, considering the bounty on my head.

"Agreed, but we might have to strategize once we get to Dane's compound. Also, as soon as we talk to the reporter, we need to leave." I would have loved to hang out on the beach, but we had work to do, and I would rather have us safely ensconced behind the shifter compound.

"I hate all this," she said. "Why can't we just live in peace?"

"We will," I returned. Having Rianne behind bars was a step in the right direction. One enemy down, several more to go. "You and I will get our happily ever after, baby doll. When? I can't say. But I swear you'll have a house on the ocean, and our kids will be free to grow up without anyone chasing us." If it was the last thing I ever did, I would make fucking sure my family had everything they deserved.

"Speaking of a house on the beach, I looked at one for sale up the road from here," she said. "It's perfect for us. But I know it's not the right time to be buying anything."

Sadly, she was right. Her place of residence was about to be a log cabin in the Catskills. It wasn't her dream home, but she and our babies would be safe. She would have more security than here and a great amount of help. I'd spoken to Greta before Tripp and I had left, and the she-wolf was ecstatic to welcome my family into her home.

My phone rang, disrupting the solitude and the whoosh of the waves on shore. I grabbed my cell off the blanket beside me.

"Calls at one thirty in the morning are never good," Layla said.

"It's Tripp. Maybe he has news on the vote." I answered, putting him on speaker, "What's up, dude? Layla's with me." Just in case he had top secret info he didn't want anyone else to hear.

"Breaking news," he said with a lightness to his voice. "I just got word from Webb that the Feds will be converging on Intech just before dawn."

Layla let out a squeal. "Hallelujah. You mean something else is going our way?"

My muscles loosened as I released the sigh of the century. We weren't anywhere close to that happily ever after I promised Layla, but we needed to celebrate each win, no matter how small. Besides, I'd always believed in the power of three. Rianne was behind bars, and the human government was about to shut down Intech. Two down, and one more good thing had to come our way. Maybe the human government would take Adam into custody and lock him up for the rest of his miserable life.

"How will the Feds deal with Roman?" I asked. "Are the humans prepared to fight vampires?"

"The Secretary of the Navy asked for our help. Viking II SEAL team has been deployed to Chicago."

Man, I would give anything to join them. "Any word on how the vote is going?"

"Webb said the votes are tied. Half want to keep our existence secret, and the other half knows we have to change how we live among humans," Tripp said. "There are still several heads of state who haven't weighed in yet."

I didn't have a chance to respond when a bloodcurdling scream tore through the night air. It sounded like it came from Jordyn.

33

LAYLA

My heart sank to the sand as I hurried to my feet—or tried. With Rorie secured to me, it wasn't that easy. My body instantly shook as Sam helped me up. Then he took off like a bat out of hell and into the house before I could blink.

I ran as fast as I could with Rorie. Maybe Jordyn had a bad dream. Seeing our sister as a bone-chilling creature would spark nightmares forever. Yet my mind flashed with its own demons. I hadn't been able to shake my conversation with Rianne and her warning about being careful who I trusted.

But those around us at the moment were people I would go into battle with. George, Rebekah, Conrad, and even the five deputy vampires I'd gotten to know in the weeks since I'd been here, although not all five were on shift at the same time. Still they were dedicated to George. Jo knew the deputies well, and considering the residents in town had been prepared to help me fight Rianne, I couldn't see them doing anything to harm me.

I refused to think the worst. But the closer I got to the glass accordion doors, the faster my heart raced. When I reached the deck, a gasp raked from my lungs before I burst into the house.

The front door was open, and one of Stan's deputies was lying on the porch.

No. No. No. My babies!

Rorie began to cry as if she could feel my fear.

"It's okay, baby girl," I said, my voice barely audible. "Momma bear is okay." I lied through my freaking teeth. I was far from okay. Bile catapulted to my throat, and the acidic taste scorched my tongue.

As if my daughter understood me, a sense of warmth traveled through my body, easing the nerves slightly as I skirted furniture in the family room before jogging to the nursery.

I skidded to a stop in the doorway, my eyes wide, my jaw hanging open.

Jordyn was passed out on the floor beside a crib with a dart in her neck, and Sam was magically strangling a familiar-looking man with his elemental powers.

"Who are you? What are you doing here? Who sent you?" Sam asked the intruder, snarling at the man as his voice thundered.

The man's dark eyes bugged out as he held his throat, his face turning red.

I couldn't believe my eyes. I had to shake my head a couple of times.

"That's Norman Collier," I managed to say. "The guardian who came looking for you the other day."

I shivered out of my funk when I remembered how he'd been staring at my children for far too long with no emotion on his face.

I rushed over to the cribs as Sam continued to interrogate the vampire. Ellie was in her crib, but Luna and Orion weren't. My heart fell to my feet. Maybe they were with George. He liked to keep the babies in his room when he babysat. But if George had them, he would be in the nursery helping Sam. Everyone had to have heard Jordyn's scream.

I crouched down over Jordyn and tapped her face. "Sis, wake

up," I said in a sharp tone. She only had one dart in her, so she shouldn't be out for that long. At least I hoped not.

I tore out of the nursery and checked every room in the house as tears poured out and my chest hurt as if someone had stabbed me several times. This couldn't be happening.

Rorie bawled in my arms, but I barely heard her over the pounding of my pulse and the ringing in my ears.

Luna and Orion were nowhere inside. Clutching Rorie, I flew out the front door. I counted five bodies—Conrad, George, and three deputies—all with darts in their necks and scattered on the porch and driveway.

What the fuck?

My legs were weak, and my body trembled as I clutched my daughter to me, stepping over bodies before scurrying to the road.

Rorie continued to cry.

"I'm okay, baby girl." I felt compelled to soothe her as best I could, but my voice cracked and pitched.

I'm having a nightmare. That's it. I'm dreaming. I have to be.

The world began to spin on its axis as I thought of my recurring dream. Bits and pieces of it flashed before me.

"Please," the boy begged. "She needs your help."

"Who needs my help?" I asked.

"My sister," he said with a slight lisp. "You're the only one who can help her."

"I don't understand. Why me?"

His green eyes were high beams in the dark of night. "Because you have the power." He tugged on my fingers. "We don't have much time."

"Who are you?"

"I'm your son," he said.

I squeezed my eyes shut for a second, then checked up and down the dark-as-sin road. Nothing. No cars. No sign of anyone.

This wasn't happening. *No. No. No.*

Tears streamed down my face, and I sucked in air when I recalled more of my dream.

The woman ahead of me tossed a look over her shoulder, her red eyes glowing like a devil from the depths of hell.

"You need to stop her, Mom," a boy of about five years old said from somewhere nearby. "She'll kill us if you don't."

A wolf howled, jarring me out of my stupor as I sobbed, holding on to my daughter for dear life.

"We'll find them, Rorie," I whispered to her as blue lights cut through the darkness.

A police cruiser skidded to a stop in front of me.

Tripp was out of the car before the driver hit the brakes. His bronze eyes swirled to black as he scanned the yard.

"Luna and Orion are gone," I cried to Tripp. "There's a guardian in the house."

Stan came around the cruiser. "What the fuck?" He got on his radio. "Mike, round up the troops. We need a search party. Have them meet me at Webb's house."

Sam dragged out Norman Collier's limp body and threw him off the porch. "This fucker won't talk. I'll need my sister to read his mind."

With vampire speed, Stan restrained the vampire with chains just like he'd done with Rianne, then shoved Norman into the cruiser.

I stood rooted to where the driveway met the road, rubbing Rorie's back, hoping the act would take away my pain and regulate my breathing.

Sam stalked up to me. "Baby doll, go inside and put Rorie in her baby rocker. Jordyn woke up. She has Ellie."

"How are you calm?" I asked through tears.

A crease dented the space between his eyebrows. "Believe me, I'm trying not to set the town on fire or rip that fucker Norman's head off. I need my wits about me if I want to get answers."

A wolf trotted up.

"Rebekah," I said. I'd forgotten about her. She'd complained earlier that her wolf needed to run. Maybe she'd seen something.

"Orion and Luna have been taken. Did you see anything suspicious anywhere?"

Bones cracked before Rebekah reemerged into human form, shaking her head. "No, I didn't. Let me put some clothes on." She darted into the house.

I hurried behind her while Stan, Sam, and Tripp were trying to wake George, Conrad, and the three deputies.

Jordyn was in the family room, holding Ellie. "I'm sorry, Layla. I tried to stop him. I promise." Her tone dripped with guilt.

"It's not your fault," I said. "But did you see anyone else with Norman?"

"I was just about to fall into REM sleep when I heard a female voice. At first I thought I was dreaming. But then, the female said, 'We need all four babies.' I opened my eyes and found Norman about to take Ellie. That's when I screamed. Then he shot me with a dart."

"So you didn't see the female?" I asked, praying she did.

"No," Jordyn cried. "What is going on, Layla? You think it's Granny behind this or Roman?"

I blew out breath after breath, and as I sat down on the couch, Rorie finally stopped crying. "I don't know." My heart was climbing out of my chest. "In my recurring dream, I saw a woman with red eyes and a little boy telling me I needed to stop her or she would kill him and his sister."

Jordyn gulped in a sharp breath. "You told me about your dream and the boy and girl, but you never told me about the woman with red eyes."

"She just appeared in my dream the night Sam rushed me to the infirmary," I said in a shaky voice.

"We know it's not Rianne," Jordyn said. "Unless she escaped."

It was impossible. Rianne was barricaded behind two feet of glass, steel bars, and a thick metal door.

"Do you think Granny took the serum?" I asked myself more than her. Those who had red eyes had taken the serum—Rianne,

Noah, and Carly. But Noah was out since he was male and didn't fit the description, and my cousin-in-law was suffering from a stroke and in the infirmary on base.

Standing up, Jordyn twisted from side to side as she rocked Ellie. "Maybe Granny decided to try it. I mean, she is dying of blood cancer, and she doesn't have anything to lose."

A wicked chill gripped my body. "Why would she need four babies, though?"

Rebekah came in dressed in a robe and holding a handful of dirty baby clothes. "Which of these were Orion and Luna wearing? I need their scent before I hunt."

I hopped up and picked through the garments before handing her Orion's jumper and then Luna's. "Did you see anything suspicious on your run? A woman with Orion and Luna?" *Please say yes.*

"I was miles from the house, and when I left, everything was normal," Rebekah said. "I should be able to track something. I'll be back." Then she took off.

Hope sprang free. Whoever took my children couldn't have gone far yet.

Sam came in, eyes hard, nostrils flaring, jaw rock solid. "The team outside is coming to." He flattened his trembling hands on my cheeks. "We will find them. We will burn down this planet if we have to." His tone was hard yet soft. "Do you hear me?"

I nodded through tears. "Then what are we waiting for?"

I fisted my hands at my sides, ready to do *anything* and *everything* to find my precious babies, and I dared anyone to get in my way.

To be continued in The Prophecy…

ABOUT THE AUTHOR

Bestselling author **S.B. Alexander** is an independent author with over 25 titles to date. She writes paranormal, new adult, and sweet romances that feature hot heroes stealing hearts.

S.B. or Susan as she likes to be called is a navy veteran, former high school teacher, and former corporate sales executive. She's a lover of sports, especially baseball, although nowadays you can find her on the golf course, swinging for that hole in one.

Her motto: "Life is too short to waste. So live every moment like it's your last."

You can connect with S.B. Alexander in the following ways:

Reader Group: https://sbalexander.com/beastsandbitches
Author Website: https://sbalexander.com
Newsletter: https://sbalexander.com/newsletter
Email: susan@sbalexander.com

facebook.com/sbalexander.authorpage
twitter.com/sbalex_author
instagram.com/sbalexanderauthor
amazon.com/author/sbalexander
bookbub.com/authors/s-b-alexander

ALSO BY S.B. ALEXANDER

Visit https://sbalexander.com/all-books/ to learn more about S.B. Alexander books and future releases. Please note release dates are subject to change based on reader demand and the author's schedule. Subscribing to the author's newsletter or following her on Facebook is the best way to stay updated with planned new releases.

GLOSSARY OF TERMS

Natural-born vampire: A human born with the vampire gene that, when activated, will turn them into a vampire.

Activation process: Those who carry the vampire gene can only turn by drinking the blood of their vampire father at the age of sixteen years or older.

Council of Elders – A group of five vampires who set the laws.

Genetic engineering: Turning humans into vampires through a process of restructuring their DNA.

Cobalt – A vampire's kryptonite. The metal will kill a vampire if staked through the heart. It will also burn a vampire's skin if they come in contact with it.

Reproduction: A natural-born vampire is born by a male vampire and a human female with a rare blood type of Vel negative.

Council of Eternal Affairs: The legal department of the vampire government.

Vampire characteristics: Sunlight doesn't burn them. Their hearts beat at <5 bpm. Skin temperature is ten degrees cooler than a human. Eye color changes to black except for a few chosen ones.

Steven Mason: Vampire and father to twins Jo and Sam Mason. He's dubbed the most powerful of all vampires because of his many powers, including his mind-reading abilities. He can only read minds when touching someone except when it comes to his children. His normal eye color is green. His vampire eye color is silver.

Jo Mason: Turned at sixteen. Powers include seeing the future through her dreams, mind-reading without touching a person, telekinesis, and she's an elemental with the ability to manipulate water, air, earth, and fire. Her normal eye color is silver. Her vampire eye color is violet.

Sam Mason: Turned at sixteen. Powers include feeling what others feel (Empath), telekinesis, and he can compel a person using a series of numbers woven into a magical spell. He's also an elemental with the ability to manipulate water, air, earth, and fire. His normal eye color is green. His vampire eye color is silver.

Guardians: Law enforcement vampires who work for the Council of Elders.

Scouts: Law enforcement vampires who are essentially detectives.